Stories That Need to Be Told 2023

GRAND PRIZE WINNER

Gerald
a memoir
Arlo Z Graves

Hey, can you tell what they're saying? Colin yells from the bathroom door to you, as you mill around the sweltering kitchen. August 2020, hitting like a convection oven.

You can't tell what they are saying. You don't know who *they* are. You have your headphones on and did not realize people are outside. Pulling the headphones off, you open the door and lean out.

Gerald, the hillbilly cabin, shakes with the concussive *buh buh buh* of a helicopter blade, and you step outside to look up.

The dry, breathless afternoon sun filters orange through the trees, thick with smoke from somewhere. It's late summer in California. Somewhere is always on fire.

And somewhere is always somewhere else.

As soon as you open the door you hear sirens and see strobing police lights whirling down the dirt roads. The helicopter lumbers out from behind the canopy so low you can see someone leaning out of it. It stops above the cabin. Evacuate. Emergency evacuation. Fire. Fire. Imminent fire. Thirty minutes. Evacuate.

Get. Out. Now.

What? The words don't land in your head. What does that mean? Fire. Evacuate. Why, how, where?

They say we have to evacuate, you call through the bathroom door, no emotion yet. There's a fire?

But the fire is tens of miles away, right? A little thing in La Honda from the thunderstorm. Right? Your phone has been warning you about it, showing you that people up by Skylonda need to be ready to leave . . . but that is nowhere near you and Gerald the hillbilly cabin.

Then, you see the wall of black smoke rising. Your mouth gets sticky and your pulse hits so hard it physically shakes you. You have to go. You have to leave. Colin is still on the toilet.

What do you need to take?

Wallet, the dog, the takeout containers on the counter—it's pho! You need to have dinner!—um . . . maybe some clothes. Shit, just grab the dirty laundry. Your Doc Martins, the bow and arrows, shit, the rental guitar, the ocarina, the dog, don't forget the dog. Her food? Nah. Colin gets out of the bathroom and you both scramble to stuff the Subaru.

He's left the toilet clogged. He says, Who cares?

Sirens scream, horses scream, birds scream, everything screams and one side of the sky has turned to night under a thick, belching cloud.

You can hear yourself breathing. Each breath dries you out, and you can taste the ash now. Beyond the redwoods you see the acrid plume of smoke with the sun behind it. It is here. The fire is here, for your home, for your everything.

No, you think. It'll be okay. They'll get it under control.

You and Colin run back and forth shoving your lives into the car. The laptops, the handmade knives, the stuffed sea lion. Don't forget the dog.

Now you turn on the garden hose, you start spraying down the backside of Gerald, your hillbilly home. Get it wet, you think. He won't burn if he's wet.

It won't make a difference! hollers Colin as you spray as high as the measly water pressure can reach.

Close all the windows. Lock the door . . . across the canyon you hear horses screeching as the helicopter lowers, skimming rooftops.

Evacuate. Fire. Fire. Fire.

Buh, buh, buh, go the blades in the smoky air. You feel them inside your chest like the bass at a Rammstein concert.

Your parents live in the house down the hill, and you see them dragging out the fire pump and hose. They built their home themselves, Big House, they call him. Gerald the trash shack came with the land. Home of draft dodgers, hermits, junkies, and now you.

You run down the hill on the little path you have taken a thousand times, a million times, a lifetime of times.

We're going to stay, say Mom and Dad. We can't lose our home. Dad, the retired mechanic with the giant brain surgery scar in his head, Mom with her Highway Patrol Top Gun tattoo. They stand in front of Iron Eagle, the long derelict blue Dodge. This is our only home, they say.

You can taste the heat of the fire in your throat. You'll burn to death! You can hardly speak. There's nowhere to hide!

Mom and Dad tell you they love you and tell you to leave.

It's going to be okay, says Dad. He struggles with mobility after the head injury, walking with one foot planted at a time, then the other, lumbering like an elderly sasquatch. The houses aren't going anywhere. It's going to be okay, he says, so calm, so sure.

You run back up the hill. You look up at your old, crooked cabin. Gerald, you named him Gerald. The recovering hoarder shack. Bad things happened in him. You were his new chance.

You have to go now, you imagine Gerald says. I have stood through earthquakes and red tags and plagues. You, little ones, must go.

And then you climb into the Subaru, squished between pieces of your life and under the rest. The dog sits on top of the bows and arrows.

You look at your cabin, your Gerald. Your rescued home. You grew up here. Here, has been your life. You are not from somewhere else, not going somewhere else. This is everything and everyone.

Will Gerald be here when we come back? you ask out loud.

I don't know, Colin turns the car on the dirt road, but we have to leave.

And you drive away.

The Subaru reaches Highway 236 and all appears unsettlingly calm. You are simply driving out, just a normal day. The woods are dark and dense and still. Highway 236 leads in a loop through Big Basin Redwood State Park. Your folks are some of the lucky few who got land up here, sandwiched in park and wilderness.

Take a breath, the fire is not here yet.

Cars cluster in a dirt pullout a couple miles up the mountain toward San Jose, so you and Colin pull over, too. Neighbors stand in the thistles looking out over Big Basin. They shade their eyes as the smoke plume rises, volcanic, from behind the Waddell ridge. The smoke seems to rise from the Butano fire road, your favorite mountain bike ride to the coast.

Jack and Judy pull up next to you. They live just up the hill from you in a lovely peach-walled cabin they built themselves and filled with plants and crystals. Nobody knows what to say or how to say it. I hope your home is safe, is repeated and repeated.

No matter what, we'll get to watch a forest regrow. Jack smiles. He accepts the wrath of the earth with a sad, gentle smile.

You do not possess such grace. You cannot lose Gerald. Gerald is a part of you.

You cannot see much from this thistle patch, so you and other cars drive on, up, up the mountain.

A few miles of climbing and you stop again on the paved overlook, the one with the concrete pit toilet. The neighborhood seems to cluster here as well, a murder of hopeful, gawking crows.

The fire doesn't look so bad from here, you think. Not a huge fire . . . some acres sure, some overgrown manzanita and brush . . . You walk a few minutes down the trail to get a different angle, and then a few minutes back.

A few minutes is all it takes.

What you see next, you can never unsee. It lives in your bones now, imprinted on the DNA of your spirit, something so integral to you it will be copied and imprinted in your meat and sinew until you return to the ground.

You see the CZU Lightning Complex crest the ridge.

How tall is a redwood tree? One hundred feet? Taller, two hundred? Taller. The coastal redwood is the tallest tree in the world.

The flames come over the ridge in a wall. Orange and snarling, leaping, and twisting into the sky the fire is three times as high as the treetops. Three times the tallest trees. It ebbs and it flares. It drinks the wind and screams, devouring the quiet green world, not a fire but a god unto itself. Gods, spirits, ghosts, you have never seen such things. Not until today.

You all watch at the overlook, your fates hang at the mercy of the chaos god of lightning and drought and a forest burdened by decades of unburned fuel.

Nothing can survive that, you realize. Heat bends the air like melting glass. Aircraft cannot even fly over it for the wild, lashing wind. Even if they could, there are none. The entire western coast is ablaze. This is everywhere.

The fire roars and snarls and begins reaching, reaching down the other side of the mountain. Reaching for the valley below where Gerald, Big House, and all the others wait, rooted, unable to run as you have run, the parts of you, you could not take.

Mom and Dad are still down there.

Gerald the shack came with the property. An abandoned junkie hoarder hell. But after spinal meningitis and the onset of autoimmune disease and chronic pain, it became clear you would not be able to work enough to move away. You had just stepped from college into the world of work, and three months was all it took to cripple you beyond restoration.

You may have been dealt a devastating hand, but it was a hand nonetheless.

And so you took your aching, broken self and learned to repair the damage. You hauled out the mountains of trash and animal bones. You washed the walls with bleach. Dad taught you how to sweat copper and hang drainpipes. Mom showed you how to frame walls. YouTube guided you through drywall, texture, and tile. You and Colin dug every single footing for a new foundation and a neighbor snuck in a septic tank for you.

You named him Gerald, for reasons still unknown. A rotting husk overflowing with literal shit, echoes of abuse and neglect, scraped and sister-boarded and puttied into a mirror of yourself, a wreck repurposed.

Gerald became a hope for a future you watched trickle away in a hospital bed. He is what Mom and Dad could give to their damaged child. He offered a chance at fulfillment that the "grind" and "hustle" had destroyed in you.

Now, the fire rolls toward him.

Even before meningitis, you learned struggle and determination. You learned to walk late, talk late, to read at fifteen. If only you had a dollar for every time a kid at school called you retard.

You are who you are through determination and spite, and so is Gerald.

But here, on the mountain, you watch the fire descend for him as if seeing your own encroaching death.

In the driveway, Mom and Dad start a generator to run the fire pump. The water tank is full, it should spray for hours.

They chain the fire hose to the front of Iron Eagle. The poor busted Dodge truck they bought forty-six years ago. His engine does not fire anymore, his blue paint pock marked, mud trekking tires flat. But he is noble and strong, American steel, and he holds that hose, raining ninety gallons of water a minute onto the roof of the home Mom and Dad built with their own hands.

With Iron Eagle left behind as the last defender, Mom and Dad finally leave. Their belching diesel truck rolls past the RIP THE LAST TRESPASSER tombstone at the bottom of the driveway. Will it be the last time?

You get them, frantic on the phone and keep them there until they reach the highway. The fire has not crossed China Grade Road just yet, and so when they clear the junction, you know they are not boxed in.

Take a breath.

You call your neighbors just to make sure. Jack and Judy, Micky, Sandy, Wendi. Everyone is out.

But what now?

Now, the roadblocks go up. Civilians are no longer allowed to enter the San Lorenzo Valley as the firefighters begin to take stands. You and Colin try to sneak in but are turned away at the summit. Too dangerous, they say. A living hell down there, they say.

Fire crawls the entire mountain range like a flow of molten lava and everything is surely gone.

And yet. Through some loophole of fate, chance, and sheer force of character, Mom, Dad, and the next-door neighbors slip through the blockade before dawn.

The fire has already entered the neighborhood, Mom and Dad see, as they creep beneath toppled trees and sagging power lines. Stew's house is nothing but rubble, but Clare's is standing. Charlie's gone, Micki's standing. Mary's gone, Jack and Judy's resolute, the deck burned off. What leads the fire to devour some and spare others? What magic spell have the survivors cast?

Branches, trees, power lines, the dirt roads a strewn, cluttered mess. But in they creep, turn by turn, and there, at the top of the driveway past RIP THE LAST TRESPASSER, Big House stands. The dormer windows look out, bright and lively, through brown, toxic haze.

At the top of the drive, Mom and Dad assess. Mom is sixty-eight, Dad seventy. They stoop a little. Dad shuffles, putting one foot in front of the other. With his balance skewed from the brain injury, that is how he must walk: one foot on the ground at all times, watching the ground, a rounded sasquatch in a Harley-Davidson tank top.

At first, they scramble, unlocking the door and rushing into the house to grab all the things they forgot in the haze of panic. Photos, paperwork, Dad's cowboy cosplay gear. Dad goes to investigate the well and the water tank, but without a generator, they are unable to pump it, no water.

Mom hobbles. With both knees injured and arthritic from injuries in the CHP, her body is stiff and painful. Still, she walks a little up the hill, up the familiar path.

And there, through the wheezing smoke, she sees the slanted roof of Gerald.

Choking on ninety-five-degree smoke and with the houses still standing, Mom unfolds a metal chair and sits on the driveway for a pause. Home is still here.

Take a breath.

And then she hears a sound, a teeny crackling of twigs. She squints around and sees nothing. But there it comes again, a snapping, a crackling, as if someone cracks dry branches for kindling.

Mom limps up the hill between Big House and Gerald, this path of a thousand trips for her and you.

Snip, snip, snap, snap, Mom squints and wipes snot on the inside of her shirt.

She sees it. Up the hill, up behind Gerald and on the other side of the dirt road, little balls of orange light trickle down beneath the scrubby oak.

Mom waddles up the hill on her stiff knees. Oh god, oh god, that's Gerald . . . oh god . . .

The fire creeps down from the ridgetop, crawling through the thick dander and underbrush and Mom gets a bucket to fill with water. One bucket at a time, she carries water past Gerald to splash on the little rolling balls.

But then she looks up and can see it isn't just a trickle, it is the entire hillside ablaze.

The roar of an engine screams through the growing, infrasonic rumble of the fire. A tractor tears down from the road, neighbor Chris wild at the controls. He stole the tractor, you learn later. Gods bless a thief.

Neighbor Chris drops the scraper, shoving brush from the gutters, stripping the road of flammable material.

He's a madman! Stay out of his way! Hollers his wife, running behind the tractor. Their home sits right across the ravine from Gerald, right in the path of the blaze.

The fire stops here, on this measly dirt road in the middle of banjo country . . . or the fire eats its way all the way to the far more defensible Hwy 9. With so few firefighters, they must make impossible choices.

Neighbor Wendi and Dad get the fire captain on the phone. We have a tractor, they beg. If the fire takes our homes, it takes everyone else.

It stops here, or it consumes the valley.

Someone listens.

You know who made the call. But they were not supposed to make the call, they were not supposed to make a stand on a measly dirt road in hillbilly land. And so they will remain anonymous.

The call, however, is made.

We're sending the inmate crew, they say.

Mom and all three of the neighbor Chris and Wendi's boys, just kids, help to put out spot fires as Chris rampages on the stolen tractor.

Suddenly the inmate crew hauls up and men pile out with axes and drip torches.

We're going to backburn, they yell. There is going to be debris, it is going to be on fire. We can do our best to send the fire back, to draw the line here, but it is going to be hot. We don't know if the shed will make it, they point to Gerald, still standing, so resolute against so many odds. Flaming pieces of other houses rain from the sky.

Do what you can, says Dad. We are grateful for whatever you can do.

The inmates begin digging, and cutting, neighbor Chris shoves junk wood out of the way, keeps doing what he can. The fire rolls and creeps, and the fighters pile up dead branches as fuel. Chainsaws snarl to life, cutting through scrub oaks and piling them up the hill.

Mom still has a bucket, pouring water one splash at a time on those little rolling balls of flame.

There is no electricity of course, but one of Chris and Wendi's boys drags over a generator to power Mom and Dad's well. Water gushes into the tank despite the power lines lying like deflated snakes along the roadways and dangling limply from the trees. Splintered and smoking black charred tree trunks crack and fall over the roads. Sparks dance like fireflies.

Mom looks to the pump shed where the pump, driven by the neighbor's generator, pulls the water from the earth.

The little pump house sits on one side of the street, the inferno roars on the other. If the fire crosses the road, the pump shed will go up, no contest, and then there will be no well to pump anymore...

The pump shed is also filled with gunpowder for Dad's cowboy action shooting hobby.

Fuck! Fuck! Fuck! Mom hobble runs, arthritic knees and all, to the shed.

The neighbor kids run, run, run with buckets, Chris makes swaths with the tractor, and Mom pauses, stricken in terror. She doesn't know if the air is hot enough to ignite the powder. Sparks rain around her. What if it explodes while she carries it?

She imagines these brave men with their shovels and drip torches trying to hold the line against a nature god when a stray ember floats past and BOOM! Goodbye, gunpowder. Goodbye, firefighters.

With the same grit that won her Top Gun in the CHP all those years ago, before women were even allowed in law enforcement, Mom throws open the door of the pump shed and hefts up the canisters of explosives two at a time. Down the hill she goes, chugging like a hobbit-sized locomotive, mind honed on the singular task. Down below the driveway, Mom flings the powder down the hill and into the creek. If the fire gets that far, it is already too late for the homes.

How hot it must be. Can you imagine? The day already pushed the high nineties, but now a backburn blazes mere yards away. Remember sitting beside a campfire? Do you recall how hot it made your clothing and skin? How dry? Consider then, all of these people fighting. The team themselves swaddled in protective gear. What temperature does their skin reach—120? 130? Death Valley temperatures?

Do they have water? How do they continue moving, working, fighting?

The flames on the hill above Gerald reach thirty feet into the air as the backburn kindles, sending out blazing meteors into the woods.

These meteors begin to fall on Gerald.

Down in Big House's driveway sits a modest fire pump. It hooks into a hydrant that now, thanks to the neighbor's generator, holds water.

Dad shambles down the hill to connect the hose. He is unsteady on his feet, especially on uneven surfaces. A few years back he fell out of the back of the pickup truck and cracked his head on a metal pipe. He required open brain surgery. He takes one step at a time, picking up one foot and placing it down before moving the other. No room for quick adjustments or speed.

Iron Eagle still holds the fire hose. Dad unscrews each segment, each section of hose . . . screws them back together on the fire pump . . . one step at a time as the meteors of fire fall.

He pulls the cord on the fire pump, it pulls just like a lawn mower or a chain saw. Once, twice, the engine catches and stutters, three times, he turns down the choke, lets it warm up.

Some things, you cannot rush.

He charges the hose before thinking, a hundred feet of hose, now filled with water, weighted with water. But Dad doesn't have time to turn off the pump, drain the hose, drag it up the hill and into position, walk back to the pump, start it back up, walk back up the hill . . .

Fire falls all around now.

Dad heaves the swollen, water laden hose over his shoulder and one foot in front of the other, drags that water up the hill, step by slow, planted step, to Gerald. The shack they used to joke about burning down just so nobody had to look at it anymore.

The eye sore, the blight. Now his child's home, recrafted plank by plank into a place of love and joy and healing.

The houses will be here when we get back, he told you.

Step by step, Dad drags water up to Gerald. A five-inch divot makes a valley in his skull. He is seventy years old, powered by spite and love.

The flames leap in the dry, crackling bramble and brush, thirty feet high, forty, lashing, biting, blackening the redwood trunks. It moans and thunders, the entire length of the little dirt road, chewing and gnashing at the underbrush. Fist-sized cinders lift from the blaze and fall, fall onto Gerald.

Fire ignites on his roof.

A sad old shack. Left abandoned and filled with trash. Your only home. His dry old redwood siding, partially straight, partially crooked . . . it doesn't stand a chance.

But he is not abandoned anymore, not today.

Mom and Dad are there, neighbors Chris and Wendi. A tractor, a generator, a bucket.

Dad hoists the heavy, heavy hose to his shoulder and opens the nozzle. And rain begins to fall.

Dad holds the hose for five minutes, ten minutes. The flames climb to the treetops behind Gerald, a wall of flame as far as can be seen. Burning leaves and debris are thrown into the air, flung like grenades toward Gerald and Big House.

Water sprays in through Gerald's upstairs window, soaking the walls, seeping down to the second floor in places. Soaking him. Washing the burning debris from his roof.

You were not there to see it. You could not get back in past the blockade. But you know Mom and Dad stood in the clutches of the CZU Lightning Complex with a hose and a bucket and said *fuck you. We're staying.*

A day of darkness comes. Between August and September, no one can get back in. No one knows where the fire stopped. You wake up one morning at the evacuation site and step into a liminal space. A great orange plume obscures the sun, not from the CZU or even the SCU Lightning Complex, but the Creek

Fire. The pyrocumulonimbus cloud covers the entire state of California.

San Francisco becomes *Blade Runner*, the air a danger to breathe. Covid masks don't work, only N-95 and full-on construction-grade respirators. But today is the day, the barricade came down.

You do not know what you are going to see when you return to Big Basin. It will be okay, you and Colin say to each other. It will be okay. We'll be okay no matter what. We'll be okay . . .

But in your heart, you know this is a lie. There are only so many times you can rebuild yourself from wreckage.

The sheriff waits at Waterman Gap, letting you know that yes, people can go in, but only residents. Eerily, the smoke covering the sun cools the raging heat. It drops to the sixties.

You drive in, curve by curve, the lush green forest suddenly gives way to the charred hillsides. The ash covers the mountains like snow, ghostly white drifts settled around black pillars and browned, crumpled scrub oak. In a terrible, cruel way, you can see the beauty in it.

Turning down your dirt road the first thing you see are the cracked pylons of Stew's house. A driveway leading to an empty hilltop. But then, you see Micki's house. One side is blackened, but not burned. Jack and Judy's stands . . . house by house you drive. Power lines hang like vines over the roads and at one point, you take the risk and drive quickly beneath a partially fallen tree, weight scarcely suspended by a crackly branch.

Turning up your road, you see black soot reaching forty, fifty feet into the redwoods. Oak has been reduced to twisted husks. The day turns darker still as the plume of the Creek Fire eclipses the sun.

The Subaru climbs the familiar dirt road, the road you have walked, biked, limped up a thousand thousand times, and everything is white with ash. The burnt pages of children's books and the melted plastic of solar panels litter the ground.

To the left on the dirt road, oblivion. The forest will repair itself as it always does, but for now, for this moment, it has become a wasteland.

Your world is gone.

You will walk up the road and see the remains of Doug's cabin, the wreckage, and the world will darken further.

By three o'clock in the afternoon, the forest will dim to the equivalency of a bright full moon. But the light coming through from above is orange, the world around you surreal, unreal, false.

You are alone here, alone in this false world, this moment that should not be. You take your time here. You know, no matter how frightening this moment in time may feel, you must experience it, you must remember.

Take a breath.

Your heart drops, for at first you see nothing as you climb the road. Ash only.

But there! The car tops the hill. Just there, do you see it? Gerald's bedroom window looking out from his crooked siding. And there, his front porch. His slanted roofs. Dark and quiet at the end of the world, Gerald waits patiently for you.

I'm still here, he says, still here. After everything. Here one more day.

You get out of the car and walk once around him. You climb up on the roof and see where embers larger than your fist fell and caught on the dead leaves, and died, blessedly died, beneath the rain of Dad's fire hose. You see blotches of cinders on the ground from Mom's bucket of water.

You open the door, and Gerald is as you left him. Water stains add new character to the walls.

The toilet is still clogged. But the plunger survived too.

Once abandoned, hated, filled with trash, and left to rot, a broken husk you rebuilt with yourself. And just like you, when he needed it most, he was not alone.

Welcome home, says Gerald.

You fall to your knees and weep.

Merit Winner: Bonus

Phantom Pain
Victoria Crane

Shane Cook lost his leg when an RPG hit the Humvee he was riding in on a sunny afternoon in Fallujah, but I didn't learn those details until much later. He rolled into my clinic wearing a tan USMC T-shirt that hung from the jagged frame of his bones but draped gently over the curve of his incipient beer gut, his body an odd arrangement of hard edges around a soft middle. There were deep gray shadows pooled beneath his blue eyes, and his arms and neck were flecked with shrapnel scars from the attack that had cost him, in addition to his left leg, a finger and his spleen. In our initial session, he described a life spent skipping meetings with his psychiatrist and his support group to play *Call of Duty* on his mother's couch. Hobbled by panic attacks, and by the wheelchair he relied on because the prosthetic was too painful, his only other regular outing was to the pharmacy, for more narcotics.

"If all that Oxy isn't touching this pain," he told me, "I don't know why you think physical therapy will."

"Then why are you here, Shane?" I asked.

He laughed without smiling. "Because my therapist told me she'd fire me if I didn't try this."

"Sounds like she knows her Marines," I replied. "Tell me about your pain."

He described some of the classic symptoms associated with phantom limbs: cramping and tingling, the sensation of having a rock or a piece of glass trapped inside a nonexistent shoe. He told me that no amount of medication touched this pain, that he could be slumped on the couch in an opioid haze, and the fire in his foot would continue to burn; he said that sometimes he just lay there with tears in his eyes, wishing he could cut his foot off all over again, wishing he could die. "How is it possible?" he asked me, and for the first time, his blue eyes bounced up to mine and held. "How can something hurt so much that isn't even there?"

"Slide on over to the table," I replied, "I'll tell you all about it."

I never tired of explaining how, because it was beautiful and complicated and more than a little bit magic. As I went to my supply closet for the full-length mirror, Shane dropped the side rail on his wheelchair and hauled his body up onto the table. Once he was seated comfortably, I started by describing all the different places his leg existed: in the flesh-and-blood limb that had been a part of him for twenty-four years; in the somatosensory cortex of his brain, which contained a neural map of every inch of his body, including the parts that were no longer there; and even in the mirror neurons of his frontal lobe, which responded to everything that happened *around* him as if it were happening *to* him. "It's only your body's response that clarifies for your brain whether a thing is happening to you or to someone else. Only your body enables your brain to know what is *you* and what is *not you*." Shane stared at me, bored and uncomprehending.

"The sensory cortex and the physical limb work together as a system," I said, "with the brain sending out signals and the limb responding through movement. But in your case, there's no longer a limb to respond. Your brain needs feedback, and ideally, that would come from your foot—you'd move it, flex it, scratch it, whatever, and that response would stop the signal. Now your physical foot is gone, but the foot in your brain still exists, and that signal keeps on coming because it's not getting any response. Drugs won't stop that. But there's another way your brain can get that feedback, and that's from your visual system. It's not ideal, but sometimes it works; sometimes *seeing* your foot relaxing can trick your brain into letting it relax."

I dragged my rolling stool over and sat across from Shane, crossing my left foot over my right knee. "Watch what I'm doing," I told him, "and tell me if you notice anything." I took off my shoe and started to massage my foot, kneading out the muscles and stretching the toes. Shane watched me with a resigned expression, sighed, shifted his leg. And then the creases in his forehead deepened a little, and he sat up a little straighter.

"I kinda feel that," he murmured.

I nodded and continued massaging. "What do you feel, Shane?"

"I feel you rubbing my foot! How the fuck are you doing that?"

"The more important question is, does it help?"

He shrugged, then shook his head. "Not really. Mostly it's just fucking *weird*."

"The brain is fucking weird, Shane." I laughed, putting my shoe back on. "That was your mirror neurons doing their job. If you still had a foot, the nerves in that foot would be silent and your brain would understand that it was seeing somebody else's experience. Without your foot, your brain isn't sure. That's what I'm saying: your body is the only thing that separates you from everyone else, as far as your brain is concerned." I stood up and kicked the stool out of my way.

"We have a lot of work to do," I continued. "Your core and your upper body are weak from sitting around, and your amputation is pretty high. We're going to have to work on strength and balance, but there's no reason you need to be in a wheelchair, Shane, we can absolutely have you walking again. For now, though, I think we need to start by addressing your pain."

I picked up the mirror and told him to turn sideways so he could stretch his leg out in front of him. "What we're going to do now is try to trick your brain. We're going to make it think that the foot it's been talking to all this time is finally listening." I laid the mirror sideways on the table, with the top edge wedged up against his crotch, the glass facing his intact leg. "Hold it there, and try to keep it straight so you don't distort the image. You should see two normal legs stretched out in front of you."

Once he had the angle right I stood back and gave him a minute. I knew from experience that this could be a tough moment, seeing himself as a whole man again after more than a year without his leg. Wearing a prosthetic can help with phantom pain—it does seem to help ease the mind into accepting the body's altered state—but I think the mirror enables people to remember themselves in a deeper way. It doesn't just look real, it is real: what remains of the patient's own body, filling the void. Shane stared at his reflection for a very long time, and I waited, until finally he shook his head as though waking from a daze and looked around for me.

"Rebecca?"

I walked around to the end of the table and started to remove his shoe. I noticed he had a Marine bulldog tattoo on the inside of his right ankle. "Normally we'd do the exercises barefoot, but it's better if you can't see your tattoo."

"I had the Marine insignia on my left ankle," he said as I rolled the sock up to cover the bulldog.

"So obviously that was a waste of money."

"Shit. Now I'll have to go get another one."

"I know a guy," I replied.

I'd first walked through the door of Punk-Ass Picasso Studios after months of idly driving by, not sure I'd ever stop. I found Ryan standing beside the giant tropical aquarium that dominated the entry, its quicksilver flashes and brilliant colors in contrast to the deep merlot of the walls and the heavy dark frames around the art that hung on them. Ryan had one green eye and one blue, and the blue one wandered just a bit to one side, so that you never quite knew where to fix your gaze when you looked at him, and when he said hello it seemed like he was watching the fish and me at the same time. He wore faded jeans with motorcycle boots and a T-shirt that read, "TATTOOS GET YOU SEX," and he regarded the drawing I'd made with none of the admiration I'd felt it deserved. After a few questions about placement and size, he quoted me a price, then handed me a clipboard and offered to take me back to his station on the spot. I hesitated for a second, and the next thing I knew, I was watching my reflection as I followed him past the mirrored wall of the waiting area, down a narrow hallway with the words "NO DRUNKS" painted in giant black letters, and into a little room at the back of the shop.

"You can fill that out while I make up the transfer," he instructed, gesturing for me have a seat at his station. "If you finish before I get back, start picking out your colors." He indicated a long rack of bottles holding inks in every color of the spectrum, with names like "Dinosaur Purple" and "Arterial Blood."

By the time he returned, I'd finished the forms and selected the five inks that looked closest to what I imagined. "Just give me two more minutes to set up here and then we can get started," he announced. I studied him from behind as he plugged his iPod into a speaker dock, pulled some supplies out of the locker, and lined up five tiny cups on his cart for the colors I had chosen. His dark hair was shaved close in the back and spiked at the front over his forehead, and I could see the black and green tips of whatever was tattooed on his back edging up from his collar. Full sleeves covered both of his arms, the right strictly black ink against his fair skin, the left a rainbow swirl of tropical fish and a giant squid, entwined in a forest of blue-black seaweed. He slid a needle into the tattoo gun, and then it was time to begin.

"How much is this going to hurt?" I asked, as though the question had only just occurred to me. I caught a glimpse of his smile as he rolled his stool behind me and swabbed my back with antiseptic.

"Most people say it's more annoying than actually painful," he replied. "But you're getting this right over your spine, so . . ." he trailed off and let me draw my own conclusion. When he picked up the needle and asked me if I was ready, I closed my eyes and let myself sink into the weight of his hands against my back, feeling the strangeness of being on this end of the transaction: being the person who breathes and holds, and waits for the pain. Being the one who gets touched. No one had touched me in a very long time.

"I'm ready," I replied.

"Here we go."

For the first few minutes, Ryan made small talk while I tried to gauge how bad this was. And it wasn't that bad, at first. He asked me about my work and my patients, and agreed that the military bases nearby had been, professionally speaking, very good for both of us. "Eagles and anchors pay my bills," he said with a laugh. "I could do that fucking Marine insignia with my eyes closed."

As the needle glided over my spine, he tried to distract me from the pain with questions. "You want to tell me about this tattoo?" he asked. "Why this, why now, why here?"

"I could give you an answer, but it wouldn't be the truth. I don't know how to answer those questions."

"Understood," he replied. "Tell me whatever you want to tell me."

"I always wanted a tattoo," I began, "and I used to think that the reason I never got one was because my ex said he didn't like them. But the real reason was that I was afraid to let people see what I would choose. I didn't want to have to own something I couldn't hide or change my mind about, so the first thing I had to do was get brave enough to pick something that was meaningful to me and stop caring what anyone thought about it. Once I did that, it was easy." He knew all about the *hamsa*, the Hand of Fatima, and its symbolism of benevolence, protection, and strength. I'd first encountered it as a gift from a friend decades before, and I'd worn it for years without knowing anything about what it meant. When it occurred to me that I could have a hamsa tattoo, I realized I was finally ready.

"Now you'll have a hand at your back for the rest of your life," Ryan said. "And maybe one day you'll tell me the rest of the story."

"Maybe," I replied. It wasn't a story that I understood, not entirely, so I couldn't imagine telling it to anybody else. A few months before, my husband of half a lifetime had opened his mouth and obliterated the marriage I'd thought I had, confessing to a string of betrayals so deep and crippling they felt almost murderous. I still held the image of his expression in my mind, seeing me react to the news, his face like a mirror where I could watch myself die. The lies stretched as far back as it was possible to go, and this—the scale of his deception, the vastness of the gulf between who I thought he'd been and who he actually was—demolished me in ways that simple infidelity never could have. If I spent the rest of my days trying to sort it all out, I would still never know what was real and true about my life or my marriage. And somehow, because of that, I was here, in this room, with the tears stinging inside my face and my fingernails sunk into the flesh of my palms. There was a path that led from point A to point B, but it was twisted and murky, and impossible to track.

Then Ryan was outlining the fingertips at the very top of my spine, and the sensation was of a razor blade cutting into my flesh, carving the black edge into my skin. I tried to breathe into it the way I always told my patients to do, but I wasn't sure I could manage, wasn't convinced I could keep on sitting there motionless while it felt like a narrow beam of flame branded the design into my back; then he paused for a second and swiped a cool wet wipe over my skin, and that instant of relief was almost more agonizing than the glassy stab of the needle.

"It's alright, darlin'," he murmured, "you don't have to say a word. Your body tells me everything." He rolled over to his iPod and scrolled through the stations until he found one that played Motown, and the oldies my parents raised me on. "This'll be better," he said with a smile, and when the needle buzzed back to life, he started to sing, his voice like melted caramel on a spoon, smooth and sweet and comforting. He sang "You've Lost That Lovin' Feeling," and "Under the Boardwalk," the deep vibrato rumbling through his arms and into me, softening the edges of the pain. Then Elvis came on, the old, fat Elvis lamenting the hardships of ghetto life, and Ryan belted out the chorus in full throat 'til I was laughing through my tears, and that was how he got me through it, until the work was done. The kindness in his voice carried me, and the warm weight of his hands was like a balm. When it was over, he helped me out of the chair and stood me with my back to the mirror so I could see the end result: a completely new landscape where my naked flesh had been, now red and welted and glowing with purple, green, and gold, like the world's most beautiful wound. The sight of it like that—simultaneously traumatized and gorgeous—was overwhelming. "That's me," I'd whispered.

"That's you," Ryan had said. "From now on."

He cleaned me up and took my money, then walked me to the door, but I didn't want to leave; I wanted to back him up against a wall, press my lips to his, feel the whole length of his body as warm and solid against me as his arms had been. I felt grateful in a way I had no words for, and indebted to him as I imagine survivors must feel about the strangers who rescue them from disaster: like he had seen me through something that had changed who I was. That he had pulled me, lifeless, out of wreckage and breathed me back to life.

I went back to Ryan again and again. Something about the process of being tattooed felt healing—an excision of grief and shame, and something else: the ghost of my husband. *Ex*-husband, I'd sometimes remind myself, but that never felt right because it was the *husband* that did the haunting, and the *ex* felt like an erasure, a nullification of everything that had gone before. *Ex* meant *over*, but it wasn't over; he haunted me in my dreams, in the forest of doubts that sprung up after his departure, in the way that nothing in my memory or my life had seemed solid or sure since the day he left.

In practically every way, my husband seemed more real in his absence than he had been while we were together, a darkness that shadowed everything else. Being tattooed was like stepping out into blinding sun: everything illuminated, everything alive. The needle's stab became first familiar, then comforting in its way, with the round, sweet melodies of Ryan's voice in steady counterpoint to the piercing rhythm of his hands, etching and wiping, etching and wiping, carving the colors into my skin, swabbing away the blood. Since the night my husband left me, I had hurt every day, all the time—a bone-deep, throbbing emptiness that nothing seemed to touch. But tattooing was a pain I chose for myself: a tangible, external suffering with a clear cause and a predictable duration. The sunburn sting of a healing tattoo became a constant reminder that my pain had a purpose, and every session brought me a little closer to the goal of becoming human again. Marked, for certain. But alive.

The Mirror Therapy was a game-changer for Shane. Within months he was mostly pain-free, even with a drastic reduction in the narcotics he'd been popping since he'd left the hospital, and when he had pain, there were things he could do to work with it. He applied his Marine discipline to doing the exercises as diligently at home as he did in our sessions, and the result was that we didn't really need to keep working with the mirror in the clinic, but we did it anyway. It was a nice respite from our other work, which was now focused mainly on strengthening his body and building skill with the prosthesis. What we did with the mirror was a different kind of therapy, aimed at making peace with the body he had now. There was a lot of pain in Shane's recovery, moves that made his scars sear and his muscles burn, undignified moments when he'd fall or fail to complete a move. So I saved the mirror for the end of each session, after he'd worn himself out.

One particularly draining afternoon, Shane pulled off his T-shirt and asked me to bring him the clean one from his pack. Across his chest, the Marine motto "SEMPER FI" was written in gothic script four inches high. Underneath it was a grinning skull, its cranium cracked by a pink streak of scar tissue.

"How original," I remarked as I handed him the shirt.

"Fuck you," he replied, laughing and looking down at himself. "I guess you probably do see a lot of these in here, huh?"

"Maybe a few. Yours has its own unique shrapnel pattern. And the incision scar from your splenectomy is a nice embellishment."

"Let me guess—you've got a butterfly tramp stamp under those scrubs? Or maybe a big rose with your kid's name and birthday?"

"Okay, now you've offended me," I replied. I pulled my scrub shirt over my head and let him see what was visible in just my tank top: a half sleeve of Japanese waves with brilliant, leaping koi on my left arm; the intricate, henna-like pattern of complex designs on my right arm with—yes—the names of my children embedded within them; the hamsa between my shoulder blades. What he could not see was the enormous mandala that Ryan had inked over my entire lower back a month before and that we were scheduled to spend several hours coloring in that very night.

"Wow," Shane said, impressed, and I held out my left arm so he could get a better look at the array of colors that swirled through the waves. "That's a lot of ink." He ran a finger down my bicep, admiring the golden-orange glow of the koi. "They're really beautiful. Almost like your camouflage."

"Hardly," I replied. "I get noticed a lot more now than I did before."

"Yeah, but it's superficial attention," he replied. "People have their own idea about tattoos, so they think they know something about you because of them. It's like being *looked at* without really being *seen*."

"That's deep, Shane," I said with a laugh, but he didn't laugh back.

"Why did you get them?"

I hated that question. I never minded being asked where I got my tattoos, or whether they hurt; it didn't even bother me when people announced their disapproval or predicted that I'd come to regret them. What offended me was being asked what they "meant," or why I'd decided to get them. It felt to me like asking a stranger about the worst thing that ever happened to them, or their favorite position for sex: a question so personal and intimate, only a handful of people would ever have the right to an answer. But Shane had become one of those people, so I told him.

"A couple of years ago my husband left me," I began. "I loved him, and I loved my marriage, so I did everything I could to save it. We spent almost a year 'working on it,' going to therapy, trying to figure it out, and every minute of that year, I felt like I would die if my marriage ended. And then one day we were sitting on the therapist's couch and he said, 'I've been lying this entire time. I'm having an affair, I want a divorce, I always wanted a divorce.'"

Shane shook his head.

"You know what's funny?" I asked him. "My body remembers it differently from my mind. When I think about that scene, I can *feel* myself fly across the room to attack him; I feel my fists pummeling him and my knee sinking into his gut, I can hear the sound of him fighting me off. But in real life, none of that actually happened. In real life, I just screamed, *How could you do this to me?* I crumpled into a ball, and I cried so hard I puked into a trash can."

Shane sighed.

"I hated the woman that happened to," I told him. "I hated that she hadn't seen any of it coming, and that she'd been a person someone else would leave. I wanted to *unmake* her, you know? And if I couldn't make her disappear, at least I could become a person as different from her as it was possible to be." I held out my arms for us both to see. "And this is different."

Then I laughed, and sighed. "That's the long answer. I need a shorter one."

"How about, 'None of your fucking business?'" Shane proposed.

"Also good." I tossed him the wet bag he'd brought along for his dirty shirt.

"I was up in the turret," he said suddenly as he zipped up his pack. "It was a Tuesday afternoon, bright as hell, but it was that late-day, shadowy kind of brightness that blinds you and makes all the dark places totally invisible. Your eyes can't adjust, so there's all these black holes, and that should've made me nervous, any other day it would've triggered all my alarms, but this day just didn't feel like that. I can't explain it, I just felt okay. I think everyone did." He shifted his leg around underneath him, trying to get comfortable, and I pulled his chair close enough for him to reach and locked the wheels. Once he was back in, he went on.

"We were leading the convoy; Casper was driving, and he was telling this story about how his girlfriend's ex got ahold of her phone and started sexting him, pretending to be her. I couldn't hear much up in the turret, except for Henderson laughing his ass off; he was right underneath me so he'd yell up the highlights. He said that Casper had sent the guy a dick pic, and I was howling, looking around, trying to see around every corner, but also imagining Casper taking a picture of his dick and then sending it to this guy, and all of a sudden there was that—*hitch*—in everything. The whole world just froze for like, half a second: not even long enough to react, just long enough for that twist in the gut that comes right before the bad thing. You don't know what, but you *know*."

"Your body meets the world before the rest of you," I said quietly.

"There was that sound, that *whoosh!*" and he punctuated the noise with his fingers, miming a little explosion. "It's a hollow sound: the sound of the empty space the grenade leaves behind."

He stopped talking and just looked at me.

"What happened to Casper?"

He mimed with his fingers again, a smaller explosion, with just the hand missing its pinky. "Poof," he whispered.

"You saw it happen?"

"When the grenade hit the Humvee, it just tore it open like a tin can. I saw Casper behind the wheel, and it was so bright, like he was driving into the center of the fucking sun. And he just blew apart. He was in the driver's seat, and then he was . . . splatter."

"What about the rest of them?"

"We lost three that day. Henderson and Garcia, along with Casper. Smalls was the fourth inside the vehicle. He made it, but he lost both legs, and he's burned over most of his body. I didn't know my leg was gone until I woke up in the hospital and they told me. I said I didn't need my leg because I was dead, and they said no, you're still alive. You were lucky, you made it." He stared down at the stump of his left leg, massaged it absently with his hands. "I think a lot about the mirror neurons," he said. "How you see something happen to someone else and your brain reacts as though it's happening to you."

"You saw your friend get vaporized."

He leaned out over his extended leg and held the stretch for three long breaths. "I thought I could only die once over there." His voice came to me muffled. "But you just keep dying again and again and again, until they send whatever's left of you home."

I felt the accumulated stories of all the broken Marines and soldiers I'd treated fall together into a picture that finally made sense. "Every time you see somebody get dropped by a sniper, or their legs blown off, or burned alive—" I stopped there. "It doesn't just happen to them. It also happens to you."

He reached out with his left hand—the one that was missing the pinky—and brushed his three remaining fingertips over the elephant on my forearm. "I think my brain still believes I'm dead," he said quietly. "I haven't really felt alive since that day."

I picked up the mirror we had yet to use and held it upright in front of him, so he saw himself reflected back.

"What are we doing now?" he asked me.

"I don't know," I replied. "Tricking you back to life."

I showed up at the studio a little early so I could sit there a while in the quiet. The atmosphere of the shop—the warm surround of the colors on the walls, the bright, mentholated disinfectant smell—made everything loosen inside me, and I savored those minutes before every appointment, waiting for Ryan to appear. I curled into one corner of the gigantic sectional couch that sat like an upholstered island at the center of the studio, binders of art and tattoo magazines scattered across the ottomans, and watched the wall of mirrors behind it for Ryan's reflection.

I heard him before I saw him, starting up the music on his iPod. A minute later he appeared in the hallway and smiled. "Come on back, darlin'." I followed him into his station, where he patted the massage table and invited me to have a seat.

"So you're going to let *me* decide how to color this?" he asked, laying out what looked like at least a dozen thimble-sized cups.

"Yes, I am," I said, and my eyes dropped automatically to his chest, and the words emblazoned across the front of his gray T-shirt: "MY MOM'S TATTOOS ARE BETTER THAN YOUR MOM'S." I tried to imagine one of my kids wearing it and found myself thinking instead of what he looked like underneath it. "So don't fuck it up."

When it was time, he turned his back so I could take off my shirt and lie down. Once I was in position, he traced a gloved finger around the outline of the mandala, triggering a rash of goosebumps that spread like wildfire down my arms. "Looks great," he said and leaned over a little so he could see my face. "Get comfortable." He smiled. "We've got a long night ahead of us."

I settled my face into the cradle and did what I always did: shut out everything but the music, and Ryan's voice, and the warmth of his hands. Over the months I'd been coming to him, I'd picked up some of his musical tastes and learned a lot about his life: about his dad, a painter whose work inspired Ryan, and whom he referred to as his "rock"; about how he learned to tattoo by practicing on oranges and grapefruits, and on himself; about his dog, Bonkers, whom he referred to as his roommate. That night, as he colored the mandala, he told stories about tattoos: the bizarre and pornographic requests people made, the surreal unpleasantness of tattooing people's genitals, the frustration of wanting a life making art but having to spend his days making only the art other people wanted.

"That's not a new problem," I said, my voice muted by the face cradle. "Da Vinci had it way back in the Renaissance, right? Artists have always had to cater to the interests of their patrons and hope they could find the time to follow their own inspiration."

"I love that you would put me in a category with Da Vinci," he replied. "But I really doubt anyone ever asked Leonardo to draw a picture of their boyfriend's ejaculating dick on their thigh."

After more than an hour, I heard the snap of a glove and the rattle of wheels as he rolled away from the table. "I think we're both ready for a break, sweetheart. I'll meet you back here in ten."

I pushed myself up from the table and stretched, then padded down the hall to the bathroom with my eyes on the floor so I wouldn't catch a glimpse of myself in any of the mirrors; I didn't want to see the mandala until it was finished. Ryan's partner, Jake, was tattooing a guy's neck in the next room, and I shot him an awkward smile as I passed their door, my arms clutching a sweatshirt over the front of my body, and a sterile drape hanging from the back of my pants. Ryan was waiting for me when I got back.

"Do you think tattooing a mandala defeats the purpose?" he asked, his back to me as I climbed onto the table. "I mean, it's supposed to represent impermanence. The monks draw them with dust and then blow them away. But that tattoo is going to be with you forever."

"Last time I checked, nobody lives forever. I'll be dust again when I die. Whoever I leave behind can blow me away."

Starting up again was excruciating; my skin felt scorched and torn apart, and we still had so far to go. I was past the point of talking, so over the next couple of hours he crooned Dean Martin and Frank Sinatra for me, the Four Tops, and Marvin Gaye. He had a voice that came from somewhere deep but not distant—unselfconscious, like he was friends with himself in a way that I'd never be. He sang like a person who'd forgiven himself for everything, and when I listened to him, I tried to imagine what that would be like.

"It's okay to cry, you know," he said after a while, when he could see the sweat shining on the back of my neck and the way my toes were curled up tight. He laid his hands lightly on my shoulder blades, and the effect was instantaneous, all the muscles there going soft and smooth. "You think you're the first person to come to me because of something that hurt you?

Go ahead and cry, sweetheart. I'm sitting here with your blood on my hands; I'm not gonna judge."

I wasn't about to cry in front of him. Instead, I breathed, and tried to settle myself all the way back into my body, and let the pain throb through me like a current. I'd spent enough time here to know it wouldn't kill me, it was supposed to feel like this, and when it was over, I would be changed. Lying there with Ryan's hands on my back and his voice in my ears, letting him console and remake me, I felt more deeply loved than I ever had, and more whole than I could remember. It was as real as anything I'd ever felt with my husband, and it was healing me regardless of whether Ryan wanted me the same way I wanted him. Wasn't that all that mattered? For those few precious hours, I could let myself believe that he loved me, and that belief would be enough. That belief would be the magic that made me someone new.

Hours later, long after Jake had left and the music had gone silent, Ryan's hand was on my bicep, and he was whispering in my ear: "Guess what?"

"Oh my God, are we finished?" I asked, blinking, rubbing the back of my neck.

"We are finished," he proclaimed, groaning as he got to his feet, "and I think you are going to be very pleased."

I pushed myself up from the table and sat back on my knees, stretching my neck out, working out the kinks, while Ryan cleaned up his ink cups and gauze pads. "How's it feel?" he asked, pulling the sterile drape out from the back of my pants and pitching it into the trash.

"Like you took a very tiny blowtorch to my back for four hours."

"More like five." He laughed as he slid another cold wet-wipe over my back and I froze, paralyzed by the intensity of the sensation, my eyes streaming with relief and gratitude and the simple, searing reality of that moment.

"Yellow always bleeds a lot," he murmured, pressing a gauze pad against the center of my spine, swiping again, blotting some more, the little pile of red- and pink- and yellow-stained pads growing on the table beside me, until finally the tattoo was ready for me to see.

"Take a look," he said, helping me down from the table and positioning me so that I could see my back in the full-length mirror. The mandala took my breath away. No wonder it had taken so interminably long: its colors seemed almost infinite, no two exactly the same, and they spread out from the center with a subtlety and precision that gave the illusion of something like movement, like the thing was actually alive and pulsing, spinning on my skin. At the center was an eight-petaled lotus flower that looked so real you could almost smell it. Ryan snapped a photograph of it on my phone so that I could zoom in and admire the details. It was the most beautiful tattoo I had ever seen.

"I think that's some of my best work," he said.

"And I get to keep it, for the rest of my life." I put the phone down and looked at Ryan, standing in front of me, not stepping away: close enough that I could feel him in my aura, and that feeling of after-the-disaster overwhelmed me again. I wanted him in the worst way; I wanted him enough for both of us. I laid one hand over his sternum—the other still clutching my sweatshirt to my chest—and held it there, letting the beat of his heart pulse through my palm, feeling the rise and fall of his breaths. And then I stepped up and kissed him, long and slow. His mouth was warm and tasted like spit, and I smelled cigarette smoke, and latex, and something human and mysterious. His hands behind me stripped off the gloves; he laid his palms along either side of my face, and I felt him exhale as he leaned against me, his body sinking into mine. I let my hand drift up the back of his neck as I kissed him, a thing I'd let myself imagine dozens of times before, and savored the way my fingers prickled over the stubble and then sank into his hair, until he stopped me and took a half-step back, his eyes still closed, his hands still cupped around my face. I braced myself then for the next thing: the sweet apology, the friendly retreat, the rejection I knew he'd deliver in the gentlest possible way. But he just smiled, kissed me in the center of my forehead, and whispered, "Hold on a second."

He turned back to the supply cart and restarted the iPod, then slipped on a new pair of gloves. Turning back to me, he waggled the tube of antibiotic ointment between two fingers and his thumb. "First things first," he said. "'Your tattoo, while healing, is an open wound,'" he whispered in my ear, quoting from the aftercare pamphlet as he spread the medicine over my back. "'Treat it as such.'" Once he'd finished, he smoothed the bandage over it, taping it all around, and when that was done, he tossed the gloves aside and ran his bare fingers lightly over the tops of my shoulders, then down my back on either side of the plastic.

He kissed the nape of my neck three times, just enough to set every part of me alight once again, and then he stepped around to face me. This time, when he leaned in to kiss me, I slid both of my arms around him, let my hands slip under the hem of his T-shirt and up the center of his back, then down over his ribs, his bare skin warm and damp with sweat. I felt the tiny ridges of scarring his tattoos had left, and tried to imagine from the outlines what they were, and why he'd chosen them. As though he'd read my mind, he leaned back and pulled his shirt up over his head, then let it fall, with mine, to the floor. We stood there in the bright light of his station, and when he looked at me with his eyes green and blue, it was almost like he was looking at two people at once, the smile fading from his face a little bit at a time. It hurt to look straight at him that way, like being seen naked on the inside and out, and I wanted to hide so I kissed him again and let the soft press of his lips and the burn at my back blot out the glare. When I opened my eyes again, I looked down at the ink on his chest, and ran my fingertips over the designs.

"So this is you," I whispered.

His body was a patchwork of different scenes: a bamboo forest in every imaginable shade of green; complicated swirls of tribal black; billowing clouds and a great full moon. I circled him, studying all of it; on his back, an elaborate, arching tree of life, hung with glorious flowers, predatory birds, and a thick, twisting vine. "Why did you get these?" I asked him.

He brushed his fingertips over my collarbones and down my arms. "I wanted to be more than I was," he said, and let his lips drift over my neck.

"You didn't feel like you were enough?" His face, nuzzled against the hollow of my throat, was just stubbled enough to make me shiver.

"I wanted to be more than enough."

He leaned down and swept a hand behind my knees, scooping me into his arms, then carried me back down the hallway, past the "NO DRUNKS" wall, out to the gigantic couch in the center of the studio. Jake had closed up the shop when he left; only a few emergency floodlights and the aquarium glow illuminated the waiting area, but it was enough for me to see our reflection in the wall of mirrors as we crossed the room. We were two brightly colored bodies twisted together, and for a moment I didn't recognize that laughing woman with the brilliant markings all over her skin. I squinted at the sight of myself, wrapped in the arms of this tattooed man, and that instant of unfamiliarity was the closest I'd felt to free since before my life had blown apart. That woman was me, and she was real, but so was the woman who'd believed in the life she was living. That person was so far distant I could barely remember her, but she flashed through my mind as Ryan swung me around to face the mirror. "Look at yourself," he murmured in my ear. "Look how beautiful you've become." I didn't hate that other me anymore; I was just sorry for what she'd suffered, and so grateful that it had brought me here.

When I opened my eyes at daybreak, Ryan was still asleep. He lay with his back to me, close enough to warm my skin, and the green branches of the tree that spanned his back stretched leafy fingers over the curve of his shoulder. I pressed my face into his hair and took a last long, deep breath of him before I climbed up off the couch. Standing before the mirror wall, I peeled the bandage off the center of my back and dropped it into the trash. The inside was stained with the colors that had seeped out of me while I slept: traces of purple, indigo spots, a vivid smear of red—the imprint of what he'd done to me, bleeding through my skin like proof. That I was still alive.

MERIT WINNER: HUMOR

The Rise of MC Menorah

Daniel Sennis

"Baldo, you're a gangster," my friend Mike said as we ran through my high school's halls warming up for track practice my senior year.

"Baldo" was my nickname, because I had a thin patch of hair on the top of my head. That was the kind of esteem bestowed upon me by my teammates, even the younger ones.

"Yeah, I am. I'm straight up gangster for real," I said.

"No doubt."

"I've got my mind on my money and my money on my mind."

"You should spit some rhymes."

"I should, shouldn't I?" I said as we rounded a corner. "How about this? *You stepping to me, fool, you're gonna go down. I'll turn you around, make your mom frown.*"

"Wow, that's some dope shit."

"Word."

"You're a Jewish rapper."

The rest of the warmup we spent discussing good Jewish rapper names, another friend Kyle joining us.

"How about Dr. Dreidel?" Kyle suggested.

"Nah, what about the Notorious J.E.W.?" opined Mike.

"Gefilte Fresh!"

"Those are good, but I think I have the perfect name," I said as we slowed down to stretch.

"Matzo Baller?" asked Kyle.

"No. Check it: MC Menorah—my raps are on fire, baby."

"Yes! It's got to be MC Menorah!" Mike shouted.

It was agreed. I was no longer Daniel Sennis, high school nobody. I was MC Menorah, rising Hebrew MC. Heir to the throne of the Beastie Boys and the significantly more obscure 2 Live Jews (performers of such raps as "Jewish American Princess" and "Oy, It's So Humid," which I listened to repeatedly on a cassette my brother purchased at the mall). Whereas other kids would try to leave their mark through epic pranks involving transported faculty vehicles or by scoring winning touchdowns, I would seek the kind of glory one can only find by kicking kosher rhymes. I would rise to the top like matzo balls in a soup bowl; I would be my high school's Jewish Pac—Jew Pac.

Humor about my Jewishness was not new. In my town in upstate New York, Jews and stoplights ran about even. Therefore, my Semitism was noticeable, and that meant it was "hunting time" for my homogeneous classmates, who smelled difference like sharks smell blood. In elementary school, my difference was a point of pride. My mom came into class, and we taught all of the kids about Hanukkah, and I felt special. But come high school, when my teammates would, unprovoked, start singing "Hava Nagila" and then try to catch me and lift me into the air, bar mitzvah chair style—the tone was not affirming. Difference in this world was ripe for mocking. But now, as I had done the year before after guys in my British lit class made fun of me for reading ahead in *Jane Eyre* and I wrote and performed for class an "Ode to *Jane Eyre*," my MC Menorah persona would transform my supposed strangeness into an advantage.

After practice that day I drove to the grocery store and bought a composition notebook. After dinner, I headed to my room.

"You going to do some homework?" my mom asked.
"No, I'm done with that. I'm going to write a rap."
"A rap?"
"Yeah. A Jewish rap."

"Oh, Okay. Sounds fun."

Fun? I think you mean "dope." You're so right about parents, Will Smith.

I lay down on my bed and started thinking of a rap. I stared absently at my poster of Pelé bicycle-kicking as I thought, what is Jewish? Dreidels? Friday night services? Bagels? Okay, well, I'm MC Menorah, so how about a rap about Hanukkah?

Christmas time is cool, I have to say.

But it doesn't match our special day . . . But Jews, we have a different way . . . But when it comes Holiday time, Jews don't play. Yeah, that's it.

This was just my kind of thing: creative silliness to craft into something (potentially) awesome to share with the world. I wrote until I had eight solid lines and then packed my notebook in my bag to bring to school the next day. MC Menorah was on his way.

As we waited for practice to begin the next day, I shared my rap with Mike.

"Wait, you actually wrote something?"

"Yeah, you think I was frontin'? MC Menorah doesn't front."

"Oh, my bad. I forgot we were talking about the famous Jewish rapper, MC Menorah. Alright, let's hear it."

"Alright, here we go. This rap's about Hanukkah.

Christmas is dope, I have to say.

But when it comes holiday time, Jews don't play.

You've got the tree, stockings, and lights.

But we're getting down for eight crazy nights.

You can't claim to have game until you've spun a dreidel.

And you can't top a matzo ball straight from the ladle.

Fried up latkes bound to make your mouth water.

Menorah lights are hot but these rhymes are hotter.

Peace!"

"Oh, snap. That's so good!" Mike said.

"You think?"
"Word. You're going to be the next Biggie."
"I'm the Biggie of the deli!"
"Huh?"
"You've never heard of a Jewish deli?"
"We live in Burnt Hills."
"Oh, yeah. Well, if you don't know—now you know, Hebrew."

As I went around sharing my rap with the team, most reviews were positive. But I also got, "You know you're white, don't you?" Or the less specific, "Just stop that." But I wasn't going to listen to these gentile grinches: I was MC Menorah, and if you didn't like it, you could suck on my matzo balls. Yeah, I wouldn't have really had the matzo balls to say something like that, but I wasn't stopping, is the point.

I began to fill my composition notebook—which I carried around with me throughout the school day in case an idea struck. First, I continued along the lines of my Hanukkah rap with Jewish songs befitting my MC Menorah persona. I wrote an inspirational rap about how Jewish people have persevered throughout history (*we rise and fall, like the tides of the ocean— our spirits stay strong because of our devotion*). Another rap was about kibbutz life. I had never been to Israel, let alone a kibbutz, but it seemed like a good subject for MC Menorah, Jewish rhyme slinger.

> *Chillin' on the kibbutz just the other day—
> doing crazy work and taking time to pray.
> It was so damn hot you could fry an egg—
> the sun didn't fail to miss an arm or leg.*

The rap keeps going on like that about the oppressiveness of the sun; it is really just a litany of complaints—in other words, though I was "frontin'" about the kibbutz experience, it is an authentically Jewish rap.

Then there was "Enough Is Enough," my antidiscrimination manifesto. This was MC Menorah's "Changes"—"Changes" being Tupac's popular socially conscious rap from the time.

For thousands of years, my peeps have been oppressed.
I think it's about time, this issue gets addressed.
The suffering is going to stop and it's going to stop now.
This ignorance and hatred I will not allow.
So listen up good 'cause I'll only say this once.
If you're disrespecting Jews, then you must be a dunce.
Our traditions are different, I will admit—
but if you think you're better, then you're full of shit.
'Cause we're all the same deep down inside—
so why you gotta front with your artificial pride?
Stop taking as fact what other believe to be true—
stop letting other people make decisions for you.
Start thinking on your own and you will see—
there is no difference between you and me.

With "Enough Is Enough," I discovered that with rap, not only could I turn my difference to my advantage, but I could, more meaningfully, speak back to the notion that the difference was something to criticize in the first place. I still know and perform "Enough Is Enough" to this day, especially when encouraging young people to treat all people with respect.

Soon I moved beyond Judaism to other subjects of interest to me—a substantial portion of which were clearly influenced by my raging adolescent hormones. I wrote a rap about the Victoria's Secret catalog, "The Secret of Victoria's." *Now you know why I can't wait another hour—those angels are so hot, I think I need a cold shower.* Yeah, you do, eighteen-year-old Dan. Then there was my inimitable rap on *Sabrina the Teenage Witch*—I had a huge crush on Melissa Joan Hart.

To My Dearest Sabrina
At nine o'clock every Friday night,
everything becomes truly alright.
Because that's when all my dreams come true—
I get so psyched for what's about to ensue.
The greatest half hour of the week—
of course it's Sabrina of which I speak.
Mainly because of one very fine dame—
Melissa Joan Hart is her name.
Clarissa Explains It All got her fame,
and now she's driving me insane!

Beyond a cold shower, MC Menorah could have used a cold appraisal of the way in which he talked about women. Of course, when it came to teenage randiness, it doesn't get more horny than the rap I wrote about matzo balls. With sincere apologies to my grandmother:

Beloved Matzoball
With spoon in hand and drool on my sleeve,
I got deep inside you and could hardly believe
how perfect you were in every way—
so warm and moist like the month of May
My lips started trembling, my head started spinning.
complete control of my tastebuds were you winning.
My lust was too strong, I gave up the fight
I had my way with you for the rest of the night.

Inspiration could come from anywhere, even the adult section of the local video store, which I visited right after turning eighteen. I went to the video store to rent a film from the notorious back room. I settled on the cryptically named *California Cocksuckers*. At the counter, I grabbed a lollipop to purchase with my video selection, underscoring the point that maturity does not abide by calendars. After my friends and I watched some California cock-sucking (which, not having seen pornographic films, made me more confused than anything—as in, why were we seeing so much penis? How is that supposed to turn me on as a hetero dude?), I took out my pad and wrote down these memorable rhymes.

Come on, baby, you gotta suck it down—
do it nice and slow; move your tongue around.
I know you probably haven't sucked a cock my size—
you just gotta concentrate; keep your eye on the prize.

MC Menorah: available now for bar mitzvahs and burlesques!

Throughout the winter, my interest didn't wane. For Hanukkah, I asked for a drum machine that I had recently scoped at a local music shop to play beats behind my rhymes. It was this small box that you hooked into your stereo that even musical idiots like me could operate. I spent hours fooling around with it, changing the tempo and type of beat, until I found the perfect arrangement to match each rap. My ability to keep up with classes like calculus and physics was pretty compromised at this time, but you had to prioritize. Raps about teen celebrity crushes didn't write themselves.

That winter I also got my first real gig. Leah, one of my track teammates, came up to me at practice.

"Hey, Menorah. Would you rap at my birthday party? It's in a month."

"Umm, sure. Yeah, I could do that. I mean—"

"You don't sound sure."

"No, Menorah's got your back fo' sho."

"Sweet!"

With only six complete raps, my ability to come up with a "set" was pretty limited, so I prepared my four best raps and hoped that'd do. I practiced my rhymes where I always rehearsed—in front of the full-length mirror on my parents' bedroom closet door. It was hard to use the term "rapper" for the lanky brace-faced white teen in a faded old soccer camp T-shirt rhyming in the mirror, but I had plenty of confidence in the rhymes themselves and my worthiness as a performer—at least performer for an audience of one's own reflection.

When the day of the party came, that confidence waned. Could I really offer myself as legitimate entertainment for a birthday party?

"*Yes, you can,*" came the voice of my inner Mike D from the Beastie Boys. "*You have to fight for your right . . . to crush it on the mic.*"

"*You're right, Mike D—and by the way:* Hello Nasty, *best album of 1998, hands down.*"

"*Thanks, Menorah. That means a lot coming from the writer of 'Enough Is Enough' and that sexy matzo ball rap. I love me some luscious matzo balls. Just remember: keep on rappin', 'cause that's your* dream."

When I got to the party, I asked Leah what I should do. "When do you want me to, uh, rap?" I laughed.

"We have a microphone and a DJ (my cousin Dave)," she said, pointing to a guy in a button down and backward cap at a small table that had been set up where the living room met the dining room. "He'll call you up in about an hour or so."

"Got it. No problem. Menorah's got you."

"Awesome. I'm so excited you're going to rap. Best birthday gift ever."

"Oh, yeah, happy birthday!"

I tried to stay calm as I waited. I must have gone up to the drink table five times to refill my soda.

"Whoa, slow down there, cowboy," my friend Mike said.

"Listen, us rappers need to stay hydrated."

"Oh, right, right. Congrats on the gig, man. You getting paid?"

"In cake."

"Not bad!"

"Now, I'd like to introduce a special guest," DJ/Cousin Dave finally announced. "You know him as Dan, but he is also known as MC Menorah, the Jewish rap phenomenon from Burnt Hills–Ballston Lake High School. Here he comes to spit some dope rhymes."

Alright, Mike D, let's see if you're right. There were about twenty kids in the living room, who all turned their attention to me as I walked up to take the microphone. I searched anxiously for a place to put down my soda.

"Here," Cousin Dave said, grabbing the cup and moving it to another table behind him. "You've got this, dude."

"Thanks."

"Get it, Menorah!" my friend Kyle shouted. DJ/Cousin Dave handed me the microphone.

"Word up, Leah's sixteenth birthday. MC Menorah in the hiz-ouse. Shot out to the birthday girl and all you homies listening: one love, homies. Let's do this! I broke into "Enough Is Enough" followed up with my Hanukkah rap, my kibbutz rap, and finished with my new Best MC rap.

> *1 and a 2 and a 3 and a 4.*
> *I am bustin' out the rhymes galore.*
> *Coming at you full steam like a thunderstorm—*
> *my talent is definitely above the norm.*
> *Hitting the bull's-eye with my lyrical darts;*
> *getting more respect than the King of Hearts.*
> *My style so money, it's truly first rate—*
> *rapping is my business, and business is great.*
>
> *You best watch out or you'll fall behind—*
> *I'm going fast-forward, I don't rewind.*

It took about eight minutes for all four raps.

"Alright, that's all I have," I said with my last bit of breath. "Peace out!"

"You killed it," Kyle said as I walked to the back of the room.

"Thanks!"

"I thought you were joking that you could rap," said another kid from my grade. "You really can. Way to go!"

"Thanks!"

"You were great," Leah said. "Thank you so much."

MC Menorah was burning strong!

Over spring break, some of my friends found me a giant Dr. Seuss hat with Jewish stars; it was the perfect hat for MC Menorah. I was flattered, though it cut off circulation when I tried wearing it while performing (apparently, it was meant for an even younger Jewish rapper). Small sacrifice for being noticed. Even one of the popular seniors, Dom, took notice of me and in calculus would ask me to "spit some rhymes." I was happy to oblige (popular kids did not acknowledge Dan, but MC Menorah was on their radar). At the winter formal, people encouraged me to rap. I asked the DJ if I could, and he gave me the microphone. I then rapped for most of the school's juniors and seniors.

As the end of the year drew closer, I had an inspiration. My final track banquet could be my chance to shine. It would be the culmination of all of my hard work finding rhymes to "dreidel," "latkes," and "Joan Hart," finding the right beats on my beat machine, and ignoring my grades. I just needed the consent of my coach.

After school, a number of runners hung out in our coach's room waiting for practice, talking running shoes, upcoming track meets, or the punk music Coach (as we called our coach) and some of the runners loved. Coach was extremely nice, yet I still felt a bit awkward approaching him with this strange request. I waited for a lull in the conversation about whether or not Coach was planning to go easy on us today.

"Hey, Coach, I have a question."

"Hey, Dan, what's going on?"

"Not much. Umm, Coach. This is kinda weird, but do you think I might be able to, umm, rap at this year's track banquet?"

"Don't let him!" my teammate Matt said. "Look at him. He's white."

"Shut up, you're just jealous."

"Of your Jewish rhymes?"

"Exactly. You don't have my challah bread freshness."

"Now just wait," Coach said, intervening on my behalf. "I haven't heard that one before, but I don't see why you couldn't. I like your creativity."

"More like stupidity."

"Matthew."

"Let's see what we can do."

"Eat it!"

I had written a rap about running, which I expanded for the performance. I found the perfect beats to go along with my rhymes and tape-recorded them along with the chorus from a rock song off one of my CDs, which repeated the lines "He's running! He's running!" to play as my chorus. I practiced over and over in the weeks leading up to the banquet. With my whole team and their families watching—and this being my last chance to perform, I wanted to get it right.

The night of the performance, I was nervous and excited.

"You're really rapping?"

"Yeah, I am!" I said with a confidence that didn't really exist.

"That is so cool."

After one runner's father spoke about our accomplishments and the great work of our coach and parent volunteers, he announced that "we now have a special treat. Daniel Sennis—I mean, MC Menorah—will be performing a rap." I walked with my stereo and set it up on a chair beside the podium. I went to the podium and adjusted the microphone, looking out on the now obscenely-large-seeming gathering at big, formally dressed circular tables: my fellow lanky long-distance runners, the muscular sprinters, the agile jumpers, the families, and Coach, giving me the thumbs-up. It was time to do my thing. This was my *8 Mile* moment. Or my *8 Crazy Nights* moment. I only had *one shot* to become a high school track banquet legend. To go where no track runner from my small, predominantly white school had ever gone.

"Okay, here we go." I went over and hit play on the stereo and the boom, bop bop, boom of my beats began. I waited for the sixth boom, bop bop, boom to wrap up and on the next boom rapped,

> *As I'm warming up, I picture my race.*
> *I see myself finishing in first place.*
> *How I'm gonna for the whole race cruise—*
> *looking real sweet in my bright yellow shoes*
> *making all the other runners look sad—*
> *and making their coaches extremely mad.*
> *I think about getting another PR,*
> *another time that is well above par.*
> *Letting everyone know who is the boss—*
> *and showing the other runnings what is loss.*
> *Never looking back till I cross that line—*
> *sportin' the short shorts and looking fine.*

The chorus came on. People started clapping.

"No, I'm not done yet!" I tried to shout over the applause. "Umm, there's more," I said into the mic when they stopped.

"Spit those rhymes, Menorah," my friend Mike shouted. I waited for the right beat to come around again.

> *As I get to the line, I'm ready to go—*
> *I have no fear 'cause I know I'm not slow.*
> *The gun goes off and I bolt like lightning—*
> *out to the front so fast it's frightening.*

As I gain speed, all you can see is smoke.
Think you can stay with me? That's a joke.
Halfway there and I'm still in the lead—
still going strong, still maintaining my speed.
Meanwhile my competitors are falling back—
they've had the training, it's the talent they lack.
Comparable only to the Energizer Bunny—
I just keep on going, my endurance is money.

I did my second verse and the clapping started again. "No, still not done!" I shouted helplessly. "One more verse."

Finally, I wouldn't be here today.
If it wasn't for Coach Button, I have to say.
He is always encouraging and never mean.
He's who gets us to run at speeds obscene.
If it wasn't for him, I don't know where I'd be.
He's the best coach we could ever have, obviously.

Finally, the clapping came at the right time, since I was done. And in this mostly smooth but maybe not-quite-Madison-Square-Garden-ready way, I went down in track banquet history. MC Menorah had reached the pinnacle of team sports performing arts, contributing a few matzo-ball-licious lines to the obscure but undoubtedly dope book on Jewish rap.

My rap career fizzled out after graduation as I began focusing on other desperate means of seeking attention, but I never left the rap game completely. I continued to rap for friends after high school, wrote a semi-rapsical entitled "Hot Jen" in college (yeah, you weren't the one, Lin-Manuel), and when I became a substitute teacher, I made a name for myself as the rapping sub with ill lyrics like *Six in the morning, hear the phone ring. Just one of the many benefits of subbing. Get up, take a shower, out the door—don't really want to know what today is for me in store.* I killed at the substitute teacher rapping game, which isn't really hard when there aren't any other rapping subs and the alternative for students to your raps is doing a worksheet. My rap YouTube videos (look for the guy looking up into the camera from below as if talking to Kareem Abdul-Jabbar) have been seen by over twelve people. But fame is not what was important in my early days as MC Menorah, and it still isn't today. It's always been about doing something I love and having the courage to tell the people who don't get why a nerdy Jewish kid from the suburbs is rapping about latkes and dreidels to go ahead and suck on your matzo balls.

Merit Winner: Passion

A Man's Yard
Robert Michael Oliver

Mr. Cabot knew that eventually he would succumb, as all mortals do, to entropy. What he did not yet perceive is the terrible swiftness with which randomness overwhelms.

As a high school science teacher—ninth grade biology, AP biology, senior seminar: genetics—he valued his commitment to facts and hypotheses. Nature, he sometimes joked, was his only god.

That, and his yards—front yard, back yard, and even his two narrow side yards—were manifestly his divinity. Or rather, because the relationship between a god and its believer is one of identification, he was their god, as in their designer, their maker, their steward. The yards were his expression of divinity and, thus, the object of his worship.

Every morning before heading off to work, Cabot inspected his yards. His journey was prescribed. He slid the backdoor open and stepped onto the eight-by-ten-foot concrete patio, the same patio on which his down-the-street neighbor, Elaine, would flirt with him when she and her husband Ralph came to dinner twice a month—second and fourth Wednesdays. Elaine flirted despite the fact that Ralph complained that his wife should stop teasing "poor Cabot" (he insisted on being called "Cabot" and not "Edwin"—his birth name—because, he asserted, "Edwin" sounded too aristocratic even though one could easily argue that "Cabot" sounded even more aristocratic, thus demonstrating that, outside the field of biology, Cabot's reasoning was flawed). In fact, that's precisely the teasing Elaine engaged in, calling Cabot "Edwin" while giggling and stroking the hairs on his forearm with the tips of her cerise fingernails, an action that sent Cabot's brain steamrolling into fantasies about stroking Elaine's hairs, not just on her forearms but in all sorts of nether places. Meanwhile, Ralph tapped her arm and whined, "Now, you stop teasing poor Cabot. You're embarrassing him."

Recently, Elaine also teased "poor Cabot" about his patio, about how dull and concrete it looked, in stark contrast to the yards that surrounded it. He had created those, she said, "with pizazz and flourish," making sure that their eruptions of color and shape were "year-round spectacular." Cabot did not mind this teasing; he considered it good-natured fun. This teasing of his patio was punctuated, however, not by a tickling of his forearm hairs, but by a playful poking of his nose, the tip of it. Every morning now, as Cabot started his daily inspection of his yards by stepping onto the pale, concrete rectangle that was his patio, he was accompanied by an image of Elaine being poked, not playfully on the tip of her nose, but passionately in those previously mentioned nether regions.

This morning was no different. Cabot shook the image of a swooning Elaine from his consciousness and replaced it with a video of mitosis, the video he used in his ninth-grade biology class's unit on cell reproduction. A microscopic cell grew and then separated into two cells with identical DNA structures, demonstrating in detail the miracle of nature. Each time Cabot viewed the clip, he experienced reverence: the only thrill that rivaled the excitement he experienced imagining Elaine being poked by no one but himself.

As he began his inspection, Cabot turned the mitosis video on repeat, restarting it each time an image of Elaine's lips puckered in his mind. He strode down the irregular, broken bluestone pathway that traveled from the patio out to the left corner of the backyard where the Alpine limestone birdbath dominated the scene. It stood next to the Purple

Sensation lilac bush, which he had planted as a shelter for the blue jays before taking their dips. In two weeks, he would plant his traditional three sunflowers, which his purple finches and cardinals enjoyed. In the past, he had planted American Giants. This year, he elected to go with a bit of color, so Little Beckas it was. Those sunflower seedlings he was cultivating in his garage hothouse under grow lights.

"Damn!" Cabot cursed under his breath, before turning and walking back up the bluestone pathway and onto the patio to turn on the faucet. He grabbed the light green hose with the multifaceted sprayer attachment and returned to the birdbath so that he could refresh its water, a ritual he repeated every Tuesday, Thursday, and Saturday. Ever since Elaine had poked his nose, forgetfulness had plagued him, a consequence that he refused to acknowledge. He blamed his recent failures to anticipate a task either on his growing old, even though he was only forty-one, or on an annoying child at school who caused him to fret while consuming his bowl of Corn Pops and lactose-free milk, another ritual Cabot engaged in with conviction.

To the right of the Purple Sensation lay Flower Bed #1, constructed exactly as he had diagrammed it six years earlier. The blueprints of his gardens, which hung in his home office, would "testify to this factoid, if asked," a line Cabot repeated when taking visitors on a tour of his gardens during the Spring Garden Festival, a yearly neighborhood event he had been selected for five years running. "If one believes in personification, that is," Cabot would add giddily, a figure-of-speech joke that usually drew a laugh from one of the tour-takers, three or four seconds after being made.

Cabot bent down and pulled the tuft of a dandelion he saw pushing its way through last year's unpainted mulch. He hated the colored chips, especially the red ones, because they appeared as if stolen from an amateur painter's latest landscape. When he planted the bed six years ago, he had attempted to rid it permanently of dandelions, digging two feet into the hard dirt and pulling out the vestiges of their infamous tap roots. Obviously, he had failed. Now, he was forced to resort to a non-systemic approach to the extermination of unwanted guests: Eternal Vigilance.

He scanned the rest of the bed for intruders. The flowers had not yet made an entrance, though several were close to the door. Planted on opposite ends of the bed were two clusters of Trumpet Major daffodils—"not to be confused with those pesky dandelions" (another quip he used on his yearly garden tour). They were the closest to blooming while not far behind were two rows of Elegant Lady tulips. Their spectacular blush-pink blossoms would obscure any sign of the trumpets having withered. On the left side of the bed, a sea of gorgeous blue grape hyacinths would arrive thereafter. On the right side, however, Cabot had elected to go with a sea of purple. In the center of the bed and needing no introduction, a lavender PJM rhododendron was but weeks away from announcing the fact that it would always be King of the Bed, another joke he used on his garden tours but most boisterously last year when Elaine had taken it.

Finding no other impostors at the king's ball, Cabot followed the path that curved around the flowerbed, which was bordered by white, bluish gray, and sometimes reddish river rocks. He had gathered the first 400 pounds of these rocks by hand, taking him a half-dozen trips to the Great Falls and Mather Gorge area of the Potomac River. He bought the last 230 pounds from Home Depot, even though he detested the idea, but a park officer had caught him stealing park property. The rocks, you see, were no longer subjects of nature's province but of the state, an idea that, as he attempted to explain to the female officer, was contrary to natural law, not the kind purported by the Catholic Church, although he didn't know if the Catholic fathers had an opinion on state ownership of rocks. His argument failed to convince the woman that the law violated the natural order. She gave him a ticket and told him that a second offense would be "far more draconian," her red lips and tongue articulating "draconian" with relish. Cabot thanked the officer for her "literate" warning and went on his way.

Flower Bed #2 began just after the teak pergola, which he had constructed himself (the blueprints were hung next to his flower bed designs). It dominated the right corner of his backyard. From there, the long, narrow bed traveled the length of his side yard from back to front, or at least that had been Cabot's original intent. First, he swept twigs out of the pergola. he kept a hand broom hung on the beam closest to the house for such purposes. Then, he cleaned the far-right corner of webs. He spent a minute looking for the web's maker. "It's best to kill the buggers or they'll build a new trap by morning," he said to himself. He found no spider, but he did find a cluster of squirrel droppings under the redwood slab coffee table in the pergola's center. Looking for the dustpan, he realized he had used it yesterday to clean up cat feces in Flower Bed #4, which was located in the front yard, right corner, nearest the street. Instead of returning the pan to the pergola's beam where it belonged, he had left it in the garage because he had been running late and needed to get to work. "No excuses," he muttered as he hustled toward his garage to retrieve the pan that he pictured resting on the table next to his grow lights.

"Objects need to be returned to their proper places. Otherwise, all hell breaks loose."

At the pergola, Cabot swept up the squirrel droppings, or what he had thought were squirrel droppings. Now, they seemed a bit large for a squirrel. Might they be the droppings of a large rat? A thought he banished from his head out of primal fear. Nevertheless, images of a large rat traipsing about his pergola and, then, lounging in one of his portable Star Gaze recliners sent chills rippling in his abdomen. Being portable, he could take the Star Gazers into his yard's open space on clear nights, as he did last Saturday evening when Elaine broke protocol and visited him while Ralph was at an investors' conference in Omaha.

She and Cabot had spent hours peering into the night sky, taking turns pointing out constellations. After naming all the constellations they knew, they made up patterns and their accompanying myths with exuberance. Their creative playfulness, something Cabot rarely engaged in, was fueled by two bottles of his favorite wine, a Chardonnay by Rombauer Carneros. This playfulness ended with a kiss, on the lips, "a solid ten seconds," Cabot later recalled. In reality, the kiss had only lasted two seconds.

After the kiss, Elaine excused herself, telling Cabot that she had to check on Ernie, her schnauzer. "He gets so cranky when he's left alone!" she exclaimed as she hustled up the rust-colored brick path along the right side of the house to the street. She did not even say goodbye as Cabot's lips tingled with excitement and his fingers, which only seconds earlier had slid along the silk of her flower-print blouse, pulsed with her breath. Irresistibly, he reached to caress those shoulder blades that were no longer there.

"No!" he blurted out before once again playing the mitosis video in his head. He hustled across the lawn to the ugly county garbage bin that was tucked behind the lacecap hydrangea whose fertile purple buds had not yet appeared. He lifted the lid and dumped both the droppings and the dustpan into the can. He was halfway across the lawn to inspect Flower Bed #2 before he realized what he had done.

"Damn!" he muttered louder than before. He turned back to retrieve the pan, checking his watch as he walked. I've five minutes, he thought, before I'll be late for work, and I can't afford to be late again. Mr. Wicks has reprimanded me twice in the last week.

Cabot picked up his pace, something that he hated to do because it reinforced the obvious: he had failed to plan out his activities correctly, not taking into account the possibility of error or difficulty.

From Flower Bed #2, he pulled three wild violets that, since yesterday, had dared to stick their crowns above the mulch. Then, he pulled a fourth. Only afterwards did he realize that, in his haste—again, something he hated to acknowledge—he had pulled an emerging tiger lily that had squeezed its top above the ground.

"No!" he exclaimed, hand trembling with frustration. "No, no, no!" He attempted to breathe, in and out. "One, two, three. I've got to do better. I've got to do better. I've got to do better."

"Are you okay?" his next-door neighbor Mrs. Watson asked, peeking her nose through the fence just to the right of "Trellis C" as labeled on Cabot's blueprint. He had pruned the President clematis of its dead and weak stems three weeks earlier, thus making room for Watson's face, topped with its early morning mop of red hair. The clematis's blue flowers were not yet there to wreath that mop in splendor.

"I'm fine," Cabot grunted.

"Well, you don't sound fine. You sound like my husband did before he went into the hospital last fall."

"I'm not your husband. First of all, I'm about a hundred fifty pounds lighter."

"Say what you want, Edwin." Watson refused to call him "Cabot." "You're stressed, and stress will send you to the hospital quicker than an ambulance."

Cabot did not respond to Mrs. Watson. He had never forgiven her—her husband, really—for not chopping down the silver maple that stood just on their side of the border between their yards. The maple's root system had caused Cabot to change his design for Flower Bed #2, which he had intended to travel the full length of the yard. Instead, dozens of ugly roots forced him to end the bed and put in fescue grass where the rest of the yard had Kentucky blue. As soon as he saw the fescue, his mistake became apparent. So he dug it up. He abhorred the idea of groundcover on principle because the purpose of it was to cover unsightly areas. Cabot's goal was to have no unsightly areas. Hence, he should never need groundcover. Additionally, groundcover, like wearing a hat indoors, only tells spectators that you have something unsightly to see. Thus, the Watsons' decision not to chop down their silver maple not only made his original design unfeasible but also made this unsightly area in his yard unavoidably noticeable.

Sure, he had done his best to make things seem intentional. After getting rid of the fescue, he put in a half circle of Mexican beach pebbles around the roots, bordered by some of his leftover river rocks, although he did sneak into Mather Gorge one Sunday morning just as it opened and rescued fifty pounds of rocks from state control. In the center of that display, which covered the roots, he installed a zodiac brass sundial.

On the night of the kiss, he confessed this whole affair to Elaine, ending his story with the fact that in the past the annual Garden Festival's selection committee had not taken off points for this "root monstrosity" when they were evaluating his yard and garden. She chimed in with "I think you've done a marvelous job with that sundial arrangement."

"You don't understand," Cabot corrected her. "The fact that they didn't take off points was annoying, but this year, this new committee with their new ideas awarded me additional points, 'for creativity' of all things. When did 'creativity' become the act of hiding ugly roots?" Not giving Elaine the opportunity to respond, he admitted he had lost all respect for the committee's integrity, and he might withdraw his entry into next year's event.

Elaine attempted to cheer him up. "Why not reward creativity? When you've got a problem and you come up with an idea to make it look beautiful, that's good, isn't it?"

"Oh, Elaine, not you too," Cabot crowed. "What is happening to our society? Problems are meant to be confronted and solved, not creatively covered up, which is what I did."

When she saw that Cabot's mood had slipped into a depressing stare, she stopped talking. She rose from her Star Gazer and knelt beside him.

He looked at her longingly. "When it comes to the relationship between me and my yards, external praise, or critique for that matter, is meaningless, or next to meaningless. My own praise and critique are all that matter, and I know that my side yard is a dismal failure."

Then Elaine tickled the hairs on his forearm once again. "Edwin, I love it when you're self-deprecating."

Cabot's mind instantly flooded with images of her being tickled, on her forearms, on her neck, on the bottoms of her feet, up her calves to the top of her thigh; and, then, advancing forward, he stretched across the Star Gazer's armrest and kissed her, full on the lips, passionately, for the aforementioned two seconds that, if Elaine had not broken it off, would have lasted for the ten seconds Cabot remembered. A startled Elaine, not knowing how to respond in that split second, did not pull away. Yet, when she felt the tip of Cabot's tongue wiggle against her lips, attempting to breach them and reach her mouth, she jerked back. She stood up. She looked at Cabot. Her mind filled with an image of her own pet schnauzer slobbering her face and, as a result, providing her with an excuse for a hasty exit.

"Stubborn prick," Cabot heard Mrs. Watson mutter as she retreated from her hole in the President clematis. Cabot listened to her clip-clap along her concrete sidewalk in her open-toed bedroom slippers. He smirked as she made her way to the tool shed, prefab Home Depot, to retrieve the hedge clippers.

"To mutilate her boxwood," he jabbed one final time, before, in a panic, he looked at his watch. Then, he envisioned his briefcase by the front door, packed and clipped shut as it was every evening before he went into the bathroom to brush his teeth and go to sleep.

"I've got to go! But I haven't finished my rounds." He glanced at Flower Bed #3 that was just to the right of his driveway. "The weeds. They'll take over."

Cabot went back and forth between briefcase and weeds. When he saw his case waiting by the door, the muscles in his right leg twitched. When he saw the weeds swarming his Limelight petunias (Flower Bed #3's number 1 resident), his left shuddered in alarm. Grimacing, he chose work over his god.

He took a step toward his used Alfa Romeo parked in the driveway. Yes, he knew that he could not afford the payments, not on a teacher's salary and not with house payments and the expense of keeping his yards in full splendor, but he had meant to do something special on his fortieth birthday, so he splurged. Then, he remembered his briefcase and hurried into the house via the patio door, which he had left unlocked.

After picking up his briefcase, he touched the front doorknob. "The water!" he shouted. "I left the water running at the faucet."

He hurried back out onto the backyard patio and turned the water off. As he pulled in the hose, staring blankly at the green snake as it retracked through the grass, an image of Elaine rushed into his head. She stood by the left, back corner of the house in jogging shorts. The sweat streamed down her neck drenching the tight, light-blue tank top that clung to her breasts. The top's fabric reached toward her bellybutton but had insufficient material to hide it and its diamond-studded button. She smiled that effervescent smile he so adored. He pulled in another loop of hose and draped it over his crooked arm, hypnotized by the mirage beaming in front of him.

"I saw your car and thought I'd say hello," Elaine said, startling Cabot out of his hallucination. He stared in disbelief:

an eternity having passed between their kiss on Saturday and his being late for work on Tuesday.

"Oh," he gulped. "You're real."

"I know you don't like being surprised. I don't know why—" She turned to go.

"No! Don't!" Cabot stopped her.

"You have to get to work, and you keep a tight schedule. It was inconsiderate of me to—"

"I do," he said. "I mean, I don't. I mean. I love you."

Elaine's jaw dropped a peg. "What?"

No longer pulling in the hose, Cabot started to repeat his declaration. "I love—"

"No!" She cut him off, the fingers of her hands spread wide and forming two urgent stop signs. "You don't! You can't!"

"I can't?"

"That's right. You can't love me. It is forbidden."

"Don't you want—" Cabot began to ask.

Again, Elaine cut the stammering Cabot off. "No, I absolutely don't want anything like that. I'm married to Ralph, Edwin. Ralph, that man who comes over with me every time I come over to visit you, remember him?"

"But last Saturday—"

"That was a mistake." Her hands punctuated her words like flashing stop signs.

"A mistake . . ." Cabot mumbled as she continued her warning.

Suddenly, Elaine's vehemence took a turn toward doubt. "But everything in my life is a mistake. So how would you know? Yes, coming here last Saturday was a mistake. I knew it before I came, and I knew it after I had come. Hell, I knew it was a mistake while I was here. Constellations? Really. And trying to console you about your stupid tree roots and having to put in a sundial. Or listening to you complain about car payments when you should never have bought such a car in the first place. It was a mistake not telling you not to buy such a stupid car. What? Are you going through a midlife crisis and need to feel sexy when you drive into the school's parking lot in the morning? It's not you! Yes, I flirt with you. It's fun. You're cute when you're flabbergasted. But that was a mistake even if I've been flirting with you the way a cat flirts with a mouse. To entertain myself. Not only is it a mistake but it's also horrible. I thought you were safe. I thought you were asexual, but I should have known better. What asexual forty-something male buys a sports car? But then my marriage is a joke. Yes, a joke and also a mistake, and you can't get any worse than that. Ralph and I don't even talk to each other. For years. We've both been having affairs. He stayed two extra days in Omaha. He's there now. It's his associate at the firm. Five years his junior and built like that model—what's her name—Megan Fox, but twice as smart. He's probably banging her brains out right now."

At that moment, Elaine checked her watch. "No, not right now. Right now, they're both asleep. That's because of the time difference, but give them another hour and you'll know exactly what they are doing. They'll be banging each other's brains out, which doesn't mean that late last night they weren't banging—you guessed it—each other's brains out. You get the picture! But Ralph and I haven't banged each other's brains out for well over a year. And that's being generous, the 'banging' part and the 'each other's brains out' part. Both parts. Not that I'm complaining, mind you. Absent the banging and the brains part, I was getting sick of his grunting and groaning. I was tired of pretending. So, I'm happy. Anyway, Alonzo down at Sweet Fitness is all I need these days. He's grade A at the banging part, and I'd give him a C+ at the brains part but that's on me. I'm distracted, always distracted."

Cabot stood there with lips open, mind racing but tongue lying flaccid on the floor of his mouth. He threw the hose onto the ground and strode right up to Elaine, his face but inches from her. She did not move, as if she were daring him to collide into her.

He grabbed the sides of her head and brought his lips to hers, kissing her passionately. She did not resist. In fact, she kissed him back, and their tongues danced like cobras to a charmer's flute song. Encouraged by the response, Cabot's hands dove down Elaine's sweaty back, pausing only momentarily before plunging beneath the fabric of her jogging shorts.

She gasped and pushed Cabot away, lips trembling, eyes pulsing.

"No! This is impossible." She suddenly sounded like a woman who had just driven her car off the road and was now watching it sink into a lake. "Totally impossible! Do you hear me?"

Cabot took hold of her waist and pulled her close to him.

"No!" she said, grabbing his hands and freeing herself. "Impossible!"

"I can be both the banging and the brains part. That's me. Both parts!"

"You don't understand." She did her best to avoid Cabot's eyes that were focused like laser beams on her retinas.

He grasped her shoulders. "Then tell me! Tell me what I don't understand."

Elaine stared at the vibrant cluster of yellow, orange, and violet Jolly Joker pansies that had erupted into bloom the week before in Flower Bed #5. A hairy bittercrest was nestled among them. "You have weeds in your pansies."

"I don't care about the weeds," he screamed. "Explain to me what I don't understand." He turned her face toward his. "I want to hear it."

She swallowed hard and summoned her courage. "It's your patio. It's horrible. It's ugly. I've always thought so, but I was willing to overlook it and not tell you. Then, on

Saturday, after you went on and on about tree roots and how covering them up was unforgivable, I still wanted to forgive you, but you don't think twice about a patio that is as gray and concrete as a prison. I . . . I can't . . . I can't accept the contradiction. I can't go through with this. I wanted to, and a part of me still wants to, but—no! It's impossible. Now, it's impossible."

She grew more agitated with each pronouncement. "No! I can't have an affair with a man who has that kind of blind spot. It's obscene. Do you hear me? Obscene!"

Exhausted, Elaine took a step back. "I'm sorry I hurt you, but rest assured. You hurt me as well, Edwin, and I will never forgive you." Then, she jogged away.

When she reached the street, she said "Hello" to Mrs. Watson, who had dragged her blue county recycling container onto the street for pickup later that day. Mrs. Watson warned her about jogging in an outfit "like that." Elaine thanked her for her advice before telling her, with breasts thrust out, to mind her own business.

As Elaine jogged out of sight, Cabot's hands flexed between spread and fist, spread and fist. "Of course, who wouldn't be upset by my patio? But I wanted to finish my yards first."

He turned toward his Lady in Red rose bush that was the "Queen of Flower Bed #5"—another remark he shared with his Garden Festival visitors, staring directly at Elaine when she was on the tour. Its winter death was losing its war against a spring rebirth: tiny green buds squeezed through the epidermis of the hard stems. Cabot reached out and grabbed the bush by two of its thickest stalks. The thorns dug into his palms and fingers. He squeezed tighter, and blood began to trickle down his wrists before dripping onto the mulch.

As he pulled up on the stalks, Cabot let out a roar that frightened Mrs. Watson as she picked up an empty Coors can from the gutter, which probably a neighborhood teenager had thrown out of his parents' Ford Rover the night before. The Lady refused to give up her bed, however; so Cabot pulled again, roaring twice as loudly, the muscles in his neck bulging as the absent red of the bush rushed into his cheeks and forehead. Finally, on the third attempt, the Lady's roots rip from the soil.

Regaining his balance, Cabot stood there like a triumphant general holding before him the severed head of his enemy. Eyes blazing, he heaved the Queen into the air as high as he could muster. She flipped several times before crashing into the alpine limestone birdbath with a bang, knocking the bath off its pedestal, splashing its water like a bomb.

Over the next 28 minutes and 42 seconds, Cabot assaulted his yards. He performed this task in a manner opposite to the manner he had constructed his divine manifestation. He went from flower bed to flower bed, pulling out a trellis here, a handful of Trumpet Majors there, and then tossing them like babies in swaddling clothes into the air, their final destiny an exploding pile of roots, leaves, and stems. When he finished, the yards pockmarked with the corpses of five generations of splendor, even the residents of Iraq's Fallujah would have thanked Allah for not having lived through that carnage.

After the annihilation was complete, Cabot sat in a lawn chair on his gray patio and surveyed his work. He knew that his principal, Mr. Wicks, would soon call, inquiring about his whereabouts. And he knew what he would say to him. He would inform him that his whereabouts were unknown. Mr. Wicks, of course, would say that he didn't understand what that meant.

"How can your whereabouts be unknown, Mr. Cabot? You're wherever you are."

And Cabot would smirk that Mona Lisa smirk and say, "I am where all mortals eventually arrive. I'm nowhere."

Mr. Wicks would wait a moment, trying to process the answer. Then, he would ask, "Does that mean you're not coming into work this morning?"

Cabot would remain silent until Mr. Wicks hung up the phone.

MERIT WINNER: DEPTH

Mayflies

Benjamin Hawley

Mayflies on a Summer's day,
Born to die
On the very same,
In a heat that never wanes.

Sun on the water
Paints the resting wings
Of a million sons and daughters,
And flitting through the air
Are the last of their fathers,
Yet to die today,
But the reaper is hiding,
Just over yonder.

Ignorant of the world,
And unfathomable seasons,
They carry out their duty
Without such faculties
As logic or reason.

Pushed to the sky
By a force unseen,
So delicate,
Like tiny machines,
Their little bodies churn,

Running on reserve,
Searching for love,
The primordial urge.

They swoop and dive,
Loop and twist,
Playfully fighting
Into winding wistful trysts
To end the day,
And start a life.

A cyclic story
Four hundred million years in the making,
And here I get to see the scene
Coming to a close,
Sunset encroaching,
Shadows being thrown,
And as I watch,
I wonder,
If their tragic little lives
Are really any shorter
Than my own.

MERIT WINNER: LOVE

Music in Absentia
Diane Rudov

My husband's Yahrzeit looms.
I hope to sit with his candle,
listening to a tape of us
playing a Mozart quartet.
But I cannot do so unless
grief's grip loosens.

Sorrow has snuffed out
memories of his cello-like
voice, and music no longer
comforts me. A violin lullaby
births weeping. My piano keys
are only touched when I dust.

The tense silence surrounding
me is too loud, like his constant
radio used to be. The dripping
of a faucet, that he could have
quickly fixed, scolds me for
pining for almost a year.

I flip on our music station,
reaching for his warm hand
out of habit. Then I push
myself to play a Bach fugue,
fingers fumbling with notes
he and I once knew well.

I risk attending a concert,
purse stuffed with tissues.
Entranced by Beethoven's
Da-Da-Da-Dum, I shed no
tears, sob when I return
to our home's hushed quiet.

Merit Winner: Love

Grass Jelly 涼粉
Isabel Li

Despite its name, grass jelly is not made of grass. The delicate leaves and stalks of the Chinese mesona plant, a member of the mint family, are peeled from their sandy beds and steeped with potassium carbonate and starch. Once cooled, you are left with a lustrous, coffee-colored jelly. Alone, the flavor of grass jelly is herbal and slightly bitter. It's a popular element in many Cantonese desserts, often served cold in sugary ginger syrup. But in Mother's stories, *leung fan* is always eaten steaming hot.

One of Mother's favorite memories to tell from her childhood is of what she calls "Yummy Street." Yummy Street, if that is even its real name, was a long stretch of vendor-occupied road in Kowloon, an overcrowded enclave on the northern outskirts of then British-occupied Hong Kong.

"Kowloon was 'the slums,'" Mother corrects over my shoulder. "You don't have to sugarcoat it with that 'enclave' nonsense."

"Mom, 'slums' is kind of an offensive word—"

"I know. But *I* lived there."

So, within that bustling city, which blazes hot all year long and monsoons for almost half of that time, Yummy Street remains a bright jewel in Mother's memory. There, Mother claims, there were food stalls and trinket booths as far as the eye could see. Vendors sold everything from pickled plum candy and medicinal herbs to fresh oysters and sweet *daofu fa*. And in the midst of it all, the central character of Yummy Street was the leung fan cart.

The leung fan cart was usually Mother's last stop at Yummy Street, one arm already laden with groceries and the other firmly linked with Pó Pó's—my grandmother. The stall was run by a lean, wiry man graying his way through his sixties. He knew Mother and Pó Pó well, which is to say that he knew their faces and their usual order. Each encounter of theirs went roughly like this:

After taking Pó Pó's order, the man would grunt his way to a large metal table connected to the serving window. There sitting on a hot plate was a mound of grass jelly, still so hot that it fogged up the plastic divider separating the man from Mother. The giant hunk was just under a meter in diameter and a quarter of a foot tall, shining glossy black under the cart's fluorescent lighting. After wrestling the grass jelly into a satisfactory position, the leung fan man would take out a gleaming knife the size of Mother's seven-year-old arm and hack off a thick slice of the dessert. The portion would then be scooped onto a Styrofoam plate and swaddled in plastic. The man would slide a tin of brown sugar syrup to Pó Pó before handing the leung fan off wordlessly to Mother, the hot jelly still sweating condensation in the confines of the bag.

"You could eat it plain," Mother tells me. "It was *that* fresh." And sometimes Mother did just that when Pó Pó let her steal a spoonful or two on the walk back from the market. Other times she would take it straight home, sharing it with her older brothers and sister and relishing in the sweetness of the syrup.

Looking back, there was always a sort of bittersweetness in Mother's tone when she recounted these stories, the kind of happy-sadness of a man talking about his love long past. Like a soldier sharing details of his home, three time zones away.

I wonder if Mother ever misses home. If "home" is still that cinderblock tenement back in Kowloon. If every morning Mother opens her eyes half expecting to wake up there, lying on that wooden bench that was her bed for over a decade. Still, she doesn't talk about Hong Kong that much nowadays, or perhaps I don't ask. But there are fourteen years waiting for her overseas, and I can't help but wonder if it hurts Mother that no matter how much she misses them, she can never go back.

"I can still go back," Mother says defensively. "I just hate flying."

My hands freeze on the keyboard. "I thought—"

But Mother cuts me off with a wry smile. "Well, there's that too." She sets down the tea that she's been nursing as she watches me work and folds her hands under her chin, contemplative.

Planes, flying, time zones . . . I guess none of that matters when there's nothing left to go home to."

Thirteen years ago—the last time we traveled to Hong Kong—we didn't visit Kowloon.

"Can we go see your old house?" I remember asking. We were taking the subway, my older sister Grace and I huddling close to Mother as she held on to an overhead beam.

"No." In explanation, Mother pointed to the map plastered onto one of the train car's walls. Her index finger tapped at an empty spot in an area labeled "The New Territories." "That's where my home used to be."

"But not anymore?" Grace asked.

I won't realize until much later how distant Mother's voice sounded when she replied, "Not anymore."

Mother and her family escaped the return of Chinese governance in Hong Kong in 1984, joining waves of other

Hong Kongers fleeing to the United States and Canada. Just three years later in 1987, the Hong Kong government gave the order to evict all of the fifty-thousand-odd residents and completely demolish Kowloon. Public officials cited the poor living conditions, prostitution, and rampant drug use in that cramped, 6.4-acre area as reason enough to tear the entire tenement city down. By 1994, ten years after Mother first left it, Kowloon, Yummy Street, and that leung fan cart were no more.

"See?" Mother crows, still reading over my shoulder. "I told you. Slums, I tell you."

"There's a park there now," I reply. "Built in 1995."

Mother looks at the pictures on my laptop screen, at the manicured green walkways and the shiny new sports center placed there. She smiles, wistful, then jokes, "There's probably some expensive tree growing where my outhouse used to be."

While crafting this story, I ask my mom where home is for her. Is it back in Kowloon? Or in the suburbs of Philadelphia, where her family had settled after? Or is it here, in my childhood house?

My mom considers my question for a minute. The notch that appears between her eyebrows tells me she's *really* thinking and not just humoring me. "I would say that my home is here. Our house."

She sees my disappointed expressions and laughs. "It's because I've spent almost thirty years here. It's because you and Grace are here."

"But what about Kowloon?"

Mother shakes her head. "The only time that that is still home is in my dreams. I have nightmares about it a lot." Mother's hands skitter nervously over the table. "In them, I'm always lost. I wander the neighborhoods of Kowloon, and everything is so familiar but not. I walk and walk these streets that I remember, but I can never go home. I know home is here, but I just can't reach it."

"That's scary," is all I can say.

Mother shrugs. "I always wake up a little sad. But then I remember where I am and where you are and then it's okay."

There's no Yummy Street in my memories, no bustling Kowloon or leung fan cart. But there is this:

Mother takes out a can from the fridge with a secretive smile. There's syrup simmering away in a small pot on the stove, the scent of ginger and Chinese slab sugar perfuming the air. She guides a can opener to the tin lip and cranks it clockwise. The lid pops open and out comes that coffee-colored jelly, glossy black under the kitchen counter's lights.

In America, in my home, grass jelly comes canned from Guangzhou. There is no taciturn vendor to slice off hunks; instead, Mother takes her glinting knife and carefully dices the leung fan into small cubes and chats with me. This leung fan has to be eaten with syrup—otherwise, it's too bitter and herbal for the palate—and it's always served cold. Mother slides a bowl to me across the counter. I retrieve the spoons. And then we eat, facing each other, a communion.

"Is it the same?" I ask.

"No," Mother says, spooning another cube past her lips. "But it's good."

Contact High
Thomas Darlington

It seems to me that humans could have evolved so that our minds worked the same way no matter what we consumed. I find it strange that we have certain substances that grow or can be manufactured that we can eat or drink or smoke that make our thinking apparatus operate differently for a while—alcohol, coffee, hundreds of different plants, and even a goo you can scrape off the back of a giant, desert toad. I understand why some folks see the possibility of human intoxication as a gift from the gods.

Deer eat psychedelic mushrooms. Elephants eat fermented fruit. Cats eat catnip. Some researchers at Johns Hopkins got octopuses high on MDMA.

I have noticed that in human culture every drug is naughty from someone's perspective and interesting or fun from someone else's perspective. The hippies used to be prudish about whiskey and the whiskey drinkers thought LSD was contemptible. The most reviled drug in recent history has been either heroin or cocaine. The common wisdom says that a person who tries one of these analgesic drugs often ends up in trouble. In my youth I sampled most of the drugs you have heard of. When I was in my twenties married to a depressive, unpleasant wife, I snorted a couple of lines of cocaine with a friend. I couldn't believe the results. I felt more pleasure than I had thought existed in the whole world.

Work and other obligations and lack of funds kept me from repeating the experience for years. By then I was in much better circumstances, living in Washington, DC, married to a more good-natured wife, and a friend of a friend, a Justice Department lawyer and regular cocaine user, invited me to do a couple of lines with him. I was surprised to feel almost none of the previous euphoria. It was okay, mildly pleasant, but not worth the aftereffects, the irritated jitteriness that lasted a couple of hours.

The lawyer was a long-term cokehead. He'd been getting high for several years, using coke in alternate months to keep from getting too dependent on the drug. It must have been pretty good coke, certainly as good as the stuff I had tried years before. Eventually, I came to believe that an analgesic drug like cocaine subjectively felt pleasurable in relation to how miserable the user's life was. In my previous, hopeless circumstances it felt like boundless joy. In relation to a more reasonable life it wasn't that special. Cocaine is an analgesic; it temporarily turns off your pain. If one doesn't have much pain to interrupt, the thrill isn't there.

That idea would explain a lot about people who use cocaine and the opioids, why some people seem to have trouble giving them up and all of the other facts associated with analgesic, recreational drug use.

I came back to Denver about the time my mother decided to move to an assisted living facility. She asked me what I thought. I said, pick a place close enough that I can ride my bicycle to visit you, which she did; it was two miles from my place. I baked bread at the time and supplied my mother with a loaf whenever she ran out. It was good bread, and I liked to think it was partly responsible for her long life. She also ate a lot of blueberries, which she thought kept her healthy.

Life went well for my mother for a couple of years, and then she became obsessed with the idea of dying. When I visited, she told me how she was looking forward to death. After several repetitions of this, it got pretty old. With each visit I found myself wanting to leave about five minutes after I arrived. I would hang on for another five minutes and then think of something I needed to do, and then as soon as her door closed behind me, I'd feel guilty about leaving so early, her voice echoing in my ears, "Don't go so soon."

My mother had never been too nurturing. She made adequate meals for her three sons. She didn't encourage our accomplishments. She expected us to do well but offered no praise when we did. I became a high school dropout without a lot of mainstream accomplishments. Somehow I managed to take a couple of courses in a Colorado junior college, then enrolled in a mediocre four-year college and did pretty well, made the dean's list, and graduated with a degree in mathematics.

I called her on the phone the evening after the graduation ceremony. She said, "Did you want me to congratulate you again?" That was painful, painful partly because it was true. I had succeeded so little up until then that I really did want some praise, and it hurt to understand that heartfelt congratulations would never come from my mother.

When my older brother got a master's degree, she said, "You should have had a PhD by now." But later my mother and I began to get along pretty well. I brought her bread and visited her, and I made a fruit spread out of rhubarb and cinnamon that I shared with her. My mother and I were the only ones who liked the stuff.

We visited amicably until she began to claim that she was longing to die. I suspected that she was actually terrified of death. It was all she talked about every visit, and my reaction was the same, either staying and listening to her for a half hour or so or leaving earlier and feeling guilty.

My mother was lonely. The residents were mostly women, and you know, old people lose their hearing in the rage of the female voice first. Plus a lot of them were refugees from Russia, so their accents were difficult for my mother to understand. She loved conversation, and I was one of the few people who spoke loudly and carefully enough for her to understand. That made me feel all the more guilty about leaving early.

Then one day I found a little packet of cocaine in my sock drawer. I rode my bicycle to Allied Jewish Assisted Living. In the elevator going up to her place on the fifth floor I dipped my finger in the coke and applied it to my soft palate. That method didn't irritate my nose the way snorting it did. I figured my mother's talk about her death would be less painful with me under the influence of the drug.

Somehow, after the drug crossed the blood-brain barrier, our conversation sparkled. Together we remembered our life in Lincoln, Nebraska. We talked about the interesting members of the Unitarian Church there. The wet, green summers of that town came back to me along with the brick and stucco house we lived in. We remembered the family station wagon stopping on gravel country roads, the sons and parents picking wild plums, half filling a bushel basket, going home and cooking them down into wild plum jelly. The jars on the shelves lasted through the fall and winter and gave our toast a tangy sweet taste for most of a year until we did it all over again.

My mother had fascinating women friends back in Lincoln who would sometimes meet with her at our place, drink coffee, and have interesting conversations. When I was about fifteen, I became able to transform into an adult for an hour or two at a time, and I sometimes joined their conversations. She had kept in touch with the long-lived friends, and she told me about their lives in her apartment that day. When I acquired an adult perspective on my mother, sometime in my thirties, I noticed that she had manifested nurturing tendencies occasionally.

Paul Simon—or was it Simon and Garfunkel?—sang a song containing the lyrics, *Get down on her knees and hug me.* Each time I happen to hear that, it makes me sad. I have seen mothers become overwhelmed with affection for a child or toddler, being driven by that feeling to drop to their knees, as if to lower themselves to level of the child and hug him or her. I don't think my mother ever did that. Each time I hear that song, I wonder how it would have felt to have one of those mothers.

Her apartment in the assisted living facility was at about the level of the tops of the trees, and it was pleasant to look out her window at the city as we scanned the parts of our lives that we had shared.

How did that dab of cocaine on my soft palate alter my mother so radically? Why were we celebrating this connection that began when I emerged from her body and continued for so many decades? How had it suspended that obnoxious habit of inviting death to come and end her misery?

When I've told friends about this event, they've said, "It was you that changed." Well, of course it was, but getting high isn't contagious, is it?

The hippies used to believe in something they called a *contact high*. The idea was that being in the company of someone stoned on pot or stoned on acid even more so, could cause a person to experience the same intoxication. I was never sure whether I believed in that mechanism. It would be difficult to explain such a thing with normal nuts-and-bolts reasoning. But I've felt it, and it seemed it was happening to my mother, and it felt really cozy at the time.

My next visit happened without any artificial mind alteration, and we were plunged back into the welcoming-death dynamic. She wanted to die, and I wanted to leave, and I felt horrible as I strode toward the door and she said, "Are you leaving already?"

Three times I prepared for a visit with the application of the magical powder, and three times our dialog continued until dinnertime. In between, the visits were as bad as they could possibly have been. The subject of those visits never strayed from her wanting to die.

My biases concerning recreational drugs had always been in line with those of the old-time hippies: Marijuana and the psychedelics were good, useful drugs, that if used carefully could bring insights, enlightenment, and acceptance. Alcohol, cocaine, and heroin were harmful and dangerous. How could cocaine give me a beautiful connection to my mother? How could it give my mother a deep bond with her son? How could it temporarily overcome what it was about death that was haunting my mother?

Don't people commit murders because of cocaine? I remember hearing about an extended gunfight between the police and the army of some Central American country over cocaine. One side was aligned with a drug cartel and one with the state, or were they aligned with two different cartels?

I was puzzled by how a little bit of cocaine on my soft palate had altered my mother so profoundly.

Indigenous people don't see mind-altering drugs as changing the functioning of the synapses in the brain. They see the plant as having a spirit, and to chew the leaves or to drink a liquid prepared from the plant is to welcome the plant spirit into your body. The coca leaves that the gringos make into cocaine the natives chew with lime, giving stamina to the user. I wonder if some of that spirit survives cooking and mixing in jungle labs, survives the flights through narrow canyons at night, survives the gunfights and the DEA raids, and can end up blessing a long overdue conversation between a mother and her son in her last year of life.

Family Portrait
Maddie Lock

There they are, six fatherless children and the spouse-less mother, all dressed up. The photo was probably taken in 1948, in a photographer's studio. The younger girls stand in a row and look solemnly at the camera. The oldest sits in a ladderback chair and holds the youngest boy on her lap. The mother, Katharina, sits in an upholstered chair off to the side. She wears a black high-necked dress, and a simple long chain as adornment. Her hands are folded in her lap. Her weary and worldly eyes are a contrast to the innocent anticipation in her wedding photo, the husband she lovingly leaned into now many years dead. The photo is the only one of the family taken together. I have it because my mother inherited it. She is the oldest, the dark-haired sixteen-year-old who holds the only boy, a two-year-old.

Flashback to a warm July evening in 2013. A group of us were in a small café enjoying *Gemutlichkeit*, that wonderful German tradition of eating, drinking, and laughing for no good reason. I was with my German cousin Michael. We were on a road trip through Germany, Austria, Italy, and Switzerland, and had stopped in the small Bavarian town where my maternal family hails from and where my aunt still lives. Her oldest son, Thomas, joined us. As we chatted over dessert, Aunt Sieglinde, a rare glass of wine in hand, cleared her throat. And changed our family history forever.

"I found my father."

Silence. Collectively we all stared, looked down confused, before looking back up at lovely blue-eyed, blonde-haired Sieglinde. What was she saying? Her father had been a German lance corporal who died on the front in 1944. Maybe she meant she found out where his grave was? He was buried in France, and the family had never learned where, exactly.

"Felix was not my father. In fact, he was the father of only the first three girls."

A delicate sip of wine.

"I was a baby made for Hitler."

We shifted in our seats, glanced at one another. *Now what?* Sieglinde's face told us she had said too much. The setting was wrong, the mood had turned. Thomas looked shell-shocked. I can't remember what happened next. The evening turned surreal. It wasn't long before Sieglinde bade us a brisk goodnight, plucked up her purse, and stepped through the door onto the cobblestone streets for the short walk home. The clinking of silverware from other tables suddenly sounded out of place.

My scrambled thoughts tried to make sense out of her words, even as they ricocheted around and around in my brain. *A baby for Hitler?* I knew my maternal grandmother and Sieglinde's mother—Oma Katharina—as the loving woman who took me in as an infant while my single mother traveled the world as part of a dance troupe to send money home to a still war-torn country. Not as someone who was involved in a Nazi eugenics program.

Thomas turned to Michael and me. "Well, now I need to talk to my mother and see if we can get the rest of this story."

He nodded goodnight and followed his mother home. It would be another three years before she agreed.

Michael and I left the café in silence, absorbing the impact on our family. All the genetics we will never know. And why did Sieglinde feel the need to bring her long-held secret into the open now? As we walked to our hotel, Michael and I kept glancing at each other. Finally, he stopped and held out both hands. And pointed to mine, so I held them out. Both sets short and graceless. We had often joked about our stubby fingers, blaming genetics.

"See, we are definitely related." Michael grinned. And we stood in the street, guffawing our discomfort away.

July 2016

As Michael and I plan our trip to Munich to hear Sieglinde's story, we take the afternoon to research Lebensborn and decide if there was any validity to "the Nazi baby-making program." We open our respective laptops and type the word into our search engines. Up pop multiple pages related to the subject. We find articles with scary titles: *Lebensborn: Secret Nazi Breeding Program*; *The Woman Who Gave Birth for Hitler*; *Himmler's Children*. There is even an interactive video game that allows players to "raise" a Lebensborn child. Called *My Child Lebensborn*, a player can take the role of a parent who has adopted a child from a program participant and agreed to raise it in the proper German way. But amid the hype we also find verifiable information, mostly from the Nuremberg Trials after the war.

Michael looks shell-shocked. I'm nauseated. Our aunt has been living with this secret for forty-six years. Now my cousins and I have to come to some kind of reckoning. Some kind of acceptance. I jot down notes and compile the facts that I consider essential and viable.

Lebensborn e.V. (Lebensborn Eingetragener Verein) became an official, registered organization on December 12, 1935. Translation: fount of life. (A fount can be a spring, a source. It can also be the vessel that gives forth something, in this case children.) Germany's birthrate had been in a steep decline for decades. World War I had taken its toll on young available men. The economy was in tatters, inflation was out of control, and food was scarce. Abortions were estimated to have reached 800,000 in the interwar years before 1935. Motherhood seemed to be the least of people's concerns. But Hitler needed soldiers.

Heinrich Luitpold Himmler provided a solution. One of the most powerful men in the Nazi Party, he created the program to help Hitler reach a goal of 120 million pure Aryan citizens for the Third Reich. His plan involved the soldiers in his elite military unit known as the Shutzstaffel, or SS. All had been vetted for "purity of blood," i.e., no Jewish ancestors, and were typically tall, strong, and fit, with blond hair and blue eyes.

Initially, programs of Lebensborn simply encouraged SS families to have more children, using incentives such as money and recognition. A gold Mother's Cross was awarded to families with eight children or more, to be proudly displayed in a window for all to see. Over time, the program expanded. SS officers were encouraged to couple with young women, in or out of wedlock, who fit the Aryan ideal of blonde hair, blue eyes. They had to be free of genetic disorders and be able to prove a clean bloodline. By 1939, SS participation in Lebensborn was mandatory, a quiet but undisputable order given along with deployment.

Himmler stated, "Should we succeed in establishing this Nordic race, and from this seedbed produce a race of 200 million, then the world will belong to us."

Munich

Michael, Thomas, and I settle ourselves around Thomas's kitchen table, fortified with food and drink for what we know will be an emotional night. My aunt sits down, a sheaf of paperwork in her hands. Her notes: Father's name and address, his daughter's name. A confirmation letter from the Red Cross, who had helped her in her search, as they had helped so many other children with questions about their lost families. All written in the shorthand Sieglinde learned as a young woman

Family Portrait ◢ 87

and still uses to write her journals. Her usually animated face looks drawn and apprehensive. She's had to dwell in the past to put together the words she will tell us.

I always felt as if I didn't belong. I would look at my three older sisters with their dark hair and sharp features. I was blonde, with softer features. I looked nothing like them except we all had blue eyes. I kept expecting my mother to tell me I was adopted. I was eight when Mutti became pregnant with HansHerbert. By then I knew that a father made babies. I got very excited when I realized she would have another baby and ran to ask her who our father was. She got angry and told me I was her child. Her child! I guess we didn't need a father. And I realized this was a secret between us. From that point on I felt close to my mother. I slept in the main bedroom with her while the others slept in the attic. I felt special.

One day—I might have been at the bakery for some day-old rolls—I heard whispering from two women. I turned to look at them and they gave me a hard look back. Even then I knew people talked about our family, especially the old women in their worn-out housedresses and scornful eyes. I ran all the way home, feeling afraid and sad. And angry. Mutti cleaned houses, and repaired the soldiers' laundry so that we could eat. She had to work hard every day and was always tired and forgot how to smile. I know now that she walked the edge, hid things about her life from us. And how important it was to give the impression of family. I asked her again and again about a father. Fathers were a mystery. And, oh, I wanted one! But I never got an answer, only hard looks.

I'll never forget the day Mutti finally told me. She had come to visit me in Sulzbach. After I married we didn't see each other much. My children came along and I was so busy being a mother and wife I didn't get to my old home anymore. We sat in my kitchen and finally I asked her again, very strongly—I demanded—to know who my real father was. She sat and shook her head, looking ashamed. Her lips were pressed into a thin line, as if she was afraid words would jump out. Finally she got up and headed to the door, as if to leave without even saying goodbye. She stopped short, and over her shoulder she told me his name, his birthdate, and the town he was from. I ran back into the kitchen to write everything down. I was so nervous I was afraid I would forget. Then she left. I never saw her again. It was 1970 and within a year she would be dead from a heart condition.

I wondered if my grandmother confessed because she knew she was dying. Or was she simply tired of the lies? Did the shame of the burden seem too large to carry that afternoon as she sat in her daughter's kitchen, probably doing what she did most afternoons: smoking and drinking coffee, her tall, long-legged torso now heavy with bloat, her golden blonde hair now a silvery gray? How often did she think about those knocks on the door late at night, the handsome and powerful man who guided her to bed? Did he whisper in her ear, did he bring gifts, did he make her feel special? Or did he demand she lie down to do her "duty"?

It is estimated that at least 8,000 children were officially born under Lebensborn in Germany, many thousands more in occupied countries. For my grandmother, no evidence was found of participation in a formal program, complete with paperwork and signatures. But I wouldn't expect there to be. As the Allies began closing in on Berlin, the Nazi agencies spent days frantically destroying all official records.

We can also assume the government-mandated program was used unofficially. With all viable men deployed throughout Germany and the occupied countries, women were left alone to tend to their families. Every day was an uncertainty. One didn't need paperwork to convince a pretty young mother to do her duty for the Führer. It was wartime. All goods were rationed, at least for the common people. If an officer were to show up with a ham, a bit of precious coffee, or maybe even a cord of wood for the stove . . . well. After all, you didn't know if your husband was ever coming home. Or perhaps you are reminded that your husband, too, is doing his duty to create children wherever he is stationed.

Sieglinde continues.

Lebensborn killed Mutti's husband Felix, the man I was told was my father. He was a soldier and loyal to the cause, but he couldn't accept his wife sleeping with other men, not even for the Third Reich. Twice he came home from the war and twice he found his wife pregnant.

It almost killed me, too.

For two years, Felix worked in Montabaur, overseeing the building of homes for the army, including his own. This was during the time Mutti and the first three girls lived in Deggendorf. When their home was finished, he sent for them and found his wife ready to give birth. To me. He told her I couldn't be his; the timing was off. He became furious and beat her, kicking her in the belly. He locked her in the bathroom and told her to flush the baby down the toilet. Me . . . I was almost flushed down the toilet!

I found all this out at Mutti's funeral. Our old neighbors told me; they were the ones who saved her. They lived behind her in the quadplex and heard her screaming. They said they sneaked food to her through the window, while Felix, a crazed man, guarded the front door. I don't know who took care of the other children. I guess Felix did. They must have been so frightened! Felix was a madman, the neighbors told me. But somehow, after a few days, Mutti was able to convince him that I was his. She begged him to believe her. But soon he had to leave again. The war had officially started.

A few years later, he came home to find Mutti pregnant again, this time with little Christel. He became incensed. He railed against Hitler; he railed against the soldiers who tended to women while their husbands were off fighting the war. Soon after, Felix was sent to France on what was called a himmelsfahrt—*a ride to heaven— which meant he was put on the front lines to die. We're not sure where exactly. While there, he put a gun to his temple, or so we were told. His grave is somewhere in France, probably a mass grave. Mutti tried to collect his pension, but she wasn't able to. She went to the army offices in town many times. I used to go with her. But they told her that because he killed himself, he was a disgrace, a traitor. So no pension.*

Young single women were also enticed to do their duty. The first official Lebensborn maternity home, Hoch Heim, was located just outside of Munich. The four-story building, reminiscent of a chalet, offered a safe place to have their children without stigma. Regardless of nationalistic fervor, sex out of wedlock was still taboo with the older generation. Testimonies from women reveal they kept their condition a secret and invented an excuse, such as work or a study program, to leave their hometowns. They had to submit to physical examinations and provide documentation of ethnic purity going back several generations. Faces were measured: the distance between eyes, eye size in relation to the eyebrows, and the nose in relation to the mouth. The women resided in private rooms with costly furnishings looted from Jewish homes. Clothes and toiletries were provided, delicious meals served.

Adoption services placed their children into "proper" German families. But first, the babies were "baptized" in an elaborate ceremony under a swastika emblem with an SS dagger held over their heads. The photos Michael and I found online depicting this ceremony are horrific in their formality and pomp. The children's lives were given to Hitler. Their value was in blood.

One photo in particular broke my heart: strollers lined up in a long row, outside in the bright sunshine. A nanny in a crisp uniform stands behind each one, smiling benignly at the tiny, wrapped bundle with a fluff of blonde hair. These are the children who would grow up in a shroud of silence as to their beginnings. These are the children who would probably feel the sense of displacement as they grew up in families—some prominent, some mainstream—who had a secret to endure for the rest of their lives. Sieglinde was one of the lucky ones; her mother was able to keep and raise her.

My aunt has clarified sounds, vague images, and the hush of whispers she remembers from childhood to a sense of understanding.

Some nights, I would wake up to someone pounding on the door. Now I know that the officers came around for "bed check," making sure everyone was inside for curfew. Sometimes one would stay. Those were the nights Mutti sent me to sleep with the youngest children in their attic room. There were other places where soldiers met with girls, perhaps an inn. One time I overheard three young women outside of a store, laughing and betting on the sex of the babies they would make. They were excited and commented on the good looks of their partners, how beautiful the children would be. Now I know it was mandated for all SS officers to do their duty to create Aryan children. But I was too young to know then that they were referring to "freiheit" or freedom, which allowed them to have sex outside of marriage. I didn't know that I was one of those freedom babies.

One night—I'm really not sure when, because the memory is so hazy. I was still very young. I woke up because I heard what sounded like a scream. When I wandered into the kitchen, I saw Mutti on the big farmhouse table on her back. Other people were around her, over her. There was a lot of blood. Red blood everywhere. On Mutti, on the table. Crimson rags piled up. I started screaming. Someone grabbed me and took me upstairs to the attic bedroom, to Christel's room. I kept asking if Mutti was dying. No, no, she would be fine. Mutti spent a few days in her bed. Now I know she had an abortion that night. Mutti was already in her mid-thirties, a still young woman with too many children. I guess she didn't want anymore.

I was able to look up an address for my father. People don't move around much, and I thought there was a good chance he may still live there. But he had moved to a town nearby. The people who lived in his old place told me they knew him and that he came by every few weeks to have a beer or two with old friends. In fact, they were expecting him that weekend. At first I planned to come back also and confront him, but I got very nervous and didn't. Afraid, that's what I was. Afraid he would reject me.

I let it go for a few years. I wasn't brave enough. Finally I got up the courage to go to his house. His daughter answered the door. I stood tall, looked her in the eyes, and said I was there to meet my father. Her face filled with hatred, and she spit out, "He did what he was told to do. Go away from here, you have no part in our family." And the door slammed. I left.

My father was a doctor who worked with prosthetics. Eventually I wrote him a letter and told him I was his daughter. I told him about my life, as a mother, and about my faith in God. That I hoped he had a good life. I wished him well. I didn't hear back. I regret not trying to meet him all those years ago. I regret my lack of courage. Later, I learned that my father had died.

Not long after, I received a call from the daughter's son. In going through some old papers he found the letter I had written to his grandfather. We talked for a while, and he seemed to be kind. He asked if I wanted a photo. Of course I did! I have it hanging in my office. At least I know what he looks like. My father is buried in Amberg, where his family is from. I was able to find his grave. I sat down in front of it and cried and cried. I shook my fist and railed against what he had done, the coldness of it all. But ultimately, I forgave him. And when I did, I immediately felt a peace in my heart. It was what God wanted from me. I wouldn't be here if he hadn't been with Mutti. I only wish he could have been a part of our lives.

Aunt Sieglinde has gone off to bed. In her typical efficient manner, she gathered her notes together, thumped them on the table for good measure, and headed upstairs. No doubt to sleep soundly. I sit and stare at my cousins Michael and Thomas. Like me, they are glassy-eyed and stunned. We are sprawled at Thomas's kitchen table littered with empty cookie wrappers, half-full glasses of water, and a bit of Grauburgunder wine. I reach for the bottle and empty it into my glass. Thomas struggles to his feet, plods down winding stairs to the cellar for another.

"I never knew my grandmother Katharina," Thomas confesses, as he returns and pops the corkscrew. "I have one clear memory of her. She came to our house in Sulzbach and sat in our kitchen with a cigarette, smoke drifting up in front of her face. I think I only remember this because she was allowed to smoke in our house, which was unheard of. This must have been the time she confessed to my mother."

He pours two fingers of wine all around. We pick up our glasses and toss it down, like pungent whiskey instead of the dry fruitiness we all complimented at first sip hours ago when Sieglinde's story began. Although I remembered hearing stories about genetic testing, Goering's experiments on prisoners—many on children—and about Hitler's obsession with a superior race, I had never bothered to look for details. Shame always crept in. It was a blight on my heritage.

"Now what?" I mumble at Michael. He shrugs, blows out a long breath. Runs shaky fingers through his cropped hair, leaving a point. An exclamation mark. Perfect. Thomas's lanky frame is draped over the corner bench as he stares up at the ceiling. This will take some time to absorb. Yet, nothing has really changed between us except our knowledge; our familial bonds have only gotten stronger.

I vow to do the research needed to understand how this could have happened with my beloved Oma. I wondered how Katharina was approached, what words were used to encourage her participation. She was living in Deggendorf at the time, a twenty-six-year-old woman with three small children and a husband dedicated to Hitler's army. He was gone most of the time. *Was* Katharina approached, or did she volunteer? Did she lay with one man or was it several?

I think back on my twenties and how impressionable I was. How I floundered about, questioning my place in the world. My purpose. A young woman, especially one with limited prospects, could easily convince herself she was doing something noble. Propaganda was everywhere: in order for Germany to claim its elite place in the world, all must do their part.

My mother, as the eldest, had to have known something was amiss. To bury the secrets a child sees and doesn't quite understand, yet intuits as being bad, would have a devastating effect. My mother suffered from chronic anxiety and depression, as did her two sisters. The memories they tucked into the deepest corners of their minds stole the peace and happiness in the lives they built, far away from the small town and the upstairs flat where the widow lived with her six children.

The family portrait. When I first saw the photo many years ago I didn't know the paternal secrets. At that time I wondered at the solemn faces, the differences in appearance. Now I wonder if this photo was taken as my grandmother's determined documentation of a family: no man necessary, only a *Mutter's Hertz*, a mother's heart. It is my Aunt Sieglinde's confession that showed me the truth. In the photo, ten-year-old Sieglinde is relaxed and smiling, her eyes engaging with the camera. She stands close to her mother. She will grow up tall and strong and healthy and smart and self-assured. She has accepted who she is, born under the ill-conceived notion of superior genetics that was Lebensborn.

When I asked my dear aunt why she confessed that night—why, after all these years?—she looked intensely into my eyes. And asked me to write her story.

"*Ich will die wahrheit!*"

I want the truth to finally be known!

Capturing Mengele
Barry Ziman

I turned eighteen on a Sunday in September 1978, when the infamous German angel of death landed next to us on Broadway Boulevard in Yonkers, New York, as we went on our way to have a Chinese dinner for my birthday.

Our 1965 red Chevrolet Impala, sheathed in steel like a Sherman tank, was ancient compared to every other car we passed on the road that evening, though it still had enough American energy and spunk to wage an attack on the recently minted yellow Volkswagen Beetle idling beside us at the stoplight.

Dad was a stoic driver, dying from a slowly growing tumor; Mom, quiet in the backseat, worn down from taking care of my ailing father. Both too old, too infirm, and too tired to capture or kill a Nazi, even one as notorious as the malignant evil we encountered while cruising down a tranquil suburban street in the purple twilight of that fading summer.

I knew the history of Josef Mengele. With a medical degree, his education was not used to heal, salve, or save, but instead to torment, torture, and murder, mostly Jews, during World War II. He had successfully evaded capture at the conclusion of that war. In the three decades that followed, he was an international fugitive. How this wanted war criminal, then believed to be hiding in South America, came to be in the car next to us was not a question for that moment.

We were just a nondescript family in an old, beaten-up car. Next to us, three imputed Nazis in a shiny foreign car. For whatever cosmic reason, our two worlds intersected at a stoplight, destinies of life and death momentously colliding. There were no other cars around us as our two cars waited for the light to turn.

Two formidable, Teutonic-looking bodyguards seemingly guarded Mengele. Dressed in dark suits, they seemed absurdly hunched over the dashboard of their diminutive German-made Beetle. Despite this awkward posture, their buzz haircuts endowed them with a certain aggressive militaristic countenance. These were the type of men easily envisioned in death-head capped, crisp black SS uniforms. I sensed the two Nazis in front were furtively armed with handguns, concealed beneath their suit jackets.

The old man in the backseat was erect, presenting an officious military profile: unabashed, defiant, aristocratic. He never turned toward us. In the small confines of the car, he kept his face forward, chin arrogantly high, too condescending to consider any threat, especially not one from a scrawny teen with two elderly parents. Despite his age, he appeared robust, with white hair thick on the top of his head, neatly combed back. That summer a recent photo of Mengele, who just had his Paraguayan citizenship revoked, was in the newspapers. In my mind, the photo corresponded with the stern visage of the man in the backseat.

Before that moment, or in the years since, I never experienced proximity to metaphysical evil—a sinister presence so manifest that its malevolence was perceptible on the skin. The hair on my arms bristled, like a physiological response to some kind of satanic static emitting from the car next to us. The intense, double-barreled stare directed at us from the two men in front and the indifferent demeanor of the old man in back seemed suspended in time. With this mutual exchange of inimical scrutiny, we waited, paused on the precipice of some physical action or for the light to become green.

The driver of the car reached into his jacket, prepared to extract a weapon, so I thought. To secure the Impala on the Bronx streets, my father used an adjustable iron rod, curved at both ends, about four feet long, that braced and locked the steering wheel to the brake. This crude but potentially lethal instrument lay at my feet, on the front passenger side. I reached down to grab it. I could envision smashing their car, cracking the heads of the two bodyguards, and victoriously capturing Mengele. On my eighteenth birthday, I felt impervious to bullets. As I reached down for the steel club their engine throttled loudly, and the Volkswagen sped through the red light. I vividly remember the terse conversation in our car.

"Those are three Nazis in the car. I think Mengele is in the backseat," I said as I turned toward my parents. I didn't need to elaborate.

"I felt they were Nazis too!" Mother exclaimed from the backseat.

"Yes, they were Nazis," Father said with succinct disgust, but not shock.

All three of us had the same palpable sense.

"The hair on my arms is standing up," I observed to my parents.

"My hair too; I felt it. I felt cold shakes," said Mother shrilly, in horror.

"I could feel the chill from them," said Dad nonchalantly, as if discussing the weather.

"Those men are Nazis and that's Josef Mengele in the backseat. We need to chase him," I implored.

"I'm done chasing Nazis," Dad firmly stated as the light turned green, and he slowly accelerated the Chevy through the intersection.

"You were stationed in Fort Lauderdale during the war. I'm certain that is Mengele. We need to get the car's license at least," I rebuked and urged.

"I am too old and too sick to chase anyone," was his nonplussed response.

Their Volkswagen vanished in the distance, blocks beyond us. We headed on to the Chinese restaurant for dinner and sat down to eat as if the entire episode was a dismissible, collective delusion. While feasting on eggrolls, fried rice, tangy chicken, and barbecued ribs, we considered a sighting that dampened our mood. We mused in dispassionate conversation, over sumptuous cuisine and Szechuan aromas, that it was an erroneous inference, a folly of projected phobia and irrational imagination.

Unspoken over dinner was my thought that the villainous, almost supernatural, appearance of Mengele in the car next to us was not entirely hallucinatory, but a conjuring wrought from subliminal fear and frustration over the cancer consuming my father and the dire condition of our fragile family. In an audacious moment, armed with a hefty metal weapon, I felt empowered to act for countless victims; I was powerless against the implacable growth buried in my father's chest.

Following my father's death, respected international news services ran stories asserting that the Nazi fugitive Mengele was indeed seen by multiple witnesses in Yonkers, New York, in the fall of 1978. His Westchester residence—the alleged hideout—not far from the Chinese restaurant. One major tabloid published a photo of the Mt. Kisco home he was reportedly using, owned by a subsidiary of his family's agricultural firm in Germany. The timing and proximity of other witnesses' sightings made our encounter credible, if not validated in my mind. The year following our sighting, as a still-elusive fugitive, Mengele reportedly died while recreationally swimming in Brazil—a seemingly idyllic demise that drowned with him any true, punitive justice for those he mutilated or murdered.

With four decades elapsed, I can reflect upon that pivotal moment when I could have perhaps captured, or killed, one of the last century's most notorious war criminals, an absolute embodiment of ethereal evil: a man responsible for metastasizing cruelty and death, a vicious cancer upon humanity itself, in a world war that ended only with an effulgent bomb blast of atomic radiation.

For those with an aching void in the spiritual soul, we seek a life infused with moral meaning and residual, righteous purpose. Justice is an envious, virtuous legacy, granted by so many, and for some at their own mortal expense. But for those like me, who will leave no progeny behind, we are unsure of our existential bequeathment to humanity. We ponder our purpose while we await the inevitable fate that will befall us all in some form, benign or not.

Of course, I could not know at eighteen what purpose I was to fulfill or fail. While Mengele's bodyguards and their bullets might have cut me down and added another to their millions slaughtered, I can now retrospectively measure my mortality against all I might have lost that day. In the imprecise calculus of whether a life has been well lived, I regretfully wish, in the random convergence of our paths, I had intrepidly acted.

That was the thing about evil back then—you could be a bystander, or you could reflexively take action, seizing a moral imperative in an inspired moment, hoping your instinct is right about what you think you see and feel, and maybe, in some small way, altering humanity for the better. Of course, that was 1978. Today, with technology, you can just facilely capture any evil before you on a phone, post it to the internet, and wait for the world to react, if it does at all, maybe creating a reprieve from the cancer around us or within that can slowly kill us.

A Story My Mother Will Never Hear
Valentina Gnup

for Eleanor Gnup, 1927–2022

In 1964 my mother bought a lifetime subscription
to *Gourmet* magazine. It cost fifty dollars,
which was a lot in those days, but she loved browsing
through the slick pages of food photos and sitting up
in bed at night copying recipes onto 3x5 cards.

When other hosts and hostesses were serving 1960s staples
like tuna casserole and salisbury steak,
her friends were dining on beef tongue in blackberry sauce
with a side of shiitake and leek strudel—
she loved her reputation as a *gourmet chef.*

Every month for forty-five years, a new *Gourmet* arrived,
always a little stack displayed on the coffee table.
After three decades of monthly magazines,
my mother began boasting about her investment—
it was the best bargain of my life!

When the magazine stopped publishing in 2009,
we all thought the subscription was over, but no,
Bon Appétit magazine showed up and continued
until yesterday, when I called the publisher
to cancel my mom's subscription.

Lydia, the woman who spoke with me offered
her condolences for losing my 95-year-old mother.
When she looked up my mom's account,
she told me (with a bit of shock in her voice)
that subscription is good until 2044.

We calculated a lifetime subscription is eighty years—
she probably received over 2,000 dollars' worth of magazines,
as the newsstand price climbed steadily over six decades.
And my mother would love this part the best—
Lydia issued me a thirteen-dollar refund.

Childhood
Shawn Bell

Childhood is Disney movies and juice boxes. It's doing homework with Maddy while eating Goldfish. Childhood is the excitement of starting third grade with Mrs. Baker, mixed with the sadness of leaving second grade with Ms. White. Childhood is camping in the tent in Emma's backyard, laughing until the wee hours of the morning. It's having a Best Friends Club that you exclude Kim from because she's annoying. Childhood is playing twelve-square during recess with fifth-grade buddies. It's the ecstasy of making it to A square with your buddy as she hands you the ball and says you can make the rules.

Childhood is your first crush. It's the agony of pure, unadulterated infatuation. It's doodles on notebook paper with your initials surrounded by hearts. It's trying out your crush's last name to see if you two should get married. Nick will never know you exist. You'll love him forever and this will be your heart's eternal torment. You'll grow up, marry someone else, maybe a nice accountant named Tim, and have a few kids, but your heart will always burn deeply for Nick.

Childhood is forgetting about Nick and dating Kyle the following year. It's starting high school with a boyfriend, which is a big deal. Kyle kisses you on the cheek, but you're afraid to kiss him on the lips. You sit behind Ella in math class, and every time Mrs. O'Brian gives you time to start your homework, you finish three problems and spend the rest of the class chatting about Ella's newest love interest. You break up with Kyle before your one-year anniversary because he's taking this whole thing way too seriously.

Childhood is church youth retreats and ropes courses. Staying up too late and telling secrets. It's testing your limits. It's forging bonds with new friends. It's working as a team and then returning to the safety and comfort of your cliques.

Childhood is wearing heart earrings for Valentine's Day. You have a new boyfriend. His name is Chase, and it was love at first sight. Chase gives you a teddy bear for Valentine's Day, a clear declaration of his undying love. You sail through first period on a cloud of incandescent joy because you and Chase are meant to be.

Childhood is sitting in math during second period and hearing firecrackers in the hallway. It's trying to understand why there are firecrackers inside the building. An ashen look comes over Mrs. O'Brian's face as she shakily tells everyone to get under their desks. She locks the door and turns the lights out. It's getting louder. It's not firecrackers. You grab the teddy bear and your phone as you crouch on the floor, your heart pounding in your ears, choosing to believe that your desk is an adequate shield.

Childhood is watching three kids film the chaos on their phones. Texting your mom that you love her. The shattering noise of the window in the classroom door. The burnt, acrid scent of sulphur fills your nostrils until you can't breathe. Everything is flashing and loud and too fast and too slow at the same time and there are screams and pops and crashes. You are not here. This is not happening. You close your eyes and hug the bear, praying out loud because you are going to die.

Childhood is lost time. You don't know how long your eyes were closed, but you hear voices. People burst into the room, asking if anyone is hurt, but you have forgotten how to speak. The eerie gray dust is illuminated in the beams of their flashlights. The police tell everyone to get up, so you turn to Ella and tell her that it's okay now, to get up and come with you. She doesn't move. Something isn't right. Nothing is right. Ella isn't getting up and there's dark liquid on the floor around her and you refuse to put the pieces together because she just needs to open her eyes and come with you. You're screaming her name because she didn't even finish telling you about making out with Thomas and now she's not moving and you're still screaming and the police are dragging you out of the room as someone asks where Mrs. O'Brian is. There's no movement from behind her desk.

Childhood is running outside with the other kids across the football field to the parking lot across the street. Your hands and feet are numb. You feel your pocket buzz. It's a text from your mom, "Love you too honey. Have a good day!" It feels like something is pressing on your chest and there are sirens and ambulances and helicopters and news crews. You can't breathe.

Childhood is more lost time. Someone is hugging you and her hot tears soak your shirt. It's Maddy. She's found you and she's saying she's so glad you're okay, but her voice sounds far away, and you're not okay. You don't know how long it's been but when you look down at your phone you have four new text messages from your mom. "Oh my god." "Are you ok?!" "WHAT IS GOING ON" "WHERE ARE YOU??" Autopilot kicks in and you quickly type back "I'm ok" but nothing's okay and people are gone and something happened. Someone did this and you are scared but you don't know what to do and you still can't breathe. You realize you're still hugging the teddy bear.

Chase.

Childhood is a stranger wrapping a blanket around you and telling you to sit down while you scream to anyone who can hear to find Chase. You need your mom and if only she were here, she could wrap her arms around you and her familiar scent could banish the darkness and make you feel safe and warm inside before the tears have even dried. But you are alone and scared and numb and covered in a strange dust and you still can't breathe.

Childhood is thoughts and prayers.

Childhood is ~~Disney movies and juice boxes starting third grade camping out in the tent playing during recess your first crush forgetting church youth retreats wearing heart earrings hearing firecrackers in the hallway watching kids running outside a stranger screaming thoughts and prayers.~~

Childhood is lost time.
Childhood is lost ~~time~~.
Childhood is ~~lost time~~.
Childhood ~~is lost time~~.
Child~~hood is lost time~~.
~~Childhood is lost time.~~

You still can't breathe.

Hoary Homage
Mandi "Monster" Hidalgo

The recent discovery of silver strands
Starting to appear near my temples
Amidst the sea of fiery locks upon my head
Has created joy in me
That I had not expected
And most do not understand.

   "How can you be excited
   About obvious signs
   Of aging and deterioration?"

      Because when I was 11 years old,
      It was the first time I ever thought,
      "I want to die,"
      And though I lacked the guts
      To ever draw a blade over my wrist,
      I began to cut myself in other ways
      Providing myself with little deaths
      And big reminders that I was alive
      And that Life is pain.

      Because at 14 years old
      I thought half a bottle of aspirin
      Might be enough to do me in
      And spent the next several hours
      Purging myself of those thoughts
      And the entire contents of my stomach.

Because at 20 years old,
Living in an abusive situation
And feeling worse than ever,
Russian roulette sounded like fun,
And after three strikes and no bullet,
I decided that Life wasn't done with me yet
And put down the gun.

Because when I was 22 years old
And going through the trauma
Of surviving an assault on everything I am,
I decided that it was time
To get reacquainted with a blade,
And I took my old friend out
And with the blade now dull
I could never work my way through
The fleshy shield on my wrist,
And though damage was done,
I never gained entry
To that main pulse running up my arm.

Because for most of my 20s
It sounded like a better idea
To slowly poison myself
With drugs and alcohol
Because a slow, numb death
Was better than failing at a quick one
Or living a long life.

Because the idea of dying
Didn't sound unappealing
Until I was well in my 30s.

Because my brain still romanticizes
The idea of going out on my own terms
And escaping this existence,
Or at least fleeing this realm.

Because I have been
So intensely committed to Death
That I never dreamed
That I would ever live
To see the day
That my hair started to turn gray.
—*You see signs of aging and deterioration,*
But I see signs of living.

Always Thought My Life as a Documentary/What Would They Say

Demetrius Buckley

He had those big beautiful brown eyes,
those kinda eyes that looked jumbled, perplexed, evil
if I must say.

It's very clear that I tried to love him
more than his mother. Why she didn't love him
I didn't really know,
but I yearned for his sensitive heart, even if
he wasn't important to anyone in particular.

She peeks at the camera with her puffy eyes—not from crying, but from waiting, from not sleeping for this interview

He put his hands on me bad one night. Lost his damn mind.
His dopehouse had got raided when I served
an undercover or some girl spurning me away
from her trick or late-night, fuck-free, dope rest
—my eye swelled around a week of mascara, my hazelnut
eye that gazed upon this man I adored,
powdered with a color that barely shaded
my beautiful unapologetic complexion. I
trusted that fool with my soul.

His hard body weighing on all my soft comforts
made it go away, but not the purple-black swell,
the pain that I could be hurt by him
whenever he wanted to hurt me again.

The night be full of many stars.
God was on my juicy tongue
like holy words you'd only hear in churches,
and I swear I was the only thing left for him to praise.
And I was. And I was. He had nobody but his demons. Had
demons nobody had. Had and have and I couldn't leave him
with his self or with them or with—the better woman
would've packed up her stuff, stepped away
from a niggah like that. You know the ones
a favorite cousin warns you of, then
fuck him as soon as you turn
him loose—those low-powered men who

fall so hard the earth trembles, like the bodies he'd stood over.

The falling out was how I learned how to get away from him.
I gathered my stuff and left no note
to find that I'd been emptied many days ago,
and to think . . .

The camera switches over to a man middle-aged, wearing a blue Polo shirt. A flashback to a neighborhood riddled with burned-down homes

I'm his best friend—used to be. What do I know about that niggah?
I couldn't tell you if I wanted to. But he was always dark,
ate the night up like a small bright.
A cloud followed him, one that was alive,
that protected him from intervention, from

consciousness. He shot
a crackhead over his pitbull, beat a fiend for giving him
fake 20s. A week later
he asked that same fiend if he needed help
not getting high.
He was like that. Too loyal almost. Too brave to stand
in a field of Jasmin. Too fool-hearted, but that
was the best part of him.
He laughed on long blocks, threw his hands up
at ice cream trucks and bought
all the kids popsicles. He knew everybody, man,
except himself.

The camera switches to a woman, short, pretty, with green eyes

Him, he different. He ran his fingers through my damp hair
the day we met,
made me feel somtin' so deep in me
I couldn't call it. It ain't love though. It's more;
it's like having to pee real bad but can't. I was with him
when you didn't see him, when you couldn't see him.
I'm the girl he picked up one humid night, found me hooking
for food, for pocket money, for car rides. I hooked
because it made me feel good to be a woman, hooked because
the man my auntie dated said I could make a man
so happy just by lying there quietly, my then 11-year-old
punani, legs far apart. Him/he
said I'm better than that,
thought I stranded that night because I was sad, beautiful—
he always called me beautiful and stuff.

Between my caramel sweet thighs
where he needs me,
I feel beautiful, tasty, delicious. He protected me from the hungry

men who'd beat and rape me. He wanted
to save everybody, I could tell, wanted to right
what he deemed wrong, but he da one needin' saving.
He could be crazy at times, but I like to stick around
to see what he'd do, then ask him why when he'd done it.
He needed
something warm with all his coldness.
And there I blanketed him with my world.

The camera flips to a field, an urban field littered with used condoms,
empty juice containers, then back to her

I lost the baby in June. Lost something in summer.
I lost a child like a heel, a phone number, a pair of sunglasses
when on top of my head. I lost my baby like an eyelash,
a pair of brand-new earrings. He don't know.
I won't tell him because he shouldn't put life
in a woman like me. We can't bring another him
into this world, another me. I lost our baby in a flush,
him to a pipeline made for a . . . him, he different.

Intercession
John Arthur Neal

So there I was, driving along, minding my own business, on my way to work, when a cop car comes whipping out of an alley—no sirens, no lights—and clips my back bumper. As I spun, my foot instinctively jammed the gas pedal down. And they say instincts are smart.

I ended up on someone's lawn, hood in some rose bushes, back wheels on a walkway. I took a breath and realized that my foot was still rammed down in "flight" mode. I had to force my knee to bend. Fortunately the car had stalled or I would have been an unwelcome guest in their living room.

I creaked open the car door and shakily got out. I smelled gas, noticed the wet sidewalk, and saw a stream spewing from my ruptured tank. Talk about pissing money away.

Panic! My car's gonna explode! I'd seen it a hundred times in movies. My first instinct was to dive back into the car to save my briefcase. Instincts—sheesh. I stopped myself and hopped away from the potential firebomb. After all, what was in the briefcase? My lunch. It was only a lunchbox-in-disguise so I wouldn't look goofy in the elevator.

I saw the police car crunched sideways against a tree, driver's door caved in. Gotta save the cop! I dashed over and pulled open the passenger door.

The cop wasn't a cop. At first I thought it was a boy with long hair, or maybe a girl wearing dirty jeans. The child was wearing a red T-shirt with some big-eyed anime character on the front.

I instinctively reached across the seat to drag the kid out, but some long-dormant brain cells suddenly fired and reminded me that you're not supposed to yank unconscious people around in case their backs are broken.

Meanwhile, apparently someone had called 911 because I heard sirens approaching. Thank God! I could leave the rescue to the pros. So I just stood there gazing at the child, trying to figure out his/her gender—priorities, you know.

Suddenly the kid woke up and looked around wild-eyed.

"Shh, shh. It's okay. Help is on the way."

He (I decided at last) heard the sirens and flipped out. He started thrashing around in high gear, found the door on his side smushed up against the tree, and launched himself toward the open door to freedom—which I just happened to be standing in.

"Outta my way, asshole," he said in a surprisingly gravelly voice for a pre-teen.

He tried to push past me, and I tried to let him, but I'm sorta big and clumsy and kept getting in his way. "Uh, you might be hurt," I said, seeing blood on his forehead.

By now a couple of other people were running up, and a fire truck careened around the corner.

The kid glared at me and our eyes locked for a few seconds. Behind his fury and frustration, I saw that he was scared—very scared.

With me momentarily paralyzed, he could now crawl out. He went nose-first into the turf, stumbled his way to his feet, and took off.

Instinctively, I took off after him. Don't ask me why. Something about him being afraid made me want to help him. Stupid instincts.

He sprinted around behind a brick house with white shutters. *A handsome Tudor*, I noted somewhere in that 85 percent of the brain we don't use. The backyard was nicely manicured and shaded by old-growth trees.

Yeah, I'm soft now, having sat behind a desk for decades, but fifty pounds ago I was quite the runner. I kept up with the little weasel despite the fact that he dodged around birdbaths and deck chairs like a pro football player. I myself blundered across the patio, shoving things out of my way.

He heard me clattering behind him, glanced back, and tripped over a sprinkler. He tumbled headlong into the side of a garden shed.

I lumbered up and asked the stupidest question in the English language: "You okay?"

He flailed, trying to get his legs under him. I reached to help, but he shied away.

"Listen, I'm on your side."

He gave me a does-not-compute frown.

The hubbub got louder—people from the front were on their way.

He got that scared look again.

"Hide in there," I said, pointing at the shed. "I'll tell 'em you went that way."

Worked for him. He unlatched the door and dove in.

I re-latched it and turned around just as a fireman and a neighbor raced onto the deck. Then someone ran up behind them and made an emergency swerve—right into a monster grill.

"He got away!" I lied, waving at the hedge. "Ducked through those bushes."

The cry was taken up—"Through the bushes!"—as more people poured into the yard. Some went over to peer into the foliage while others ran back around to the front.

"He's in the next yard!" I heard, followed by, "Who is?"

"Stay put," I murmured to the shed. "Gotta take care of the car. I'll come back for you."

As I went to deal with coppers and tow trucks and paperwork, I wondered, *What the hell am I doing?* The kid was obviously a fugitive, and stealing a police car was a felony, no doubt—as was, I suspected, aiding and abetting. Was I really prepared to lie to the authorities—commit perjury—to help some tough delinquent escape his well-deserved punishment?

I guess I was, for I spent the next twenty minutes giving a false statement to the police. You have to understand, I'm a law-abiding citizen. I don't do things like that.

The good news is, the firemen sprayed foam under my car so it didn't blow up. The bad news is, the tow truck guy thought the chassis was bent, which meant the car was totaled. He accepted my credit card and off went my vehicle to await the insurance adjuster. But not before I pulled the first-aid kit from under the front seat and hid it in my briefcase alongside my lunch.

I borrowed a cell phone from a spectator (I'd forgotten mine back home on the charger) and called my wife. "Hi, hon. I've been in a little accident. No, I'm okay. But the car isn't. I need a ride, so could you pick me up?" I finally explained enough to get her settled down enough to give her the address. "And, um, would you bring the cash we've been saving for the trip? And any other cash you have?" Yowza. Talk about pushback. "Listen, I'll explain later—I'm on someone's cell—but please, just trust me, okay? I'm, uh, following my instincts on this."

I let her absorb the implications of that. I'm not an instinct-following kind of guy. I'm reliable, predictable. This was definitely weird. "Okay," she said at last. God, I love her!

"And would you call the office and tell them what happened, that I'll be in late?"

Finally the cops got called away on some other emergency and the neighbors got bored, so I "casually" meandered back to the backyard. Fortunately the homeowners weren't home—no doubt slaving away to pay for said home, which was, admittedly, very nice.

I tapped on the shed door. "The coast is clear," I said, opening it.

The kid was huddled behind the lawn mower next to a bunch of rakes and shovels and whatnot. He'd been crying. Another hook in my heart.

"I screwed up," he said. (Paraphrased—he actually used the F-word.)

"Yeah, well, stuff happens." (Also paraphrased—I was trying to build rapport by sounding as streetwise as he obviously was, not the middle-class dweeb I really am.)

"I killed someone."

Whoa! But I was proud of myself for keeping my cool. "Heavy."

Since I just squatted there on my heels like a lawn gnome, he apparently felt the need to fill the silence. "My mom's boyfriend. He beat her up a lot. And last night he got drunk and grabbed my butt. I . . . I cut him. They're talking man-two." He awaited my judgment.

It took me a moment to translate—manslaughter 2, or manslaughter in the second degree—something like that. I wasn't sure what it meant, but I'd heard it on TV. "Uh, sounds like the asshole deserved it. Self-defense."

Who was I to act as judge and jury? And subvert the legal process? Beats me. But I knew that the Wheels of Justice turn slowly, and even if he did get off eventually, he'd spend months if not years in juvie. He'd get indoctrinated into that whole prison scene, taught lessons you don't want to know by fellow inmates. Basically, I was afraid he'd get chewed up by the penal system and spat out a hardened criminal.

"Listen, my wife's bringing some cash, and we could drop you off at the bus station. Is there someplace you could go? Some cousins or something?"

He stared at me for at least five seconds with an expression of wonder. Then he said quietly, "Yeah, there's someplace."

Using the hose, I wet the napkins I'd filched from the food court when I'd slipped out of the office for some pizza (don't tell my wife) and helped him clean up. A little antibiotic and a bandage strip and he was good to go. I gave him my sandwich, too, which he promptly scarfed.

As I went to close the shed door, I noticed a pair of scissors hanging from a nail, no doubt for snipping spent flower blossoms and so forth. I had the boy use the hose to wet his hair and gave him my comb to untangle the snarls. Then I chopped off the long straggles around the back of his head and over his ears. With his hair slicked back and clipped off his neck, he looked like a different kid. Not bad for a three-minute job. I let him keep my comb, too.

I raked up the loose locks with my fingers, pitched them into the compost bin, and rinsed my hands. "Uh, I think the bus station has a gift shop for magazines and snacks and whatnot. If they have any souvenir T-shirts, buy one and get rid of that red shirt. First thing. The cops are probably on the lookout for it."

He nodded soberly.

I replaced the scissors, secured the shed door, and wished there was something we could do about his grungy jeans, but—oh, well.

Keeping to the shrubbery beside me as I walked around the mini-mansion, he snuck to the front to wait for my wife's arrival.

Glancing sidelong at him, I wondered if I was following divine guidance or something. Or maybe I owed him karma from a past life. All I knew was that it felt right, even if it was wrong.

The Commies
Doug Bost

When I was sixteen, I found out about the Commies, they got my best friend, and they almost got me.

I had tenth-grade social studies with Mr. Schoenberg. I don't remember what day it was exactly, must've been early spring, there was a knock on the window of Mr. Schoenberg's classroom, by the door to the hall. I think it surprised all of us that Sammy Paddock was there. He was looking sideways into the room, motioning for me to come out. Mr. Schoenberg gave him a scowl and then he gave it to me, too. "Make it fast."

In the hall, Sammy was already walking. "I have to show you something."

Sammy was taller than I was, athletic, blond hair, square jaw, like a picture-postcard German teenager. Sammy had acne before most of us, and by tenth grade it was at its worst. He was the funniest kid I knew. And just about the smartest, except for some of the girls in our grade. Sammy and I liked all the same movies. He was my best friend.

As we walked, I kept asking Sammy what it was I had to see. What the hell was so important I had to annoy Schoenberg about it? But Sammy didn't really answer, just kept talking under his breath and walking through the hallway and the gym and then the boys' locker room and then outside, into the parking lot of Orono High School and off toward the tennis courts.

Sammy circled around back of the courts to the far end of the chainlink fence, where you couldn't be seen from classroom windows, off near the start of the woods. I stopped. "Come on."

Sammy looked around and came back to me and reached into his waistband and, just like it was something he'd done a million times before, Sammy pulled out a gun.

It was a revolver, a dark silver and brown thing with a surprisingly long barrel, and Sammy held it pointed at the pavement.

"Holy shit, Sam," I said. I took a step back and he kept looking around to make sure nobody was coming.

"You can't tell anybody."

"What the fuck, man, what are you doing with a gun, man?"

"I just got it yesterday."

"Where did you get it?"

"I can't tell you," Sammy said.

I'm sure I asked, "What are you gonna do with it?" and "What's it for?" but I can't even remember exactly, because I had every question. There wasn't anything I didn't have a question about, nothing about this gun made a bit of sense, it was completely forbidden and lethal, and it changed everything just to have it suddenly out in the open right in front of me.

"Do you want to hold it?"

Did I want to hold it. Well, yes, I did. But no, I did not want to hold it.

Sammy held it out carefully, like you see on TV, with the handle pointing toward me and I couldn't help it, I just laughed, it was so wrong and we were so close to the school I laughed and after a few seconds I took the gun from him.

It was heavy, and I said so. I kept my finger away from the trigger but there was something instinctive that made me raise my arm and point it out toward the woods and I'm sure my face was red from the fear. The other thing, the worse thing, was that it felt good in my palm, like it was crafted to nestle in my hand and settle there, and I knew that's what handguns are designed to do—feel absolutely right in your hand.

"I shot it this morning," Sammy said. "Way down past the cul-de-sac, in the woods."

"Oh my god."

"I know," Sammy said. "It's not that hard, though. Actually. I mean, I hate it but it feels really, really good, right?"

I kept the barrel pointed at the ground and tried to figure how to hand it back without the thing going off.

"You can't say anything. Like, not to Maddie, not to your brother, nobody."

"I won't," I said. "But c'mon, you have to tell me where it came from. This is crazy."

"I can't."

"Did you buy this?" I asked, trying to imagine that. Sammy borrowed his parents' car a lot, a boxy gray Buick Regal. Or sometimes his grandmother's car. He could have driven down to southern Maine. Gone to a gun shop off 202 and bought it there, I guess. But he was sixteen, did that even happen? Maybe. "Come on."

"They gave it to me."

"They. Who, they?"

"I'm working for these guys. I do jobs for them. They pay me."

"Who?"

"They're drug dealers. In Bangor."

"Drug dealers in Bangor. You work for drug dealers in Bangor."

"Shut up. Yes. I did a job, I guess they think I did it okay, and they like that nobody knows me and I have my own car, so I take drugs from one house to another house."

"Holy shit, Sam. You do that?"

"And they gave me this yesterday, because some of these guys are really bad people."

"So they gave you a gun? To defend yourself?"

"They said I should have it in case."

"Who are these fucking people?"

"I can't tell you, at all, I can't tell you. You don't know them. I call them the Commies." Sammy laughed at what he'd said.

"You call them what?"

"The Commies said I might need protection. So."

"Like, they're Communists?"

"That's just what I call them."

"Holy shit, Sam." It was about the twentieth time I'd said that in five minutes. "Here."

Sammy took the gun back by the handle and opened the chamber to show the bullets slotted perfectly inside, waiting to be fired. "Totally ready to go."

"Jesus."

"You felt it too, right? Like, it feels good and bad at the same time."

"You gotta get rid of that thing."

"Yeah, well, I can't."

I tried to picture Sammy making the rounds of drug dens, delivering bags of cocaine or something else somewhere in Bangor. Where would that even be? Who was doing drugs in Bangor? It was hard to even imagine it. But here was the evidence.

Sammy tucked the gun into the back of his waistband again. "Okay. That's it."

"Are you going back inside?" I asked.

"Back into school? No. I'm supposedly at an appointment, so no. I got a note," he said.

"Where do your parents think you are?"

That didn't seem to matter.

"But you should go back," Sammy said. And there was this thing in his voice, this sound, like he felt sorry for me that I was going to return to class, but he was going back to running drugs and shooting guns or whatever the hell else I didn't know about.

"You go, Schoenberg's gonna be pissed," Sammy said. "I'll call you after dinner."

I shook my head and started toward the school and Sammy headed the other way. From behind, you could kind of see the bulge at the back of his waistband if you were looking for it. He walked around the fence to another part of the parking lot. Sammy looked back at me. He gave me a wave.

That night, we did talk. We talked a long time on the phone, but I didn't get any more details or explanations. Nothing.

And what was unusual in the weeks after that was that I didn't see Sammy so much, even though there were calls some nights.

Sammy skipped school or he'd be gone right after the last bell.

And I was busy. Debate. The school play was in rehearsals. Homework.

I thought back on how long we'd known each other. Since we were babies, really. Our moms were friends. Our dads taught at the university. Sammy and I went to preschool together, then we went to kindergarten together and we were just naturally buddies, you didn't have to think about it.

In kindergarten, we both skipped the same day together because it was K day, and we knew all we needed to know about the letter K. So we just left the class that day and walked to Sammy's house and his mom was out in the front yard and she looked really concerned and she wanted to know why on earth we were home, so we told her, and she thought about it for a minute and then she said, "Do you want some sandwiches?"

One time Sammy and I stole matches from over his family's fireplace, the long wooden matches, and took them out behind the fence in back of his house to light leaves on fire. His mother saw the smoke and came out running. She was really mad. I asked her if she was going to tell my mom and she said no, I was going to have to tell my mom myself, but Sammy was grounded. So I started to go home and Sammy caught up with me in their driveway with a desperate plan: I couldn't tell my mom, we both understood that, but if my mom ever heard about this thing with the matches and wondered why I hadn't admitted it right away, I should say I had been watching *The Mod Squad* and I'd gotten so distracted that it slipped my mind. We both thought it was a smart plan and I kept going and when I got to Forest Avenue there was my mom, just walking home from work, and she was so glad to see me and she asked me if I'd had a good day at school and she held my hand and I never said anything about the matches.

So Sammy Paddock and I had known each other forever. And talked all the time, all the way up to tenth grade. Which made it strange when we didn't talk so much.

It was something to try to figure out.

I couldn't tell anybody about the gun, but Sammy told Maddie almost right away. And Beth. And they came to talk to me.

Maddie and Beth were just about our only friends that year, and Sammy was the topic of endless speculation for us, even without the gun or the Commies.

Where did Sammy go all day? Why did he say that thing he said? How did the Regal get dented? Did he have a crush on Maddie or was he just pretending to? Was he gay? Was he straight? Why did he talk about time and death and suicide and plane crashes and joke about harming himself, why did he talk about that all the time? Why was his favorite, constantly repeated joke "I'm gonna take my own life with a rusty handgun"?

Sammy was the kind of person who, as soon as they leave the room, everybody else turns to each other to see if they all just saw that.

About three weeks after he showed me the gun out behind the tennis courts, I was in another class. English, maybe. And once again, there was Sammy coming to see if I could walk out. And the teacher allowed it.

On this day, Sammy was sweaty. He looked different. Dark face. He didn't talk this time, and his hair was damp. He walked me through the cafeteria and the carport to where his dad's car was parked and we got in.

And Sammy didn't look at me but he lifted his shirt and there was blood.

There was kind of a lot of blood.

It was all over his stomach and it had stained the top of his jeans and the dark-colored shirt he was wearing but it didn't seem to be gushing. It seemed to have stopped, mostly. I put my back up against the car door and got as far away from him as I could and I must've yelled and asked him what the fuck happened and why wasn't he in the hospital and Sammy said it was okay and nobody was trying to kill him but things had gotten bad and he went to see some doctor who the Commies trusted and the doctor gave him some painkillers and told him to come back in two hours when he could see Sammy privately.

And I was thinking, this is insane.

I was thinking, there are no Commies.

This is Sam.

This is a situation where he either tried to kill himself or he accidentally let the gun go off carrying it around in his pants like he was on *Miami Vice* or some shit, and this was not at the point anymore where we could all pretend it would be fine.

"Is the bullet in you? Do you have a bullet inside you right now?"

Sammy said it went right through him, it went in right here, and out a few inches back from there and that seemed to be true, because I could see these two punctures that were both bloody wounds and he said the doctor told him he was lucky it didn't hit anything major and he'd patch him up no problem this afternoon, and I just said it's not no problem, there is a big fucking problem.

"I don't want you to die, Sam."

And Sammy said, "I don't want to die either, Doug."

Sammy started the car and said I should get out.

"Are you gonna go see the guy right now, please? Or go straight to the hospital? Please?"

"I told you I would, don't worry."

"I'm totally worried."

"See? You're a good friend," Sammy said. "I just wanted to tell you about it. Now you gotta get out."

So I got out and I closed the door and I stood there a second.

Sammy drove away in that boat of a car and I ran into the school, into the main office, and I asked Mrs. Cobb if I could use their phone and she gave me a little room off the guidance office and I called Sam's house. Sam's mother answered. And I told her what I'd seen, what had happened, that Sammy had a gun, that he seemed to be shot, that he needed to see a doctor right away. And his mother was quiet but I could hear her saying, "Oh. Oh," on the other end and she thanked me very much and she said she would take care of it right away. And I hung up.

And then—nothing.

Sammy wasn't around for about two weeks solid after that. I told Maddie and Beth. But I don't think I ever told my parents. No idea why. What could they have done, really?

And of course we speculated.

Maddie heard he was in Eastern Maine Medical Center, but that was a rumor.

Beth heard from her parents that he was out of state. We didn't get anything confirmed, no news we could be sure of.

It was just like it always had been—Sam's closest friends furiously talking about him and wondering and guessing.

And school went on, homework and weekend debate tournaments and play performances or something and all the spring business of being sixteen.

Two weeks later: boom. There he was. Back in class. Hanging out after school. Flirting with Maddie. Driving me places in his new car, a red VW Rabbit he'd bought with money he saved last summer.

He didn't want to talk about it. He didn't acknowledge the gun or the blood or the conversation in the car or the fact that I'd called his mom. It was like a blip that happened and we'd never be referring to that blip again.

It made sense, sort of, to all of us. He'd been caught, exposed, there wasn't a way to make drug-running or self-defense or Commies credible anymore. That part of his story had to be over.

But, of course, we just kept wondering.

It was the kind of thing we talked about whenever Sammy wasn't there. My long evening phone calls with Sam turned into long evening phone calls about Sam, with Maddie or Beth. And there were never any answers. Only more questions.

So about six months went by.

We finished tenth grade, we had a summer of riding bikes and watching movies. *WarGames* was a big deal. Driving to the coast on weekends. I had a job at the mall that I hated but it was good to get paid.

And then that September my parents and I were going to take a trip to London and Scotland but before we left I wanted to get some new music for my Walkman, so there was a Saturday afternoon when I asked Sammy if he'd drive me into Bangor to the record store that had a much better selection of cassettes. We went and got some good stuff and then we got into his ruby Rabbit and started driving back to Orono. Maybe a twenty-minute drive.

As we turned out of the mall, we stopped at a red and there was a little thump, just a small one, but the car right behind us had hit us, just barely, and Sammy looked into his rearview and said "Jee-zus" and took the right and I probably said something clever like "Drive much?" to the idiot behind us.

And we kept talking about whatever, but Sammy was checking the mirrors and after a while I turned around to look out the back and I said, "Is that still them?"

And it was.

That same car was still behind us, right on our ass.

I looked a little more carefully now. It was a black car, or maybe dark blue, and it was bigger than ours, maybe a Chevy Caprice, and as much as I looked, I couldn't see the faces of the people in the car. But I could see there was more than one of them.

"They're fucking following us," Sammy said.

And I said, "No."

But then off Hogan Road, that car made the same turn we did, toward Orono.

When Sammy went faster, they went faster. And when Sammy started to make a turn, they started, too, and when he suddenly stayed on the main road and didn't make that turn after all, they were right with us.

"Those assholes," I said, but my voice caught a little bit. Sammy told me to put my seatbelt on. And I said, "Who is that?"

And then I started feeling a rush of blood to my neck and my head and I was panicking.

"It's the Commies."

And I said, "That's crazy," but I kept looking in my side view mirror and there they were. Jesus Christ, right there.

"What do they want?" I could feel my voice getting higher and getting more desperate and Sammy made a fast turn in Veazie on a street we never took, headed downhill toward the Penobscot River.

"They want me, they don't want you," Sammy said.

Another turn, faster, a speed bump on a quiet street and the bottom of the Rabbit scraped the pavement and jolted us up and I was braced against the dashboard and another turn took us back up out of these dead-end streets, back to Route 2, and that fucking car had stayed right behind us the whole way.

"Don't worry," Sammy was saying. "I'll get you to London. You'll get on that plane. It's okay, Doug. I'll get you to London."

Across the railroad tracks again and out past Gass Horse Supply and the Penobscot Valley Country Club, Sammy was flooring it now, and I was trying to think how we could get out of this without fucking dying—could we go to my brother's place? Could we make it as far as my house or Sammy's? And if we went there, would we be putting all of them in danger when these Commies got out?

"This is when I could use that gun," Sammy said, and I said no no, but also, y'know—Yes.

This road. It was a little road, really. You just don't drive this fast on this road. But we were doing it.

And then I had an idea that was actually a good idea. To this day, I still think it was a good idea. "The State Police barracks. Pull in to the State Police parking lot, it's up on the right, the cops'll be right there, they wouldn't dare follow us, but if they do, we got help!"

So we topped that next hill past Willow Drive and then Sunset Drive and we were going so fast that you could feel that moment of almost weightlessness and you could see the sign: Maine State Police. The gray and black cars the troopers kept out front.

Sammy made a hard right into that parking lot and I was holding on to the back of my seat and all my new cassettes were sliding around on the floor mat now, fallen out of the bag.

I had my window down on the passenger side.

And as we cut in and leaned deep into that turn, almost 180 degrees, I craned out to see if those drug dealing killers would be stupid enough to follow us in here.

And that car behind us slowed down.

That Chevy Caprice or whatever.

They didn't turn.

They slowed down. Their windows were down, too. And now as they rolled past the State Police barracks, I could see their faces. Two guys in the front, another guy in the back.

Goddamn.

I knew those guys.

Maybe not by name, but those guys were from our high school.

And the guy in the passenger seat—Jesse something, maybe?—he reached out his arm and flipped us the bird and laughed and you could hear all three of them laughing and shitty music cranking out of their car stereo. Not a fucking care in the world, and there they went, they just kept on going. Just a bunch of assholes from school. Joyriding in a car that probably belonged to one of their dads. Maybe they recognized the Rabbit, or maybe more likely they were just gonna fuck around with anybody who'd been pulling out of the mall that time today. There they were, and there they went, and Sammy pulled to a stop, breathing heavily, put it in park.

And I looked at him.

And Sammy said, "Fucking Commies." And let out a big sigh.

Sammy started to settle down. He turned his whole body halfway around to look out back and make sure the car was gone. He hadn't seen their faces like I had.

"I told you." He let out a big laugh, a huge laugh, a big square-jawed, blond German handsome red-faced laugh where the veins in his neck started to show.

"Jesus!" he yelled, and pounded on the steering wheel. He turned to me. "You okay?"

"Yeah," I said.

He pushed his hair back.

"Are you okay?" I asked.

And Sammy made a face and he shrugged and said it really loud when he said, "Yeah, I'm okay!" And he was still kind of laughing, even then. And he said, "For now, anyway."

Maps
Faith Shearin

In a college geography class my professor
explained *No map tells the truth;*
there's always some distortion,
some point of view. Behind his head:

a slide of Babylon
sketched on a clay fragment
showing far away and unknown lands
where a bird could not safely

complete its journey. He showed us
an antique map inside a cartouche
on which four heads blew winds
from the corners of the world,

opened a moral map from London
in which each house was color-coded
by income: *yellow: wealthy,*
sable: low-class, vicious, semi-criminal.

There were maps etched on mammoth tusks
and animal skins indicating
spiritual realms, constellations, myths;

I remember a colorful one
with the heavens remade
as a box with an ivory lid.
A map is an act of persuasion:

each kingdom placing itself at the center,
all dragons asleep in the middle distance.
I think of Ptolemy's hippos
and cannibals, a basilisk

sunning itself off the coast of Africa;
I think of Roman cities sketched
along trade routes: diagrams
of parallel lines, branching roads, sprawl.

If I made a map of my life
there would be monsters
and individual trees. As a child I attended
dinner parties with men who collected maps,

as if they understood scale.
Just yesterday my mother told me
the story of a woman who listened

only to her station wagon's GPS—paying no
attention to topography—a smooth voice guiding her
down a boat launch into the sea.

Passover
Gina Soo Golden

I caught a fly
under the edge of a penny
I found on the floor.
I felt it under there—
It must've been slow
or I, as a child, was a zen master.

As I watched it struggle,
The day's occasion occurred to me.
The table set with white
dishes with their simple black
swirl in the center
Like the insects paths
Traced in children's books

The pristine white
Table cloth draped
down to the chairs
The sun poured in
The glasses sparkled

And I alone at the table
with the fly
on my perfect white napkin,
thought for a moment
what if I pressed . . .

And let it go.

January Wedding
Amy Brunson

It is June 15, 2010. I have been eighteen years old for exactly three days. I'm sitting on the porch of a dilapidated two-story yellow house on 15th Street, right off of Pike Avenue. Raccoons live in the walls.

I live here, too, with my boyfriend and six other grown men who want to live more like Jesus did. They've decided the best way to do that is to rent a drafty house in the poorest neighborhood of North Little Rock and change nothing else about their lives.

On the porch with me are Tom and Nick—my boyfriend and the one friend of his who follows him everywhere. Tom and I just got back from Bonnaroo. My mom paid for my ticket as a graduation gift and I paid for Tom's because he couldn't. There, three days ago, Tom bought an overpriced beer from a festival vendor and said, "I got you a birthday present!" As I opened my mouth to say thank you and accept the drink, he said, "I've been sober for a whole month, just for you! Month's up! Happy birthday!" He chugged the beer. The Avett Brothers came on stage. I wept as they played "January Wedding."

Now, on the porch with Miller High Lifes in hand, Tom, Nick, and I shoot the shit as usual. The porch is tiny—more of a stoop—barely big enough for a few folding chairs, which we don't have. There is a gallon-sized mason jar of spare change at my feet, which Kayla, the sex worker from down the block, helps herself to regularly.

Staring at the change jar, I hear Tom say, "Will you marry me in January?"

I look up. "Which January?"

"This one."

He holds out his hand to shake mine, as if making a deal. Because he is. And being a firm believer in the sanctity of the handshake, he pauses—mid-proposal—and solemnly asks Nick to be his witness. Nick solemnly agrees.

Here's where I have options.

Option 1

Convince Tom that we won't go to hell if we fuck out of wedlock. And then just do that instead.

What I don't know at the time (and still don't fully know, to be honest, but since then the evidence has stacked up) is that Tom isn't afraid of hell. He is afraid of himself and of what he might learn when he finally feels the inside of a woman: that he simply doesn't prefer it.

But let's just say I do convince him to go ahead and fuck me already. It will happen in the back of his "rapist van" (a term that will feel totally innocuous until an incident after a party at the Thrasherdome in 2013).

The sex we have in this van will not be good. Parked in the backyard, away from the prying ears of our New Monastic housemates and the thin walls that separate us from them (not to mention the one we share a room with, the three of us divvied up between two twin mattresses on the floor), we make it work. Knowing each other in the Biblical sense, that is. And maybe—just maybe—it quells his misguided desire for a legal union long enough that I have a chance to grow up a little bit, talk some damn sense into myself, and get the hell out of dodge.

Option 2

Get the hell out of dodge. Immediately.

I have a full-ride scholarship to the most expensive and most progressive liberal arts school in the state (the state being Arkansas, so take all that with a grain of salt). My freshman year isn't starting for another couple of months, but I still have one parent who will allow me to come back home without too many questions or lectures about the fact that I moved to "the ghetto" with a bunch of "dirtbags" before I was legally allowed to make that decision for myself.

It goes like this: I drive my new Toyota Corolla and my one suitcase full of clothes the seventy-eight miles back to my mom's place in Western Addition. I cry. A lot. But my best friend Sadie gets me into just enough trouble over the summer that I practically forget, with alarming quickness, the fever dream that was my month with the raccoons.

I go to Hendrix in the fall. I make out with the senior who chaperones my orientation trip (he's so nice! So normal! And the cabin has a fireplace!). I live in my assigned dorm room with my roommate, Audrey, and her sexy, small boyfriend, Adam Jacuzzi, of Jacuzzi tub fame. He doesn't go to school here. He's just a loveable punk with nowhere better to be.

I change my major to anthropology. My life goes on.

Option 3

Say yes. Shake Tom's hand. Commune with the raccoons for another six months.

Go on my college orientation trip and don't even once think about making out with the nice, normal, senior chaperone. See that Audrey and Adam have duct-taped my bed to hers when I go into the dorm room mid-semester to collect the few outfits and canister of instant coffee I brought for the two nights I was required to sleep there.

Make plans for a surprise wedding at our church on the evening of January 2, 2011, where no one knows Tom and I are getting married except for the pastor, Jack, because we need someone to officiate and Rowan, our twin mattress roommate, can't get his shit together enough to mail in the four-dollar check required to receive his certificate as an ordained Dudeist Priest with the Church of the Latter-Day Dude.

Have a sex dream about Jack a week before the wedding. Question everything.

Confide in our trusted pastor (Jack) that I am having doubts. His wife and kid are away for the weekend and although I do not tell him about my dream, my dream comes true. He is wearing a lab coat for some reason (he is not a doctor or a scientist). He pins me against the wall of a room filled with books and beakers (sure, I guess his Hillcrest duplex could conceivably contain a room filled with books and beakers). He absolutely blows my mind.

Now, I am no longer a virgin. Now, I have an insatiable thirst for much older men (much older than my already inappropriately old fiancé). Now, I have a secret to keep. Because the wedding is still on.

But do you remember Rowan, the almost–Dudeist Priest? Rowan finds out about me and lab coat Jack. I'm not exactly sure how he finds out, but of course he does. And he tells everyone. The wedding is off.

Audrey and Adam rip the duct tape off the dorm room beds when I appear for the spring semester with my suitcase full of clothes and instant coffee, which I will never actually drink. Shelly stays with Jack because she's the staying kind of woman. And Tom? Who fucking knows. But I do know that the night he finds out, he runs drunk in the streets waving a pocket knife at God screaming, "Why?! Why?!"

What Really Happens

To save me some time, please read Option 3 again until you get to the part where I have a sex dream about Jack.

Okay.

The dream happens but it doesn't come true. Instead, I fantasize about it during the post-vow prayer he leads to close out the ceremony. All heads bowed, all eyes closed, his left hand on the small of my back. The small of the back of a married woman. And that's that.

Confessions of a Barfly
Heather Jarvis

I think my inauguration from barely legal fresh meat to barfly happened while I was busy snorting a pill in the bathroom stall. Maybe it was when I was outside in the gravel parking lot, barefoot, trying to fight some girl for god only knows what reason. But if I really had to bet on it, it was a night in the beginning.

I sat at the local sports bar staring at the memorabilia, built into the bar just like me. Them bound by polyurethane, me by poor decisions.

I needed a drink.

Crown Royal sat proudly on the throne of the top shelf while all of us regular subjects scurried messily around the bar. Jim and Jack stared back, taunting me with their thick bourbon eyes. The girly Ciroc and fruity-flavored vodkas danced like vixens, seducing me with the oblivion they would provide.

I really needed a drink.

My wallet was empty—my new normal. The bartender saw me for what I was: desperate. She looked at my earrings and raised her eyebrows questioningly. For a moment I gave it a second thought. I imagined how she must see me. I had always put high value in what others thought of me. I had always been timid and awkward. But I wanted to be approachable, I wanted to be social, I wanted to be everything I wasn't. I admired the girls who fit the mold effortlessly. I longed to be somebody else, anybody else. I wanted to sit at the bar while men pawned over me. I wanted women to be in awe over my charisma. Alcohol gave me the attributes I longed for.

God, I needed that drink.

I pushed my shoulders back, took a quick glance around, inhaled a shallow breath, then pulled my inhibitions out of my ears and handed them to her to pay for a swig of cheap liquor. That was the moment I left my candid ideal in the wind and started living for the tilt of a glass. My decency that night barely afforded me a bottom-shelf Solo cup.

It didn't take long for me to start using my sexuality as a tool to take advantage of men. I grew bold. My couth washed down with each swig, I became scandalous. I quickly learned tricks of the stool. I would leave some liquor in the bottom of my hustled-up drink, not wanting to appear desperate for my next.

"Have you ever had a chocolate cake shot?" I would ask whatever lonely man was at the bar. Nobody ever had. Manipulation at its finest. Most of the time, *whoever* would buy us both a shot. Women weren't exempt from my escapades. I learned to spot desperate girls, anxious, overweight, lonely. I'd be their friend for a drink. I did anything for a drink.

The bartender appeased my hustle. I entertained her with my mischiefs—at least at first. Inevitably I had to graduate to the big leagues. One night I turned on the barstool and looked around. I saw a dark man who looked like a ball player. He saw me look at him and nudged his head up.

BINGO.

I smiled, stood up, and pushed my shoulders back to expose my cleavage. I purposely made my boobs bounce a little with the music seductively. *Sexy, I have to be sexy*, I said, pep-talking myself. It only took minutes for him to approach me. I naively thought I was controlling my surroundings. I didn't realize I was slowly losing control. I was like a speeding drunk driver—there was no way this would end well.

"Hey, ma, let me buy you a drink?" he questioned.

"Okaaaaaayyy," I said innocently.

I finished off the last little bit in my cup. One drink led to another. I sipped myself into oblivion. I ignored his hand on the small of my back, I ignored the hardness in his pants as he danced behind me. I ignored everything in me that screamed I would regret this. I threw shot after shot back and gave in to the darkness.

I came to naked on a bed with him on top of me. He was covered in sweat. I could tell he had been at it for a while. My inhibitions came back to me, but it was too late to go back. He didn't buy my drinks all night for nothing. He was making sure he got his money's worth, with or without me awake.

The next time I saw him at the bar, I smiled, hopeful he would finance me for the night. He whispered to his buddy, laughed, and pretended I didn't exist. A lot of men at the bar pretended I did not exist in those days. I was less to them than the ice melting in the bottom of their glasses. I had become worthless and a pest in the bar scene within weeks.

Sometimes I would wake up after a night I couldn't remember with my panties inside out. I would not know who, just what. Other times I wouldn't even have panties on.

New Year's Eve is a barfly's dream. Once, I woke up covered in piss in my best friend's bed. I had dicks and random gestures written all over my legs like a bathroom stall. My best friend blow-dried the bed, irate, not at all sympathetic, shaking her head.

One night I looked around the bar assessing the situation as a fight erupted. All the staff ran toward the commotion in the pool room. Only partially tipsy and broke, I seized the opportunity. Nobody around to witness, I bent over the bar reaching for the tip jars. My ass hung out my cheetah print skirt as I emptied all three jars into my purse. I stood, pressed my skirt down, flipped my hair, and walked right out of the front door, over to the bar next door.

I have stolen, so it will be no surprise to you that I've starved to buy booze. The only things regularly in my stomach were beer nuts, cheap liquor, and, if I was lucky, ramen noodles. You should know I don't even like Reuben sandwiches. So why I was locking eyes with Ronnie, another regular, as he bit into the stacked corned beef sandwich with a longing that made me feel I would die without a bite, I will never understand.

I stared. He crunched. Some grease slipped off the sandwich, hitting the wax paper with a tat-tat. I wanted to lick it off. My stomach rumbled. My eyes got big like a puppy's. I was trying to get him to give me a bite, making convo, complimenting the sandwich more than his ego.

I silently prayed to god.

A drunkard, a beggar, a pathetic girl sitting at the bar soused, drinking melted ice. My only ambition in life to lick the thousand island dressing off poor Ronnie's lip. He finally offered me a bite. I thanked him with my handiwork in the gambling room.

I have also trashed the place.

I left a trail of Doritos from some random person's kitchen all the way to me, passed out on the living room floor after Super Bowl Sunday.

I flunked out of college because I was too hungover to go to class.

I never meant to become a fixture at the bar. I never wanted people I have known my whole life to cringe when I stumbled toward them drunk. All I wanted was to be liked, to fit in and be comfortable in my own skin. I am ashamed of the things I can't remember. I am haunted by sweaty men who treated me worse than dirt on the bottom of their shoes after they were done with me.

I stare at the ground.

I can't keep eye contact.

I am silent.

I seem standoffish, but really I am terrified of social situations.

I worry I will sound stupid, so I awkwardly do not speak at all.

I will myself invisible but go nowhere.

I feel like everyone stares at me.

I have disassociated to the point I don't know how to come back but I want to come back. I want to be present in my own life.

That is why I need this confession. This story needs to be told so I can move forward, so I can forgive myself. I am slowly figuring out how to embody the uncomfortableness that sobriety brings.

That is what I wish I could tell the past me: It's fucking uncomfortable to be human, so deal with it. It's not just you, you're not the only one. No amount of oblivion will complete you. One day you are going to want to live and feel touched. You're going to want to make love but you will feel tainted and dirty. You are going to remember the most disgraceful things you have done and wonder how anyone could love you.

You're going to remember being butt naked on a pool table with the old man who owns the bar on top of you. You are going to remember his hesitation and how he stopped right before he fucked you to ask if you had diseases. You don't. You came out clean. You are not dirty. You are actually a badass individual. You made it.

You're going to have to learn to laugh, learn to love, learn to smile, basically learn to breathe all over again, but you're gonna do it. You're gonna learn because eventually you have to look up. Eventually you have to say something. Eventually you get to the bottom of the bottle, the liquor store closes, and you have to face yourself.

So just do it sober, grin and bear it. It's worth it to be alive. It's worth it to remember what you did last night. It's worth it to remember his name and who won the game. It's worth it to be yourself. You are enough. Everything you ever wanted to be is already inside of you.

To all the barflies out there losing more of themselves every night, if you don't listen to anything else here, keep your earrings! They look better on you. Life and sobriety look better on you.

McPherson Kids
Logan Rose

Every Friday after school, the children of Flagstaff, Arizona, go ice skating at the Jay Lively Activity Center. The nerds, like myself, pant around the rink, getting blisters from their rental skates and pausing for greasy slices of lukewarm pizza on the rubberized flooring that smells like socks. Our biggest dramas of the evening are watching other kids fall down and finding out who will dance with who during the couples' skate. The McPherson kids always come inside for the couples' skate. It's kind of a big deal.

Usually, I sit out of the couples' skate, the unforgiving metal bleachers feeling especially cold on my bum. As I mentioned before, I'm a bit of a nerd. My name is Samantha, and I don't go by Sam. Plus, I'm the smartest girl in English class, and nobody likes that girl. Well, some people do. I have friends called Joey and Liz, and on the best nights, we skate together as a "couple," all of us holding hands. I guess that would make us a throuple, but we're all virgins—unlike the McPherson kids.

I suppose I should tell you about the McPherson kids. These are the cool kids, the ones who really qualify as "teenagers." They drink and have sex and do drugs, and they do it all at McPherson Park. When the McPherson kids' parents drop them off, they go inside, but they don't rent skates. They buy black coffee from the vending machine and change clothes in the bathroom. They wear their sluttiest, tightest, most ripped-up clothing under their sweaters and jeans. It's kind of genius.

Then, the McPherson kids go outside. They sit in the park no matter how cold it is, and if you look closely, you can see the glowing ends of their cigarettes from the frosty windows inside the rink. I don't know what you have to do to become a McPherson kid. All I know is that I am never invited to the park. I am kind of friends with one of the girls, Dora, but she just smiles at me, her lip ring hitting her teeth as she goes outside and lights up. Funny enough, Dora is dating my ex-boyfriend, Jason. I can hardly call Jason my ex-boyfriend because all we had was a sweet summer romance at camp. I taught Jason how to swim, and we promised each other we'd be one another's first kisses, and then we weren't. I think Jason's first kiss might have been Dora. Man, she's so pretty. She's so cool. I wish I could go outside with the McPherson kids just once.

On this particular night, Dora and Jason come in for the couples' skate. Dora looks sweaty, and her eyeliner is smeared. She sits next to me for a moment, breathing slowly and deeply. I can see the beads of sweat at the top of her Hollister camisole, and when she looks at me, her pupils are huge. She smiles at me, like always, but her eyes are watery. She pushes back her hair and wipes away the eyeliner under her eyes. She takes one final deep breath, pats my leg, and goes off to find Jason, who is coming out of the men's bathroom.

"Are you okay?" I ask her, too late.

Joey comes to find me on the bench, holding hot chocolate from the machine and a pack of peanut M&Ms. Tonight, we deserve sweet treats because tonight, Liz has found someone to dance with—an older boy from another school but not one of the McPherson kids, thank God. Still, Liz might be the first of us to get an actual boyfriend. I always thought it would be me.

As we pass the sugar-water hot cocoa back and forth, I watch Jason and Dora skate around the rink. She clutches his arm, as if she's holding on for dear life, and he looks like he's ready to shake her off. This is confusing because Jason has always been so in love with Dora, and Dora's always been, like, the coolest cat at school. When my mom comes to pick me up and spots Jason and Dora cuddling in some corner, she always says, "That boy is smitten kitten." Then, we laugh, because we both knew Jason when he was just a fair-haired little boy with buck teeth and blue eyes. Sometimes, Mom asks me why we're not friends anymore. "You grew up together," she insists.

The truth is, I wish we were still friends. I wish I was cool enough to hang out with the McPherson kids, but apparently my D.A.R.E. training was a waste of time because no one has ever even offered me drugs. Instead, I lose myself in Jane Austen and make detailed story maps of how all the characters are connected in *Great Expectations*. Ms. Manning thinks I will study Dickens when I go to college, but honestly, I just hope I go to parties in college.

Anyways, I pretty much forget about the Dora/Jason thing because I'm so jealous of them both, and I have to focus on school. But after a few weeks, Dora stops coming to school, and Jason looks bad—like really bad. Jason and I are kind of friends, so I ask him what happened. He looks at me like he wants to tell me the truth but then decides against it:

"Something happened in the park."

I know better than to pry, so I just ask, "Is Dora okay?"

"Yeah, I mean, she will be."

Jason gives me a hug, which is super out of character and could probably ruin his whole social standing, but I accept it. It feels good to be touched. I can tell that he needed the hug more than me so I say, "Let me know if you want to talk about it."

He smiles at me, somehow with the same mannerisms that Dora has, then he hangs his head and sulks off.

Later, I hear some mean girls gossiping. They're not McPherson kids, but they all go to some Christian camp every summer, so for some reason, they're popular.

"Did you hear that Dora's pregnant?" one of them says.

Suddenly, I understand everything. Poor Dora probably thought she would lose her virginity on prom night. That's where I plan to do it. To be honest, I was hoping to do it with Jason. I always thought he'd come back around, and I always thought we'd have plenty of time to lose our virginities to each other because we messed up the first kiss thing. After all, we're fourteen, and we don't attend "abstinence class" until we're sixteen. All the older girls joke about it. They say that at the other schools, a sexy lady puts condoms on bananas. I wonder if Jason put a condom on *his* banana, but I don't want to think about him like that. I always thought he was more of a gentleman, and if Dora's pregnant, I guess he didn't.

Mom says abstinence-only sex education is a "crock of shit," but maybe it's not if everyone ends up so traumatized. I think of Dora's smeared eyeliner and the way the light has gone out of Jason's bloodshot blue eyes, and for the first time, I am glad I'm not a McPherson kid.

What I Did Right

Miriam Murray

I often wonder how I got here,
strong again and without fear,
without pain and without flooding anger,
with a heart full of beauty—
breathing it in every day.

What did I do right?
When my thinking went bad,
I trained myself to catch it
as early as possible.
Moved my arms to say stop,
stretched my legs, shook my head.

Thinking cannot fix thinking
but action can. Take a deep breath.
Eat something healthy. Drink something hot.
Go outside and look up at the sky.
Fill your eyes with beauty.
Read a book—especially books by women—
Biographies, poems. Read

What did I do right?
I told my story over and over again.
I went to therapy every week.
I let out the pain, the terror.
I took the medicine they offered.

What did I do right?
I believed in myself,
in my worth, in my heart.
I let out the pain and the anger.
I wrote about feeling broken.
How did I get better?
One small step at a time.
That's how I got home.

Library War
Christopher Santiago

"Library call!" I announced to the prison living area. **"Sign up for the library!"** It was my first day as inmate librarian for Riverbanks Correctional Institution's mental health program. The prison's main library, located in a separate building, had closed its doors to inmates from our unit, so the staff helped us put together a library of our own. It was set up in a dayroom on the upper tier of unit F2, the building where the South Carolina Department of Corrections warehoused its mentally disabled prisoners.

The F2 library was inferior to the main library in every way. There were no computers, no law books, no alphabetically organized shelves, and no library cards. Inmates could borrow up to three books at a time, but we had no library officer. It was entirely up to the inmate librarian to check books in and out. Worst of all, our shelves held less than half as many titles as the main library. We desperately needed reading material.

Reading is linked to good behavior and mental health. Think about it. Inmates absorbed in books are not getting into trouble. Even if they read only to distract themselves from prison realities, they are still taking in new information, educating themselves. Reading contributes to their rehabilitation.

It should come as no surprise that there are organizations on the outside that donate books to prison libraries. During my first day as librarian, I mailed letters requesting book donations for F2 to several such library projects. They replied quickly, assuring me that books would be shipped to my institution within the next few months. It seemed all I had to do was wait. I had no idea what I was up against.

> "Knowledge of the enemy's dispositions can only be obtained from other men."[1]

Several months passed, and no books had been delivered. I was starting to wonder whether the library projects had forgotten my requests when it occurred to me that maybe the books had arrived but were being withheld by the prison mailroom. I would need to ask the mailroom supervisor.

Riverbanks was a maximum-security prison. Across the yard from the housing units stood a small brick building that contained the mailroom. No prisoners were allowed inside. We sent and received mail through a window in the brick wall.

One particularly hot summer morning, I was waiting in line outside the mailroom for a chance to speak with the mailroom supervisor when I met the inmate librarian for Riverbanks' main library. There were about ten other prisoners standing in line with us, our bright orange uniforms glowing in the sun. We must have looked like a row of carrots.

"Hey, you work in the library, right?" I asked.

"Yeah," he said. "You live in E dorm?"

I nodded. It was a lie, but if I said I lived in F2, he probably would have ignored me. Most guys from the other buildings treated inmates from the mental health unit as less than human. If I could keep the conversation simple, I thought, maybe I could pass as neurotypical. "I was wondering . . . Where does the library get its books? Do they, like, write to people on the outside for donations?"

He smirked. "Actually, we don't have to anymore. Now we just take the books marked for F2. Those window lickers can't read anyway, you know?"

Someone in line behind us laughed. I wasn't sure if he was laughing because he knew I was from F2 or because he thought the "window lickers" comment was funny. I didn't find any humor in it. I wanted to say that many of us could read quite well. But I just stood there like a smiling carrot hoping my face and ears weren't flushing beet red.

I kept pretending to be "normal" until I could no longer resist the urge to withdraw from the conversation. Having already learned what had happened to our donations, I fast-walked back to my building without ever speaking to the mailroom supervisor. As soon as I returned to F2, I wrote a formal request to the main library. In my request, I mentioned that they might have received some donations meant for F2 by mistake. I politely asked that those books be sent to the F2 library.

"The opportunity of defeating the enemy is provided by the enemy himself."[2]

Instead of our donations, I received a box of dusty books marked with Riverbanks' main library stamp. When I opened the box, a stale odor assaulted my nostrils. Inside was a stack of old paperbacks with missing or damaged covers, their pages yellow and brown. Some looked like they had been dipped in tea. Others contained mold. They were books the main library wanted to throw away. After all the donations they had stolen from F2, they were sending us their garbage.

I was used to being treated differently on the basis of my disability—such discrimination was partly the reason F2 inmates were excluded from the main library to begin with—but this stack of trash made my blood boil. Atop the pile was a coverless English translation of Sun Tzu's *Art of War*. I picked it up. Sun Tzu, the introduction said, wrote his classic book of military strategy 2,500 years ago. I flipped to the second chapter. It was titled "Waging War." Okay, I thought, if it's war the main library wants, it's war they'll get. Right then and there, I mentally declared a library war. The main library wanted to exclude us, steal our donations, and send us their garbage, but I was determined to make our library the best on the yard. It was on.

From that day forward, "Library call!" became my battle cry. I made sure the library opened on time every week. On weeks when the officers wouldn't unlock the library, I collected and distributed books on a pushcart. And when my friend K returned from the psychiatric hospital, we rebuilt, reorganized, and relabeled every section of the bookshelves. We were both serving life sentences. There was no way we were going to do all that time with an inadequate library.

> *"According as circumstances are favorable, one should modify one's plans."*[3]

We still needed books. Since we couldn't get donations from library projects, we would have to find another way to build our collection. Prison policy allowed individual prisoners to receive up to three books at a time from legitimate book distributors. K and I figured if we could convince enough F2 inmates to order books through the mail, once they were finished reading what they had ordered, they might donate an amount of reading material sufficient to fill our library shelves. The books would be mailed directly from distributors to the inmates who ordered them, so there was no way for the main library to intercept them.

First, we helped people order from major distributors like Amazon and Barnes & Noble. Then we handed out catalogs for booksellers such as the Hit Pointe, Books N Things Warehouse, and Edward R. Hamilton. For inmates who couldn't afford to buy books, we gave out the addresses of book programs that mailed free reading material to prisoners. Anyone behind the walls could write to these programs to request books by subject or genre.

Before long, packages were coming in from bookstores across the country. Each week, books arrived from free book programs like those based at Lucy Parsons Bookstore in Massachusetts, Bound Together Bookstore in California, Bluestockings Bookstore in New York, Downtown Books and News in North Carolina, and Left Bank Books in Washington. The donations were adding up, and for a time, the library shelves were almost full. But there was a problem. The new books seemed to disappear from the library almost as quickly as they were donated.

Tackling theft would prove to be our most difficult challenge. In prison, snitching could get you seriously injured or killed, so even when we identified some of the thieves, we never reported them. Besides, correctional officers couldn't care less if library books were stolen. Most officers showed up at their jobs to perform the absolute minimum amount of work required to earn their paychecks. They didn't want the additional task of hunting down thieves. They might even punish us for complaining about the thefts. We had to solve our own problems.

> *"He will win who knows when to fight and when not to fight."*[4]

Something odd was happening in the F2 library. The guys who couldn't read were checking out the most books. Their favorite excuse for not returning them seemed to be, "I'm not done reading them yet." And then there was Reggie Brown. Reggie was illiterate, yet he hoarded dictionaries. At any given time, he had at least twenty dictionaries squirreled away in his cell. And he was a frequent visitor to the library. Whenever he showed up, he would bring a dictionary from the reference shelf to the checkout desk. Once, he tried to pick a fight with me.

"You can't sign out the dictionary," I told him.

"Why not?" It was the same question every time.

I answered without looking up from what I was writing. "Because it's a reference book. Those are for people to read while they're in the library."

"I want to read it in my cell," he insisted.

"Sorry, but you can't sign that one out."

"Why *not?*" He took a step closer to the desk.

I looked up at him. He was more than twice my size. If I was a carrot, he was a pumpkin. "I just explained why not," I said. "Why don't you use the dictionary on your tablet?" Every inmate had a prison-issued tablet with a Merriam-Webster dictionary app that could define more words than most printed dictionaries.

He leaned over the desk, put his face in mine, and cocked his head to the side. "Is you racist, mothafucka?"

"No." I had been doing time since before Reggie was born; I wasn't about to let him intimidate me.

He raised his voice. "Then why I can't sign out this dictionary? It's 'cause you racist!"

The library suddenly got very quiet. Everyone was watching to see if we would fight. K had my back, but if there was a fight, an officer would probably show up to close the library.

"It's because I'm not allowed to lend out the reference books, but you're welcome to read it while you're up here." After I said this, the silence was so intense, it was almost like we were in an actual library.

Reggie feinted a punch over the desk.

I didn't flinch. (Okay, maybe I flinched a little.)

"I'ma read it in my cell," he said as he turned and walked out of the library with the dictionary in his hand.

K breathed a sigh of relief.

"Well, there goes that one," I said, wiping the sweat from my forehead. But it was no big loss. According to Sun Tzu, *"One who is skillful at keeping the enemy on the move maintains* deceitful appearances, according to which the enemy will act. He sacrifices something, that the enemy might snatch at it."[5] In the F2 library, we always kept the good dictionary in the desk and left an old one on the reference shelf.

Unfortunately, not all our books could be protected in that way. Most thieves had no interest in dictionaries. Magazines and comics were usually the first items to get up and walk out of the library, never to be seen again. Manga and roleplaying games were next to go, followed by best-selling novels, and so on. To make matters worse, we had underestimated the lengths to which convicts from the other units would go to steal our books. Despite having a superior library of their own, prisoners from units B2 and E were paying food items to indigent F2 inmates to steal our best library books and smuggle them out of the building. Once those books hit the yard, the chances of recovering them were slim to none. This was the reason illiterate inmates were checking out so many books without returning them. It was their side hustle.

Sun Tzu was whispering in my ear, *"A wise general makes a point of foraging on the enemy."*[6] Since the other dorms were stealing from our library, why shouldn't we steal from theirs? But I didn't want to pay people to swipe back our missing books. That would just create a cycle of theft. We were fighting a defensive war; the other units were the aggressors, not us. All we needed was to find a way to stop the thieves.

> *"You can ensure the safety of your defense if you only hold positions that cannot be attacked."*[7]

Every prison library develops its own strategies to combat kleptos. The main library, for example, secured its most sought-after titles in a locked cabinet. But the F2 library was a simple room with only bookshelves, tables, and a desk. There was nowhere to keep reading material that thieves couldn't get into. We needed to expand our operation, and that meant bringing in new recruits.

A group of F2 inmates agreed to store the most popular books in their cells, where they would be safe and readily accessible. K and I kept an inventory of the separately stored books, which we would lend only to prisoners who had shown themselves trustworthy with library material. The result was a network of cells, each holding different genres of books in an unofficial secondary library. My friend Carl, who was obsessed with the occult, kept a cell full of books on magic and witchcraft. His unofficial religion section looked like it belonged at Hogwarts. A few nerds secured the fantasy and science-fiction novels, roleplaying games, and comics. Our resident otaku held the manga, and our jailhouse lawyer maintained the law books. I even convinced Reggie to be our "dictionary man," a title he was proud to adopt.

Here's how our system worked: When someone we trusted asked for a book that wasn't on the shelves of our official library, we would check the inventory list to see whether that title was in the secondary library. If it was, I would deliver it to the requester after the official library closed. My own cell served as the drop box for both F2 libraries. I hung a sign that read "Return library books here" above the food slot on my cell door, and people dropped their borrowed books through the slot to return them.

Once the secondary library was established, whenever we received book donations, the best titles would be stored in cells while the rest were sent to the front lines—the library shelves. Like the books in our official library, all secondary library books were stamped with "F2 Library" in hope that if they were lost, they might find their way back to my drop box. By not putting all our eggs in the one basket of the official library, we had found a way not only to reduce theft but also to ensure that the best books could be borrowed and returned even when the library was closed.

"We cannot enter into alliances until we are acquainted with the designs of our neighbors."[8]

Eventually, the secondary library grew so large, it became difficult to keep track of all the books. We could have moved some to the official library, but that would have been no different than handing them directly to the thieves. Instead, K and I sent kites to the other buildings to negotiate an exchange. We had books the other units wanted, and they had books we wanted. If we could establish trade routes within enemy territory, that might lay the groundwork for some kind of peace accord. After all, if the other dorms had a way to get the books they wanted, they wouldn't have to pay thieves to steal from our library anymore.

The book exchange started small. At first, only a few titles were swapped between E dorm and F2. But soon we were moving boxes of books from one building to another. Once the other units took notice, they all wanted a piece of the action. Even the main library joined the exchange. After that, we started seeing books from the previous year's stolen donations entering the circulation. Those first shipments of books were finally finding their way to F2.

That's when things started looking up. Not only did the thefts become less frequent, but some of the books that had been stolen magically reappeared on our library shelves. As expected, prisoners in the other buildings had stopped paying people to steal from us. They had already read all our best books. A few sticky-fingered inmates still occasionally swiped books for themselves, but theft was no longer the problem it once was. The secondary library was now obsolete. It was safe to move all the reading material from our cells to the shelves of our official library.

Maybe F2 would never have the best library on the yard, but through teamwork and determination, we had vastly expanded our reading selection and ability to access books. I would like to think we changed the culture of the prison, that we were victorious in a pivotal struggle against discrimination. But even if we weren't, at least we had plenty to read. In the end, the real victory was winning roughly equal access to books for all Riverbanks inmates, regardless of their mental health status.

Due to an overabundance of books, K and I decided some reading material should be moved out of F2. We simply did not have the shelf space for so many titles. So, I sent a request to the library officer, and he granted permission for me to bring the main library a box of donations.

When I arrived at the main library carrying a cardboard box full of books, the inmate librarian was standing behind the checkout desk. I wasn't sure if he recognized me from our previous encounter. "Special delivery from F2," I said as I placed the box on the desk and slid it over to him. He thanked me and opened the lid. Inside the box, on top of all the other books, was Sun Tzu's *Art of War*. It was brand new.

Notes

1. Sun Tzu, *The Art of War*, trans. Lionel Giles (Pax Librorum, 2009 [1910]), 13:6, paxlibrorum.com.
2. Ibid., 4:2.
3. Ibid., 1:17.
4. Ibid., 3:17.
5. Ibid., 5:19.
6. Ibid., 2:15.
7. Ibid., 6:7.
8. Ibid., 7:12.

Longs Pass
Doug Emory

I
I sat on the tailgate of Jacob's Jeep, lacing up my boots. He waited, at the trailhead already, his trekking poles rapping the ground. I slammed the hatchback with an echoing boom then craned for Hank, our team's third member. He balanced precariously in the dirt of the road shoulder, one arm extended above the diminished remnants of the Teanaway River's North Fork, the stream flowing from the slope above through scattered boulders and pines white with dust.

"Butterflies." He held a palm upturned, like he coaxed a shy dog near, and spoke so low he might have spoken to himself. Black beneath his fingers, the water pooled. "They weren't here last year. I didn't think they came so high."

I peered into the shadows. Butterflies danced through a withered garden of iris. They flitted so near that Hank's fingers flinched, but none lit on his beckoning hand.

"Let's go," Jacob bellowed. He carried flowers of his own, a bouquet thrust through his pack's ice ax loop, a splash of orange and yellow against the earth tones he wore. Grimacing, he bit down on a hair tie while yanking his thicket of graying hair into a ponytail.

"Our master calls." I clasped Hank's hand and tugged him up, the dirt collapsing under each step. "You can play with your pets when we're back."

Jacob took off soon as he saw us approaching. At the trail register, from ancient habit, I waved Hank ahead and signed in.

Once, we'd been a climbing team, bonded, in the corny mountaineer's phrase, by "the brotherhood of the rope." In that brotherhood we'd followed one order without exception: me at anchor, Hank in the middle, and Jacob leading. Jacob led, always. Nothing deterred him, not endless miles of trail, not whiteouts or uncertain handholds on ice-glazed stone. He was unbreakable until his son Ramey's death on Mount Stuart broke him, sent him over a cliff from which he would never stop falling.

Those twin falls—Ramey's and Jacob's--dragged our team into oblivion with them. One might have mistakenly believed tragedy would strengthen our bonds. Jacob and I both had lost sons to mourn, mine to divorce and his to the mountains. Hank was a counselor. He helped me when my wife packed up, and he offered the same salve to Jacob. But our friend slipped from our grasp, never reached out except for these memorial hikes to Longs Pass. Hank and I trooped along as mere role players, Rosencrantz and Guildenstern, accompanying Jacob through the weak October light, reprising the morning three years ago when we'd tried to save Ramey and failed.

Hank had gained some distance while I signed the register, but I caught him quickly. The trail's angle of ascent was unrelenting, and he'd lost his conditioning, his belly soft over his pack's waistband. He rasped in a breath. "We still gonna talk to him?"

I glanced uphill, ensuring Jacob was beyond earshot. He moved into sight and out again, cut by branches and tree trunks, hunched forward as if striding into a gale.

"I'm not sure it's a good idea," I said.

Two nights earlier, Hank had called me with a proposal—let's get the team back together. Immediately my mind conjured memories: not the surreal alpine landscape so much as the clattering of ice axes at sunrise, the idiotic jokes at one another's expense, and stories repeated a thousand times that never aged. Our past days felt flooded with light, our camaraderie perfect, our accomplishments, from the safe front room of my undistinguished apartment, fantastical. But after agreeing to Hank's request, I'd considered the details of what talking to Jacob entailed.

He shot me a sideways look. "Seriously? Why?"

"Don't you think it's selfish? How exactly do I phrase this pitch? Jacob, we want to start climbing again. Let's all return to these spectacular places that killed your son."

Hank tugged off his knit cap and stuffed it in a pocket. "Gonna drop a layer."

Sweating too, I shrugged off my jacket.

"Brett, man, I'm not doing this anymore. Either we climb, and an annual memorial becomes part of what we do, or I skip this trip to the graveyard. This is what we were. Now we only see him this one day a year. It's unhealthy."

He gave a hop, straightening his pack. "Besides, nothing's that simple," he said. "It's selfish and it's not. Sure, I miss what we had, but what about Jacob? What does he do now, hour after hour and day after day? Over those years together, didn't we develop a responsibility to him?"

"We've tried," I said. "We've always been open to whatever he wants. I worry we've been so respectful of his feelings, we're disrespectful. If that makes any sense."

Hank gave me a look, then laughed. "You want to lead?"

"Nope. Tradition must be observed." Although the world, I'd learned, could surely warp us into any form it desired, I would retain my ceremonial role as anchor. I climbed last, to give our team that extra split-second to react when trouble inevitably came.

Hank drew ahead while, beyond his hunched shoulders, I watched Jacob. When we'd been a team, I'd developed a metaphor for how Jacob moved: like a cable car, an effortless glide upward, powered by an irresistible mechanical force. Today, though, he labored. He was far too human, leaning heavily on his poles and stabbing the earth in desperation.

Slowly as Hank and I moved, Jacob couldn't gain on us. Before, he would have been a dark smudge nearing the horizon, pausing only to cajole us or, in one of his odd quirks, help us through difficulties. I remembered once, when I had arrested a slide but jabbed my ax through my pinkie in the process, he had called down, "Hey, you! Stop bleeding all over my mountain." Then he'd descended, cradling my hand in his, repositioning that torn, fish-belly flap of skin and bandaging me with a gentleness far greater than I experienced in the emergency room afterwards.

Jacob had been invincible then, and who would I have been without him? Just a middle-school English teacher who had driven his wife away, who woke alone in the night, believing his distant son cried from his apartment's spare bedroom. I could have been forged from the predictable disappointment of Christopher's custody visits, hurtling to the airport, my head filled with illusions of his timid smile breaking open like a dam at the sight of me. I could almost feel his head pressed against my chest, his arms hanging limp at first before rising into an embrace that would hold me forever. Who I met instead was a slouch-shouldered boy taller and skinnier than I remembered, his hair lengthening to veil his eyes and one foot invariably trailing, as if ready to spin back for the bridge onto the jet.

But in following Jacob, in kicking into the marks he left in scree and snow, I become someone besides that pitiful creature who wept over photos of vanished happiness. Physically I gained strength, could post-hole through knee-deep snow and ascend nine thousand vertical feet hauling a pack overflowing with gear. I could rise predawn and still be moving when darkness returned. My reward was imagery straight out of Norse mythology: sheer cliff faces, impossibly delicate rock spires, and ice etched by black lightning-bolt scars of crevasses. From summits, I stared through my dangling boots to black patches of forest a thousand feet below.

Certainly, I was exhausted often and on occasion scared, but I pressed ahead, succeeding at tasks most people couldn't comprehend. I owed that parallel version of my life to Jacob.

Now, although he and I never spoke beyond these forlorn memorial hikes, I thought of him frequently. I had grief all my own, but I wondered how he bore his greater one, how he forced himself from bed, engaged in small talk at work or made sense of mowing the lawn. In my imagination, the impetus that drove him upslope had shifted, fitted now to a different objective, that of forcing himself to believe drawing breath was worth the effort.

Our trail climbed. The sheltering pines gave way to stubby alpine firs. I dropped my head, watching my feet, angling my boots out for purchase when scree littered the trail. I skipped around larger exposed rocks. At tree line, we pulled alongside a chute that avalanches had scoured clean, a wide gulley filled with hard pack, crumbling shale, and Krumholtz circles. Above us, horseshoe clouds drifted toward the ridge.

I caught Hank at the trail junction, sprawled against the weathered sign where the Ingalls Lake Trail branched north. Jacob stood a few strides farther on, tossing back a handful of Gorp. Silver flecked the stubble on his cheeks.

I dug into a pouch hanging at my side. "Anyone want half this?" I slapped a chunk of energy bar into Hank's upraised palm.

Jacob shook his head at my offer. "You make any significant tops this summer?" he asked.

"Finally made Hinman." I mumbled through a mouthful. "Camped below in Necklace Valley in a biblical plague of mosquitoes." With a gulp of water, I washed the dust-dry bar down. "Then I drove to Denver, slogged up some fourteeners, and bagged a peak in the Wind Rivers on the way home."

"You do all of this alone?"

I raised my eyebrows at Hank, anticipating one of Jacob's standard risk-versus-reward lectures, his reflexive admonition against climbing alone. "Yes, Dad. All by myself."

He unrolled the hair tie from his ponytail and his hair exploded like he'd grabbed a jumper cable. "You know how I feel. At least you're staying active. I've always wondered how you esteemed school district employees fill those breaks we working stiffs fund."

I re-centered my ball cap on my egg-bald head. "You know, you could raise pigeons in that nest of hair you've somehow held onto. Or maybe share a little with Hank and me."

Jacob laughed under his breath and turned away. "You let your partner sit there much longer, we'll have to commission a crane to lift him. Time to move." Poles clacking, he started away, and I extended Hank a hand.

"How are Emma and Christopher doing?" Hank said as we headed out. "He make it out this summer?"

I shrugged though he couldn't see. The divorce decree required Christopher to split summer vacation equally between me and his mom. "He came out for a week. He's fifteen, so he spent all his time staring at his phone. Can't fight that."

"Here's a crazy idea, man—you could skip the Rockies and camp out near his mom's place instead. That boy will need his father."

"I could bust into his mom's house, put a hood over his head, and drive him to the mountains. Or I could accept the reality I don't interest him all that much."

"You make your reality, Brett. You work with kids that age just like I do. All of them eventually want their parents whether they admit it or not."

I changed the channel on the subject. "How about you and Alma? Going on, what, three hundred years of bliss? Any marital drama yet?"

"Still boring. Oldest is starting college next year, so approaching the trauma of an empty nest. It's not like we don't have our issues. Last night, she informed me I'd been stacking the dishwasher wrong for a decade."

"All happy families are alike; every unhappy family is unhappy in its own way," I said.

Hank laughed but didn't reply. He sucked in another ragged breath. Ahead, the trail turned a shallow arc away from the avalanche chute then began switchbacking steeply to the pass, visible now as a shallow scoop in the ridge another three hundred feet above. Jacob had slowed but kept moving, kicking his boots in and timing his breath to the movement. Hank stared up and rested, hands on hips.

"A few easy steps more," I said. "Just take it steady."

At the pass, Jacob's figure hovered silhouetted against the gray sky. Hank nodded briskly and resumed his upward trudge. Mount Stuart remained hidden until our final steps and then emerged more fully with each stride, its shattered crown of summit pillars followed by the scars that etched its mile-high face: deep-cut couloirs, talus ramps, and drifted snow reflecting light from high ledges.

I shrugged my pack off and caught a strap as it fell. Jacob knelt, rocking back on his heels, constructing a pyramid of stones to hold the bouquet he'd carried.

"This view." Hank shook his head. "It's always overwhelming."

"Like a blow from Thor's hammer," I said.

Jacob pushed up and batted the dust from his knees. His flowers seemed bigger than they were, a splash of brilliance contrasted against a universe of blacks and grays.

Jacob's hands folded over one another, clasped tight to his chest. "Might I say a few words?"

"As long as you need," Hank said. "Anything you want to say."

Jacob bobbed his head at us then faced the mountain. A breeze shuffled the tangle of hair across his shoulders.

"Dearest Ramey." His voice was low, and I strained to hear. "In our kitchen for your twenty-first birthday, we three gave you a rack of protection. Son, I'll hope till I'm with you again, hope forever, that you understood the intention behind those cams and slings and pickets. We intended both to welcome you into the community of climbers and to keep you safe. Many nights since, I've doubted the wisdom of that gift, but then I remember the joy these great summits brought us. Long days of a father and son in the hills. A time to hear your thoughts, watch you grow, build friendships and become the brilliant young man you are."

"Amen," Hank said. Swiftly I mouthed the word after him.

"As your father . . ." Jacob's voice quavered, but he pushed on. "As your father, ironic as it seems, you gave me life. You showed me the world. That was a rebirth, seeing this world's beauty as you saw it. That was a gift I can never repay."

Hank had eased forward without my noticing, and he laid an arm across Jacob's shoulders. At the touch, Jacob's knees buckled just an instant, his boots scraping the ground for balance. Then Hank turned Jacob and drew him to his chest.

Jacob's head tilted back. His eyes pressed tightly closed and his shoulders shook, but no sound escaped him. Nails digging into my arms, I hugged myself. Across the valley, Stuart stood, heedless as ever of us, and futilely I traced its face for the point where Ramey's boots had lost their grip on the earth.

As with most climbing accidents, details were vague. Ramey had been with a girlfriend from the rock gym. They'd climbed unroped, probably traversing an ice-packed ledge. In the movie my imagination created, the girl fell, her speed breathtaking, the air hissing, ice crystals thrown aloft and dazzling like sequins against the sky. She didn't have time to scream. And the Ramey I knew? He dived after her clawed fingers, extending his arm in rescue though he lacked any hold himself.

In my vision's periphery, Jacob set both palms lightly against Hank's chest and shoved him away like the man had been crowding him. He dragged a rough hand across his face and took me in with an unflinching look.

"Your son was a special young man, Jacob," I said. "Thank you for bringing him into my life. He held up his end of the rope, even when he was a tiny punk. He was unique. Not a day goes by I don't think of him."

We didn't linger after Jacob delivered his eulogy. We just stood a handful of minutes without speaking. Then we hoisted our packs in tandem, as if an inaudible signal had simultaneously summoned us all.

Jacob waved Hank ahead. "Lead us to glory, Henry. First time for everything. Pretend we've returned to the days we were passably accomplished at these adventures."

Relieved at finally heading downhill, Hank took off like an antelope, gravity hustling him along. Jacob didn't follow. He blocked my way forward instead.

"You said 'unique,'" he said.

"I'm sorry, Jacob. What's the question?"

"'Ramey was unique.' Your words. Remind me how. Some days, I have a hard time picturing his face."

"Remember how he told us we were old and slow before we were old and slow? He could righteously talk some smack."

Jacob shuffled ahead, his steps compact and quiet so he could hear.

"But think about his tattoos. Most kids would have gone bad-ass macho, sleeves of Forbidden Peak down one arm and Liberty Ridge the other, but Ramey? He picked his favorite flowers--bear grass and paintbrush. He had a gentleness you don't find in a person who could drive the way he could."

Jacob held that desultory pace, his head still cocked to hear.

"He treated my Christopher the same way. He was ten years older. He could have blown off and left the little kid behind, but he picked up every rock and stick Chris pointed out as special. By the time we made the car, he carried twenty pounds of rock and enough wood for a bonfire."

Jacob laughed. "They were brilliant together."

"I don't know I've ever been happier than when we were out with them." Then, suddenly remembering that Jacob and I had once been special too, I asked, "How are you keeping these days, my friend?"

"Honestly? I feel like I never quite wake up, like I pry one eye open each morning but the other stays dreaming."

He lifted his chin, his stubble-covered face appearing in profile. "How long has Chris been away with his mom now?"

"Five years last July."

"So how are *you* keeping? I've got my Kerry, a wife of thirty years. Ramey's older sister flies out to keep us company. But you? I expect you're lonely, no child in the house and no one lovingly pointing out your manifold faults."

"I'm in a classroom full of kids all day." The words caught in my throat, like I'd been discovered lying and scrambled to disguise it. "The quiet's a relief, and there's always grading and lesson planning to keep me out of trouble."

"Here's hoping you've managed to teach one or two how to write a sentence instead of maintaining your Sisyphean career. But being in a classroom isn't what I mean, is it."

I listened to our boots scraping along the trail until he spoke again.

"You still seeing that woman who called you her 'no strings whatsoever' experience? The one you were with when we drove out after Ramey?"

"Turned out she wanted strings. Plenty of them. She was a Romantic in disguise."

"Ah, and that would never have aligned with the cynical likes of yourself."

"She decided what I did that night was a grand gesture— like I'm a guy capable of grand gestures. It awoke all sorts of romantic illusions. I expect she's been married ten times by now, chasing after Sir Lancelot."

"Weather's coming in." Jacob lifted an arm, gesturing across the western valley. Clouds were breaking over the Esmeralda Peaks, their summit rocks materializing in veiled gray images before fading like memory. A curtain of dust swirled upslope, toppling back on itself before reaching us.

"Let's catch Hank," Jacob said. "It will never do having him beat us back. He'll develop the misconception he's a mountaineer."

When Jacob accelerated, I at first matched his pace, then braked, skidding, knocking a stone loose and sending it down, a dark point spinning high before disappearing. Then I looked back up to Longs Pass, the ragged outcrops of shale black with lichen and the naked slope gray under the clouds.

II

I thought back to my son hiking with Jacob's, Ramey naming every flower and freezing Chris with a hand on his chest whenever an animal crept into view. For the hundredth time, I regretted giving in when my ex refused to allow Chris to fly home for the funeral. The boys had been so close, so perfectly aligned. Despite the passage of time, Chris would have wanted to honor his friend.

What was easy forgetting now was that it took death to reconcile Jacob and Ramey. Until then, only climbing bonded them, a sole point of connection in a relationship otherwise colored by perpetual drama. Ramey was a middling student who attended college but left after six months. He was between jobs as often as he was employed, and every romance he toppled into proved ephemeral as smoke. But in the mountains, from four years old on, he was a savant. The trail lightened his steps, nearly floating him skyward like a helium-filled balloon. At age eight, we taught him to self-arrest. I had a picture from that day, the boy bracing an overlong ice ax across his torso, his teeth bared in a ferocious grimace while his father grinned broadly over his shoulder. Two years after that, I tightened his harness straps and roped him in for his first glacier crossing.

During that evening Jacob had recalled at the pass, Hank and I had arrived instants before Ramey left with friends to celebrate his birthday. I handed out cans of beer from a grocery bag while Hank sneaked Ramey's present under the kitchen table. Loudly, we demanded Ramey take a seat and Jacob reignite the half-eaten cake. Kerry snapped off the overhead light, and, after Ramey drew a theatrical breath and extinguished the candles, we slapped a conglomeration of every imaginable type of climbing protection onto the tabletop and slid it forward. Ramey glanced up and whispered a barely audible thank-you. His eyes brimmed. In that flickering candlelight, his face glowed like a comet.

Truth was, by the time we gifted Ramey that gear, he had far outstripped our adult team's capabilities. He ditched us for a rotating menagerie of younger, stronger partners, and I followed their exploits on Instagram. Ramey and his team perched on platforms kicked into icy slopes so sheer my head spun with vertigo. Goggles blackened their eyes. Their smiles were open and undaunted. How could such wild, audacious joy fail to infect a person? I felt it myself, safe on my couch at home.

For our aging team, Jacob's climbing philosophy never altered. He weighed risk and reward. His favorite saying, repeated ad nauseum, was, "There are old climbers and bold climbers, but there are no old, bold climbers." His proudest moments occurred when a summit was within reach, but he judged conditions too risky and turned us around.

When speaking of Ramey's conquests, though, his views transformed. He focused on the creativity of route selection, the technical skill and physical determination Ramey demonstrated. I expect, like most of us, he wanted the world to join him in understanding how extraordinary his child was, and that desire blinded him to the ethic he had followed for years.

I felt pulled by Ramey's contradiction, felt both the wonder of his triumphs and the terror of his routes. They were intricate, detailed as a Vermeer painting. Often, he told me, he couldn't sleep beforehand, just lay in bed, visualizing each landmark, each twist in direction, each movement. Too frequently, he led, soloing, ignoring the rope. He spent overlong minutes traversing beneath thawing ice cliffs and crumbling spires of volcanic rock. Those insubstantial structures would creak with an almost comic groan, but then projectiles would break free with such force they generated their own windstorms and shook the climbers on their stances. Ramey had reduced the climbing game to pure chance, a chaotic lottery where the outcome lay beyond anyone's prediction.

Over pints, I tactfully tried expressing my concerns to Jacob. The rules set for us, he informed me, simply didn't apply. Climbers at Ramey's level possessed skills I failed to comprehend. When Ramey himself visited my apartment, he assured me he was safe, but then added, always too soon after, "Man, you should feel that rush, Uncle Brett! One life, right? Can't let it fade off into the middle-class void. It's the only one we've got."

The night he went missing, he left Jacob a static-distorted message just seconds long: "Dad, we're still up here. Stuart . . . we're . . ."

But Jacob's phone was charging at the time, and Ramey's words went unheard for hours. After midnight, Jacob woke, buried in blankets but shivering like he lay outside. He listened to the message, immediately called Hank and then me. The woman beside me rolled over and propped her head on her palm, studying me with wonder as I filled my pack with gear.

I told her she could stay, but she walked with me to the parking lot, leaving the warm arc of light from the building entrance and stopping before condominium windows blank with night. Her Honda sat alone in a visitor's stall, its windshield reflecting the icy security lights like frozen stars.

"What's he expect you to do about it?" She balanced uncertainly on the curb.

"Moral support mostly. Maybe they'll want us to sign on with search and rescue."

"I have to confess surprise. Out the door at three a.m. on a non-climbing weekend. I wouldn't have thought you gave that much of a shit about anybody."

Two hours later, outside the ranger station in Cle Elum, Hank, Jacob, and I waited, hands folded around truck stop coffee cups until the Forest Service showed up. Jacob chased the ranger into the office, a half step behind her, his arms flying, haranguing her about beginning a search. Hank and I leaned against the Jeep, the broad main street empty, hugging ourselves against the cold.

"Wait till afternoon. See if you hear," the ranger said, but we knew better. We drove to the trailhead, bearing packs that would make Jesus weep. Jacob and I each carried ice axes, rope, harness, medical supplies, and extra clothes. We would scale the mountain, charging up and down each of its dozen routes until we rescued Ramey. As ever, Stuart remained hidden until those last steps to Longs Pass. Then it soared remorselessly into view, revealing both its reality and ours: Stuart was a two-mile high maze of rock and ice. We were three minor creatures, transitory as dust, fragile as glass. The mountain rendered us powerless. Exhausted by the sight of it, we sank on top of our packs, waiting hours on helicopters above and rescue parties below.

After the funeral, Hank and I drove to a memorial at Jacob's house, where he gifted Ramey's remaining climbing gear to the boy's friends. Hank and I stayed till everyone else had gone. As we left, Jacob clapped our shoulders like a thousand times before, as if nothing between us had changed.

But from then on, he screened his calls. Days passed before he responded to my invitations out for drinks, invitations he invariably declined. When I emailed, inviting him back into the woods for anything from mild lake hikes to our standard climbs, he never responded at all.

Several weeks after the memorial at Jacob's house, I stopped by unannounced on a Thursday after class. He popped open beers, and we sat across the kitchen table from one another. He folded both hands around his bottle and only answered me in clipped replies. At any sound outside, his head would suddenly lift, his eyes alert. Before the accident, Kerry had frequently wandered in to poke fun as he and I pored over maps, calculating distances, routes, and elevations. Now she stood at the window, pulling back the drapes as though she suspected intruders in the yard.

Our relationship had been cast in its new form. I reached out less frequently, then stopped altogether. Months passed. I never expected to see Jacob again, but when his name flashed on my phone's screen, I picked up instantly. I don't know what I anticipated—a return to a golden age, the days before Ramey had fallen? I was utterly naïve. If I'd only considered the date, I would have known Jacob's motivation before a word was spoken—we were returning to the graveyard, to be humbled again by Stuart and memorialize his son.

I picked up speed on the trail. Neither Hank nor Jacob had waited for me at the junction, so I marched on alone. I ducked back into the firs and pines, leaving the wasteland of tundra, and ran my palms over the porcelain grace of their needles. On an instinct built from thousands of miles of hiking, I sensed trail's end approaching. A car door slammed, faint, muffled by distance. The clearing where we'd parked showed in a flash through trees. Not far below, my friends' voices rose, a wordless murmur, familiar and comforting as rushing water.

Jacob, I'd assumed, had given up on our climbing team, but I couldn't shake the remembrance of him as my friend. I'd resigned myself to his abandoning us, but I wondered now whether his actions absolved us of our responsibility to him. What if Hank was right about what we owed him? During our days in the mountains, Jacob was even better than me at defying basic human needs: fatigue, blisters, or bone-rattling cold. What if, in his now-diminished strength, hypnotized by that eternal looping vision of Ramey's fall, Jacob had simply lost the capacity to tie himself into the rope?

At the trail register, I signed us out then stepped onto the dusty roadside. Hank sat perched on the tailgate, prying boots from his swollen feet.

"Nice of you to show up." Jacob ducked his head into the car.

"My liege, a mystic vision appeared to me." Like a street preacher, I lifted my arms skyward. "I wandered the wilderness alone, ditched by my asshole friends. And in that emptiness, lo, a pint of the North Bend Brewery's finest IPA materialized from shimmering air and called me to a quest."

Hank's boots thudded into the hatchback. "Not on me to reject a message from the gods. Especially one commanding me to drink beer. Jacob, brother, you in?"

Eyeing me suspiciously, Jacob remained blocked behind the car's open door. "I have to get home."

"Bullshit," I said. "You don't. It's barely noon. How about this, you cheap bastard? For the pleasure of your company, I'll even buy your beer."

III

The brewery sat right on Main Street. Traffic was heavy for an early afternoon, so Hank pointed Jacob to a parking spot a couple of blocks away. Jacob clambered from behind the wheel like arthritis afflicted every joint. He lagged behind as we jogged for the bar.

I swung through the door first then waited on my vision to adjust. Malt hung in the air, sweet and heavy, and the room gradually took form: upturned barrels near the windows, long tables lining the interior, and, framed between bowls of golden light on the far wall, the bartender drying his hands on a towel. We were his first customers, and he gave us a brisk wave over.

With three pints squeezed unsteadily in my hands, I crossed the room, futilely trying to keep from spilling. Hank had chosen one of those barrel tables, right under the window overlooking Main Street, and I doused its rough surface liberally as I set our glasses down. Jacob stood while I draped my jacket over a chair, and when I sat he didn't move. Something outside had caught his attention, and I followed his gaze.

"What's up?" I asked.

"We need to beat traffic home," he said. The traffic light beside us was out of sync. Each time it turned red, cars lined up beyond our sight.

I took a swallow and rapped Jacob's sleeve. "Get comfortable and admit it, man. I had a great plan."

"First time for everything."

Hank returned from the bar bearing a plastic bowl of popcorn. He snagged a fistful and slid it between us. He took a prodigious gulp of beer. "Ahhhh, Jesus that's good," he said. Then he launched into his favorite current story, one I'd heard already, about a student who'd asked about attending massage school after graduation.

"I don't get it," Jacob said. "Why is this worthy of our discussion?"

"It's funnier if you let me reach the punch line." With a sharp clink, Hank tipped his glass against Jacob's. "He wanted a massage program where he didn't have to touch anybody. Too much anxiety, so he couldn't manage any physical contact. He wanted to connect with and heal clients, but only telepathically. I told him I'd thumb through our college catalogs for a program like that."

The corners of Jacob's mouth upturned ironically, raising the shaggy outreaches of his beard. He sipped hesitantly from his pint, smacked his lips, then drank more fully.

Hank scooped up another load of popcorn. At my elbow, a car honked. I slopped yet more beer across the table and craned looking for napkins.

"Here." Hank dropped a napkin into the pond pooling in front of me, then caught my eye and mouthed, "You're on."

I coughed to loosen the frog suddenly formed in my throat. "Jacob, we—"

"We?"

I waggled a finger from Hank to me.

His thicket of eyebrows arched. "I might have guessed."

"*We* were thinking. The three of us climbed, a couple of weekends a month, for twenty years. I remember almost every step we took, even from the first. Those were the best parts of my life. All our stories. So much craziness and joy." I paused an instant for breath. "Then it all went up like smoke."

Jacob's head rose from his glass, an overlong gaze taking us both in in turn. "You understand the reason for that. This morning should have clarified that for you."

"Yes, Jacob, yes. We know. We respect what happened, but—"

"We're just asking you to join us again, a few times a year," Hank mercifully cut in. "Put our old team back together. It would be healthy for us all."

"Of course. Simple, isn't it?" Jacob wagged his head. His wild hair swung, obscuring his face. "And 'healthy,' my god. Not for you two alone. You'd likely end filling yet more body bags for the Forest Service. What would possibly be on your proposed mountaineering dance card? A hike to Snow Lake with half the population of Seattle?"

"Whatever you're comfortable with," I said. "We were thinking glacier travel, basic Class Three climbing, that sort of thing."

He rocked back on his chair legs, eyes following a group of customers coming through the door. His voice lowered, like we were a married couple who couldn't resist arguing but didn't want anyone to overhear. "You could have just called me, you know. You left me night after night alone. No need to bribe me and pressure me over a quiet drink. We're long past that."

"Jacob, I did call. I called a dozen times a week."

His chair dropped forward, the legs scraping the cement floor. "*A dozen times a week.* Truly? Our phone records must differ."

"Help me out, Hank, would you?"

But Jacob didn't let Hank utter a word. "You understand, old teammate, that life's most important lesson involves looking in the mirror. I, for instance, am an engineer who uses repetitive calculations to solve inconsequential problems. You," he flipped an upturned palm at Hank, "are a high school guidance counselor, and you, my rhetorically challenged friend, teach advanced placement English."

He took a sip then centered his glass precisely on the table. "No shame in what we became, none. The shame comes from fooling ourselves into believing we were something more. That's what cost my son. He believed the fantasy we created."

"Jesus, Jacob. Are you serious?" I leaned nearer, like I struggled to be heard over the wind. "We didn't trick anyone. If Ramey had stayed with us, he'd be sitting here right now."

He scoffed with a harsh, metallic bark. Jacob might have weakened in the mountains, but he sat across from us now in all his former passion, his expression locked in that narrow corridor between scorn and anguish. "Don't dare tell me we kept Ramey safe. Every tale we told glorified recklessness. The Terrible Traverse. The Northwest Buttress, those icy ramps we crossed in rock shoes because we were too pressed for time to switch back to boots. That ridiculous tale where you charged into a whiteout, lamenting Emma's leaving with your boy."

Jacob's speech at Longs Pass, I understood now, had been governed by context, delivering the necessary, ever insufficient attempt to convey his love. But every morning when he struggled from bed, he delivered the speech we were hearing now, a well-rehearsed sermon to the person confronting him in the mirror.

"You understand, don't you." His voice sank, as if in my silence I conspired with him. "At best we were braggarts. Aging men, going against the mountains, fooling our sons into loving us by pretending we were gods."

Hank didn't appear to be listening. His fingers folded contemplatively over a few more popcorn kernels. I shook my head. "No, Jacob. The accident's made you forget. We were just guys who went into the woods and fell in love with the spectacle of it. We learned how to move on challenging terrain. Rock and ice. We loved being together. It's that simple."

"Nothing is that simple. I've done the forensics, you see. I know where responsibility for this lies."

"It's your life. You believe what you want," I snapped. "When I visualize the accident—and believe me, I've replayed it a thousand times—I see Ramey's partner losing her balance and him reaching to save her. That's who your son was, Jacob. That would have been his every instinct. Would you change that?"

"Now? After what I've endured? Of course I would." He dug for his hair tie in his pocket, pinned it between pursed lips, and yanked his hair back. A beat passed, the room stifling, choked with silence. Then Hank leaned forward, one hand on Jacob's forearm and the other on mine.

"Jacob, what if Brett's right and an accident is only an accident? Prying emotions apart can be hard, Jacob." He raised two intertwined fingers. "Grief and guilt can blur. They're this close sometimes, but they're not the same. Allocate responsibility if you need to, but be fair to yourself. You can honor one emotion without indulging the other."

His hand left my arm for Jacob's, as if he needed both to hold our friend in place. "Look at me, Jacob. Do Ramey the honor of respecting his choices. Imagine his life in a cocoon. What a deprivation that would have been, to never have been split open by the view from a summit, never to stand beside friends and take in an ocean of peaks. Never to have stories of foolishness and triumph to tell." He drew his hands away carefully, palms flat on the table. "You wanted to spend time with him and teach him to value what you value. That's what a parent does, Jacob. That's just love. That's what love is."

Jacob's shoulders slumped. His head fell onto the chairback, and he blew an exhausted sigh toward the Christmas lights twined through the ductwork overhead. His pose reminded me of my nights rocking Christopher in his nursery, slouched back as far as the chair would allow while I counted and recounted the luminescent constellations we'd affixed to the ceiling. A minute passed. Jacob at last began speaking again, his words floating upward, each syllable worn smooth from the journey of the past three years. "I don't want to see anyone, but I despise being alone. For my pride, I wanted to mold Ramey in my image, wanted him to see me as a hero, and now I have no one. And never, never will this end."

"Fathers have wanted worse for their children," Hank finally said. "Here's the other side of pride, my friend. What's the first rule of the mountains? Our will only carries us so far. We control what we control, but the mountains make the final determination. We pray they'll be merciful, but the choice is theirs."

Jacob straightened. Tears worked through his overgrown thicket of beard. They dangled above the weathered wood like crystals of refracted light. He swirled the swallow of beer left in his pint, the foam sticking to the glass, a microcosm of clouds on sky. "So, what are you thinking?" he asked. "Where are you thinking we should go?"

Hank gave me a nod of permission, and I answered carefully. "Maybe start working the Backcourt 100, back to those scramble peaks along Teanaway Ridge."

"The ones we halfway finished years ago?" He laughed and wiped his eyes on his sleeve. "You're like a living, breathing cliché of a peak bagger. No peak you've failed on you won't try again. There's a vast irony in that."

He and Hank exchanged a sudden look, like all along the two of them had been leagued together and I the outsider. Jacob angled himself slightly, cutting me out of the conversation entirely.

"I know today is your doing." He tapped a finger beside the popcorn bowl. "Brett, that poor oblivious bastard, would never have understood how to invite me back. You're the counselor here. You've demonstrated your emotional voodoo. Now exercise your powers to get the whole team back on the rope. Prevent our living another tragedy of fathers and sons."

Hank emptied his pint and belched softly. "That's a high bar just to get you back. My counseling talents have their limits, and I'm grossly underpaid. We'd need an overnight backpack to wake this boy up and address all his issues."

Jacob caught my questioning look reflected in Hank's eyes. He angled back toward me. "Even now, you sit here like a stump, blind to the obvious. My Ramey is gone, gone forever. You have a hope I've lost, but you refuse to recognize a glimmer of it."

"Exactly what type of hope is it you two think I'm missing?"

"Call Christopher, Brett," Hank said.

"You call your son to hear his voice on his voicemail," Jacob said. "You pitch a tent on his front lawn. His response isn't the point. You're the parent here. It's your decision to create a future or lose it entirely."

He bent close, his rough hand overlapping mine and grasping so hard my bones cracked. "Do you understand?" he said. "Finally?"

I sat without speaking. Jacob's eyebrows knitted in concentration. His face wore that same look of patient concern as when, after my fall, he'd bandaged my hand all those years ago.

"I've known you long enough to understand there's a cost for any advice you give me, good or bad," I answered slowly.

"Let me buy the second round too. A down payment to make up for all the disappointments I've caused."

"It's a small gesture," Hank said. "But your recovery has to begin somewhere."

I swept their empties clattering in one hand and caught mine up in the other. When the bartender glanced over his shoulder, I bobbed my head. "Another round," I said. Then, while he stared into the first glass under the tap, I stepped outside.

The flooding light caught me off guard, and once again I blinked my eyes clear. Cars still lined the street, waiting for the mistimed stoplight to turn. A half block away, a mother and her little girl debated at the crosswalk. The woman wore a summer dress, too light for the season. A sweater hung draped across one arm. Her skirt swirled around her knees in the chill wind, and the girl fluttered like a butterfly, grasping for the orange flag her mom had pulled from the canister attached to the light pole. Cautiously, the woman held the flag out, but the girl snatched it and broke away, parading into traffic with her arm upraised, like that scrap of orange plastic would shelter her from every evil this world holds.

But then her mother, skirt sweeping back and heels clacking, gave chase and caught her hand. She swung her daughter up under one arm, the girl's legs kicking and her howl of protest transforming into peals of laughter.

Puzzle Man
Clare Olivares

I watch as his thin bony fingers shake
picking up the puzzle pieces
his brow furrowed
as he tries to discern
the proper placement
my impatient hands wanting to reach in
fit the pieces swiftly and precisely
breathe, breathe into stillness
it is not necessary to speed up his play
or armor yourself for his decline
relax into his quivering hands
moving at a marionette's pace
clippetty clop clippetty clop
his mind's rhythmic tune
the pace more trot than gallop
What's the hurry he asks
we're not getting any younger fella
clippetty clop clippetty clop
at this pace we'll reach heaven at sundown
What's the hurry he asks

Ripe Tomatoes
Mario René Padilla

The wheatfields under turbulent skies, I made a point of trying to express sadness, extreme loneliness ... what I can't say in words. ... For myself, life presumably must remain lonely. ... I must seriously advise you to smoke a pipe, it does you good when you're in a bad mood, as is often the case with me. ... I've always considered it idiotic that painters live alone.
                    —Vincent Van Gogh, Letters to Theo

I harbor few memories. Vague, indeterminable thoughts from the past do exist. I'm only human. I ignore them—as one might hear a passing airplane without glancing toward the sky. They move on toward other horizons. Disappear unrecognized.

For me, the past no longer exists, as it must for sentimentalists or dwellers in what-might-have-been. I'd make a poor fiction writer. As for the future—it's nothing but a daydream. For me, only *now* exists.

Like now, standing at the Kröller-Müller Museum in Otterlo, eye to eye with Vincent, his loneliness reflected in his self-portrait, in the strained and troubled expression of his pitiable stare from beneath a straw hat, me in my coppola, unruly strands of long gray hair sticking out. And in this moment, I realize my relationship with Marie, as it exists back in LA, is slowly going to hell. Another relationship gone.

On my return, she'll say it's me. I'll argue otherwise, show fault in her expectations of me, place it at her feet, as I crawl back into my cave of composition.

"Loving someone like you is like loving a ghost," she chastised in the car to the airport. "All form but no substance. You are a formidable, interesting man, Marco, when you choose to be, but for me you never fully materialize."

Yes, I confess to Vincent. I am more comfortable inside the cozy confines of melodies, keys, notes, sitting at my Steinway—burrowed like an animal, snug inside the dark walls of my imagination.

"Your real relationship is with that instrument, inside your studio, fondling your Pro Tools—avoiding messy flesh and blood emotions and my feelings." At the airport curb, she sighed. "I may not be here when you get back."

She didn't get out of the car.

The recreation of an ideal is impossible, Vincent's eyes retort.

Vincent, that just might be the definition of hell.

Like this morning. The chaos I witnessed on the Nederlands stage. So disturbing to watch. The dancers' movements, stiff and awkward. Unable to capture the intricate Afro-Latino rhythms, dance the twelve-eight clave beneath the pagan indigenous drums of my score. I attribute it (unfairly, of course) to them being Northern Europeans.

I look at Vincent's eyes for reproach.

Let's be realistic here, these rhythms don't course naturally through the DNA of Norse Vikings. But they've been passed down to me through generations. My ancestors drummed for better crops, danced for success in battle—into delirium before sacrificing maidens to ward off demon naguals and pagan spirits of destruction.

Oh, what the hell am I talking about. It's my fault. Me. I arrived two days late with the music. But I had to make those changes, Vincent. You understand. The thought of leaving them in—those *imperfect* chords—was unacceptable.

"Marco, the dancers may not be ready by Friday," Hans Bauer, the Nederlands Dans Theater choreographer, warned. "We could have used those two days."

"Perhaps my late arrival is a good thing, Hans. Less rehearsal time makes a better performance. As I see it, the dancers have two fewer days to think about what they are doing. I don't want them overthinking their movements. I want them natural and spontaneous—strutting like jungle animals. Savage. Dancing purely from instinct and not from a count."

Hans's sharp look stopped short of saying "nonsense," his reputation for patience with experimental composers on full display.

"We'll do our best, Marco. I want you to be satisfied with our production of *The Jungle*. You'll get instinct alright. This I promise. Perhaps more than you think us possible. Of course, some stumbling may be involved." He laughed, good humoredly.

"That's perfectly acceptable . . . after all, they're moving in a jungle."

I left rehearsal early. Came to see *mon inspiriteur* at the Kröller-Müller. Ninety or more of his works in one building. It's overwhelming. And who knows when I'll ever come back to this country. I'm not a traveler. But for my European premier—I had to come.

Your eyes look tired, Vincent. Weary. Sad. Such a lonely, unhappy life all the biographies say you had (and I've read many). Your suffering. Your failed attempts at love. Unfulfilled ambition.

Failed? Yes, I failed to recreate the illusive ideal my boy. I failed at that.

But for me, your sunflower will always be the true sunflower.

The dancers of the Los Angeles Ballet found their way into my rhythms alright. As did the Alvin Ailey Dance

Company in New York. "Musico salvaje," the *New York Times* reviewer wrote, knowing of my Mexican heritage. "Powerful indigenous drumming, congas, tumbas, timbales behind a string orchestra and horns scored unconventionally with complex time signatures. An exhilarating performance one can only experience in the gut."

Since that review, choreographers worldwide have been wanting to schedule a performance of *The Jungle*, or anything else I've written. But my previous works never received this kind of response. The reception is everything I'd hoped for. I should be happy.

I'm not.

But when have you ever been happy? Vincent's eyes remind.

Yes . . . I feel bad for Marie. I know she loves me. Has tried to, at least. Will it always be like this with love, Vincent?

Go to the next canvas. Gaugin said it was one of my best.

Standing before *Bedroom at Arles*, something flutters inside my subconscious. An image rising from its depths. A forgotten experience, suppressed, now recognized.

A melancholic memory? Oh no, not one of those. Normally, I block such sentimental intrusions into my present. Not this time. I must plumb its purple depths. Rehearse its re-creation.

I remember. Vague details are gradually coming into focus, like looking into a wind-agitated lake, the image becoming mirror-clear with the passing of a storm. I see the room again. It was my first studio. I'd just moved into the space—really, just an illegal garage conversion I'd got cheap. How old was I? . . . Twenty-five. Yes. I see me. A young man, sitting at the Steinway I'd just purchased with unused college tuition money. Thick black wavy hair, thin muscular body in a colorful African shirt, filled with boundless energy, a desire to make music, compose melodies with intricate rhythms—swirling inspirations—the kind only young hands can create.

"Like your stars, perhaps," I whisper to Vincent.

Museum patrons move away.

I remember. I had a day job then, selling recording equipment and instruments at Guitar Center to musicians with their own ambitions. I was jealous. Envious of their seeming natural talent on the keyboard, listening to them test Korg workstations and Fender pianos.

I was always uncertain of my abilities, Vincent. Perhaps every artist, at first, feels like a fake.

I did, the eyes in his adjoining self-portrait express. *Eight years painting. One work sold.*

But you destroyed so many, painted over those that didn't meet your expectations.

Yes, Vincent's eyes relay. *I did. The refusal to submit to ultimate satisfaction is like absinthe—it keeps the impossible possible, the unattainable ideal attainable.*

Museum patrons are getting annoyed. They want this dark-skinned foreigner, mumbling to himself and monopolizing the central view of *Bedroom at Arles*, to move on. To them, I must look a little crazy: unshaved for days, tired jet-lagged eyes, my hands plunged into the pockets of a long black wool overcoat in spring. I ignore them.

Stepping back, I sit on a gallery bench, close enough to observe *Bedroom*. To reminisce. Diving deeper into the past—as in a submersible, sinking into the sea of my subconscious.

It was twenty-four years ago. Yes, I'll soon be fifty. I remember disapproving roommates in a beachfront apartment in Playa del Rey. They accused me of becoming antisocial. Staying in my room—always playing my rental spinet. No fun anymore was their verdict. But I'd discovered I wanted to compose. I was tired of selling instruments, of being a tanned piano player at random studio sessions, living the LA beach-party life of a rock musician. I even entertained the possibility I could be a serious composer—an *artist*—though at the time, I had no idea what that meant, or what it would demand of me. First, I had to get away from beer parties on the beach, volleyball games, twenty-somethings in board shorts chasing slim young girls in bikinis.

I devoted all my free time to reading music books from the library. Studied orchestration. Harmony. Ranges of orchestral instruments. Musical score notation. I listened for hours to Stravinsky, Berlioz, Varése, Stockhausen, Jarrett, Miles, Tito Puente. Studying their styles. Learning. Imitating.

My new garage-studio space was very small. It had no stove, only a hot plate. It had a mini refrigerator and a small bathroom with a shower. But I had no other needs. When they delivered my used Steinway A, it took up half the space. At an antique furniture store, I bought an old wooden table with two woven rattan chairs. I found a single wood-framed bed to replace the king size waterbed I had in my beach apartment. I even bought a ceramic pitcher for the table. Just like yours, Vincent.

I added several large white pillows for my bed and covered it with a red blanket.

Whatever happened to that red blanket? I've blocked it out.

No, it's her I've blocked out. But I see her now. She was my next-door neighbor. My Scheherazade, standing in her backyard beside a pool, dressed in a white nightgown—like a vampiress from a horror film.

So difficult, extracting reality from a dream, you say.

Oh, I know. I know. But I'm not dreaming this, Vincent. I'm sure of it. Our conversations. I see her dark eyes, the beautiful olive-skinned face of this sad and troubled fifty-year-old Armenian woman.

Yes, I see her. Clearly . . .

My first glimpse of her came in early evening, not quite twilight. I was exhausted, having moved furniture all day. I stepped outside feeling a bit moody, to smoke one of my grandfather's pipes and consider my plan—the reality of my decision sinking in. Cypress branches above the studio were shifting in the wind—so different from the constant crash of surf onto shore. I heard a screen door open. I glanced over and saw, above the four-foot-high white picket fence that separated our yards, a woman exiting her house. All she had on was a long white nightgown. Thick long curls of black hair flowed down her back to the waist. She walked unsteadily toward her pool's security gate, entered, closed the gate behind her—carefully—and stood at the edge of the pool. She looked down into the water as if she were contemplating going for a swim. But she wasn't in a bathing suit.

This ghostly apparition, so fascinating. I moved closer to the picket fence on the pretext of smelling the scent from the honeysuckle vines that covered it. I felt guilty spying on her, but I couldn't help myself—this mysterious woman in white, so lovely in the night. She wavered, but caught her balance, then lit a cigarette from a pack in her hand. I remember thinking, it's too early to be in sleep attire. Her form beneath the sheer fabric, silhouetted by pool lights, revealed the shape of long legs, full hips, and large breasts—like a statue of some fertility goddess at the edge of a Roman villa peristyle. She took a drag from her cigarette, exhaled toward the pool, from which she never looked away.

I heard my mind say, "She's old."

She spotted me standing at the fence. I had to speak.

"Hello," I said.

She didn't seem alarmed, as maybe she should have. Her eyes focused on my voice. Seeing me, she calmly said, "Hi." Her voice sounded odd—statues don't speak.

"I hope I didn't startle you. I thought we should meet. I'm your new neighbor, Marco."

"Oh . . . yes . . . I thought I saw someone moving in today . . . Sure."

She walked through the security gate—closed it carefully again—and, on bare feet, walked across the grass toward the honeysuckle fence.

Arriving, she switched her cigarette to her left hand, held out her right across the tendrils. "I'm Sonia. Nice to meet you."

Grasping her soft hand, it felt like I'd slipped on a calfskin glove. I liked her accent.

"So, Old Solomon finally rented the place," she said, slurring some of her words. "I was wondering what he planned to do with it."

"You mean I'm the first to rent it?"

"It was his wife's painting studio. I'm glad someone's making use of it."

"Well, it's a music studio now. I should warn you I play piano at night. But just let me know if the sound carries to your house and bothers you . . . or your husband. I can close the windows."

"You play piano?"

"Yes."

"Is that your job?" She drew on her cigarette.

"Well . . . no. I'm an accompanist for a theater, for their musical productions, but daytimes, I work at Guitar Center, the one in West Hollywood, selling instruments and recording equipment. It pays the rent."

Exhaling the smoke away from my face, she said, "Nothing wrong with that. But that's quite a drive for you."

"I know. I'm looking forward to when I can quit. I'd like to just compose music full time."

"I see . . . No, your piano won't bother me. I like music." She looked up at her two-story modern house of stucco and glass. "I wouldn't know if it bothers my husband. He doesn't live here anymore." She tossed her cigarette butt into the grass and looked at me. "Play as late as you want." She grabbed the fence to catch her balance. "I'll look forward to hearing your music. Good meeting you, Marco."

"Nice meeting you too."

I watched her, shoulders erect, cross the lawn to her house. And though a bit unsteady, her legs moved effortlessly, as if, at one time, she'd been a dancer.

"I wonder how old she is? I thought. "Forty maybe?"

When she reached the screen door, she paused, glanced back toward the pool, then entered the house. Moments later, a blue TV light illuminated an upstairs window—the only light in an otherwise dark mausoleum of a house.

Mr. Solomon gave me permission to plant a vegetable garden. It was something I'd always wanted but could never have living in an apartment. Whenever I wasn't working or composing, I worked my garden, weeding and tilling the little patch.

As a child, I'd watched my grandfather work his garden under a coppola: harvesting basil, Swiss chard, lettuce, potatoes, peppers. But what I remember most was his large, perfect tomatoes—the biggest, most delicious tomatoes in our Italian neighborhood.

Early on, I was told I had my *nonno*'s double-jointed thumb. In Italian folklore, a thumb that curves backward means the owner creates with his hands, a craftsman, a gardener, good at making things. Whenever my mother left me with my grandparents—often because of my father's drinking—I remember feeling such peace in the house. I'd wake up mornings in a place without shouting or raised voices in pitched battle. From my bedroom, I smelled my grandmother's coffee brewing. Entering the kitchen, she'd kiss and hug me against her large breasts, my cheek against her gold crucifix. *"Buon giorno, figlio mio. Hai dormito con gli angeli, pataniello mio?"* I'd watch her sip her coffee while preparing breakfast. Outside, through the window, I could see my grandfather digging in his garden.

During breakfast, there were few words. After eating, my grandfather would light a pipe—hold it with his curved thumb—the room filling up with the sweet scent of Prince Albert, his favorite tobacco, which is now the brand I smoke. After he left for work, Grandmother would put on her cassette tape of Pavarotti and sing to her *Favorite Neapolitan Songs*. I'd watch her mix flour, water, and eggs into pasta dough.

"Marco," she'd say, "go down to the fruita cellar and bring upa some ripe tomatoes. Two, aspetta . . . no, three of the biggest ones. Makea sure you feel them like I show you."

I loved going into the fruit cellar. It was my cave of treasures, where I played with my toys. It had a dank, musty smell. The aromas of freshly picked garden vegetables ripening on the shelves, baskets of fruit, trays of my grandmother's cut pasta drying on wax paper. Stepping on an apple box, I'd pull the string I could barely reach and turn on the overhead light, then choose the largest tomatoes my small hands could handle. I liked the religious statues she stored there too, not having room for more upstairs, their faces, moving in and out of shadows from the swaying light. They became my porcelain playmates. My favorite was the tall statue of the Virgin Mary—almost as big as me. Thinking of it now, Freud would say I'd half-fallen in love with her. She had a beautiful, sculpted face with long black hair and dark mournful eyes that comforted me—the pity I felt in them. Even as a boy, I felt her sadness—her son nailed to a cross and all. I'd recite a Hail Mary and head back up to the kitchen.

Watering my newly planted garden one Sunday morning, Pavarotti blasting through a speaker balanced on my windowsill, I looked next door. Sonia was there. This time, she had on a one-piece black bathing suit with a towel over her arm. I watched as she walked through the security gate. Again, she closed it carefully and walked to the edge of the pool, looked into the water, but did not go in. Her fixed, unwavering stare unnerved me. Was she afraid to go in? Did she even know how to swim?

She laid the towel down and settled onto a chaise lounge, her long shapely legs stretched out. Looking up, shading her eyes, she noticed me standing with the water hose.

"Hi, Marco." She waved, got up, and walked toward the honeysuckle fence. I turned off the hose and met her. "I like your garden," she said with a smile as she approached. She had not smiled at our first meeting. She looked younger. "I saw you planting it. Gardens take a lot of work."

"Yes. More than I realized. I wanted to plant seeds, but I went for plants instead. Too impatient for results I guess."

"No shame in that. I'd do the same." Her eyelids closed and reopened at odd moments. "Each spring, I say to myself, I'm going to plant one, but never do. I love the taste of ripe tomatoes right off the vine, when you can taste the sun in them."

"Exactly."

"But gardens take a lot of work," she repeated, pausing as if she'd run out of other expressions. "When I was a child, all the houses had gardens. They weren't just hobbies."

Her comment bothered me. It reminded me we were from different generations.

"I think I'll have a lot of tomatoes," I bragged. "More than I can eat. When they're ripe, I'll bring you some."

Her eyes brightened. "Oh, that would be lovely. I'd really like that."

The conversation we were having was not the conversation going on in my head. I couldn't take my eyes off the full shape of her figure. So much more appealing than the young thin bodies at the beach apartment—their tanned lower backs exposed between the bikini top strings and the bottom fabric that barely covered their butts—their nakedness always on full display.

"I hope my piano hasn't disturbed you?"

"Not at all. I *really* love hearing you play. I danced when I was a teenager. I remember instructors at the studio always searching for music we could dance to." Her hands made a movement, a kind of flourish. "The music you were playing last night would be great for dance."

"Really?" I said with a light chuckle. "I've never even seen a ballet. Though I like listening to Stravinsky's *The Firebird*."

"No, I don't mean *en pointe*. Your music is more for contemporary dance—barefoot. Anyway, play as late as you want. Oh, I like your Pavarotti too. Are you Italian?"

"Yes. Half. On my mother's side. Her parents immigrated from Naples, Italy."

"I thought so. You know, Italians and Armenians have a lot in common."

"Really? Are you Armenian?"

Nodding her head, "First generation. My parents immigrated in the forties."

Again, I felt a sinking sensation in my gut. Worlds apart. "Exactly where is Armenia?"

She smiled. "Most people couldn't tell you where it is. It's close to Turkey and Iran. It was once a part of the Soviet Union . . ."

As she spoke, I realized how little of the world I knew.

"It's an independent country now," she added.

"I like your pool."

Her face changed. She caught herself. "The pool was not my idea. Like I said, I prefer gardens. I planted the honeysuckle along this fence."

"Is that what this is? I love the scent."

"We had lots of it in our yard in Worchester, Massachusetts. My father planted it everywhere. I love when it turns golden." She paused. Her mood changed. Plucking a few tendrils of honeysuckle, she turned abruptly. "Nice chatting with you, Marco."

"Yes, have a nice day."

Over the next few weeks, there were days when Sonia made it clear she didn't feel like talking. She looked strained and pale. These might be the days I heard her dumping bottles in the recycling bin. But one night, returning home around ten after a theater rehearsal, I saw her standing again at the edge of the pool, dressed in long slacks and a white blouse. Lit by pool lights, she seemed so alluring, smoking, staring down into the water. I didn't feel comfortable disturbing her meditation on God-knows-what. So, I continued walking toward my studio.

"Oh, Marco. Wait a moment," she called out. She walked through the security gate, closed it, and weaved herself toward the honeysuckle fence.

"For a second, I thought you were about to jump in with your clothes on," I kidded.

She didn't laugh.

"I can't swim," she responded seriously. Her words came out slow and deliberate. "Just needed some fresh air is all. What was that you were playing last night? Such a haunting melody? It reminded me of something my father used to play on his duduk."

"Really? Was your father a musician?"

She inhaled. "No." Blew her smoke into the air. "Not by trade. But he loved playing his duduk at the Armenian Club."

"It's a new composition I'm working on." I didn't say it was called "Lady of the Floodlit Pool." "What's a duduk?"

"A very old Armenian instrument. Ancient really. Sounds like an oboe, I guess. Or maybe a clarinet." She weaved a bit. Held on to the fence. She began blinking as if she were about to tear up. "My father would have loved your music." She inhaled again. Thought for a moment. Then exhaled. "He was a painter. Did portraits and landscapes. A wonderful painter, actually," she added, as if there were doubts. She paused. I let the silence have its space.

"He died when I was twelve."

"Oh. I'm sorry to hear—"

"He lived such a hard life," she continued, speaking now almost to herself. "He grew up in an orphanage after his entire family was massacred in the genocide. He was two years old. They spared him for some reason. Nuns raised him." Then, with heightened emotion, her mouth twisting with disgust, she spit out, "And the world let the Turks get away with it." She grabbed the fence again. "They were never punished."

She didn't bother to explain the genocide. She assumed I knew.

"At eighteen, they forced him to join the Soviet-Armenian army. Horrible people. The Nazis captured him. He spent two years, *two years* in a prison camp. Horrible people. After the war, he immigrated to Massachusetts. There's lots of Armenians in Worcester." She inhaled her cigarette, paused again. Exhaled. This time, I felt uncomfortable. I was just about to speak.

"That's where he met my mother," she continued, her mouth twisted again. "Just one tragedy after another."

Sonia never stopped to gauge my reaction. She threw her cigarette into the grass. Lowered her nose into the honeysuckle. Straightened up and said, "I love honeysuckle."

"It has a great scent. I'm glad you planted—"

"My mother's life was different. Her family escaped the genocide. They entered the US with all their money. And I mean lots of it. My grandfather built the largest mansion in Worcester. She had private schools, balls, horseback riding lessons." She smirked. "It hurt her terribly when I refused to live that life, the life she had planned for me—a pretty Armenian debutante." She spit out the words as if they tasted foul.

Her eyes went unfocused for a moment. "My father painted beautiful portraits. But no one wanted portraits in the States. So, he did landscapes. Sold them cheap at art fairs. But to make money, he had to paint houses.

"You mean he actually painted houses?"

"Yes. My mother was embarrassed. Ridiculed him for it. Imagine, such a wonderful artist having to paint houses. He became depressed. Started drinking—more than before—so she left him."

"That's awful."

With both hands holding the fence, she looked back at her yard. "You just never know when you leave someone, if you'll ever see them again . . . Goodnight, Marco," she said in lower, sadder tones. Turning, she began to weave her way toward her house. After a few steps, she stopped, looked back at me, and smiled. "Don't forget, you promised me some tomatoes."

And though she smiled, I'd never seen anyone so sad in my life.

A few days later at Guitar Center, I ate lunch with Don, a coworker, and decided to mention my neighbor. Don was in his mid-thirties, I liked him because he seemed to know more about things. And he had a good sense of humor.

"But you said she's old, right?"

"No, I said she's middle-aged."

"Look if she's over thirty, she's too old for you, buddy." He paused. "Alright, thirty-five. But that's it."

"But she's . . . very complex. Mysterious. Like no one I've ever met. Certainly not like those girls at my beach apartment."

"Yeah, I've seen them. They looked fine to me."

"But she's so exotic and intelligent. She's . . . Scheherazade from *One Thousand and One Nights*. That's who she is. She's got these dark, consuming eyes like the Sargasso Sea."

"What the hell are you talking about?"

"You don't read, do you?"

"Apparently not what you read. Listen, man, the reason she's not like those girls at your old apartment is because," and he leaned in close to my face, "she's a middle-aged woman, dummy." He sat back down, smiling. "Jesus, man . . . Does she have any children?"

"I don't think so."

"And besides, you said she drinks. You really find that attractive?"

"Of course not."

"How about her ex-husband? Seen him around?"

"No."

"Wait. How do you know she isn't crazy? I mean, maybe she killed him, and he's buried under the pool you say she stares at. Better ask your landlord when that pool was built."

When the tomatoes ripened, I followed through with my promise. I picked several of the largest ones, filling a grocery store bag, and carried them through the ficus hedges that separated our front yards. Set them against her door. I didn't stay.

That evening I went out on a date. After my conversation with Don, I forced myself to ask out one of the actresses from the theater. I was bored all night. We talked about her acting, her technique, her new 8x10s, her old boyfriend, how serious actors should be in New York, how she was moving to New York. Being from Ohio, I told her don't move in winter. I knew she'd never go to New York. At the end of dinner, she invited me back to her apartment. The whole time I kept comparing her to my intriguing neighbor. Yeah, Sonia was middle-aged. Maybe even a little crazy? But *her* drama held my interest. She was probably even a better actress. I went in, but I didn't spend the night. Besides, three cats sat about the bedroom staring at me the whole time we were in bed. Fortunately, it went quickly.

I got home around two a.m. Looked up at Sonia's house. I saw the blue TV light and wondered if she liked the tomatoes.

All Saturday, I composed. At twilight, I went outside to water my garden. My grandfather had instructed that the best times to water a garden were early morning or right before sunset. I heard Sonia's screen door open. She bypassed her pool and walked straight toward the honeysuckle fence. From the way she was walking, I could tell she'd been drinking, but she wasn't as bad as I'd seen her before.

"Marco."

"Hi. Sonia. So? What do you think?"

"Oh, your tomatoes are delicious. I ate a whole one today. I looked for you last night to thank you, but you weren't home."

"Did you taste the sun in them?"

"Absolutely! Just as I remembered. So good . . . Listen, I thought I'd make a big salad with some of your tomatoes. Could I bring you a bowl for your dinner? Have you eaten?"

"No, I haven't."

"It's the least I can do."

"A salad sounds great. Thank you."

I don't know. Maybe it was her Scheherazade eyes, the sweet honeysuckle scent, the balmy evening, her dead father, last night's date. Spontaneously, I said, "Sonia. I've got an idea. Why don't I give you a head of lettuce from my garden. You can make a salad and I'll come over. We can eat it together on your patio. It's such a nice evening. What do you think?"

She seemed stunned, reacted as if she'd been tasered. "Well," she stammered. I—"

"That's if you don't have any other plans this evening."

She laughed good naturedly. "Me? Other plans? Hardly. Well . . . okay. That sounds good."

"I'll even make some pasta. My grandmother taught me how to make capellini pomodoro the Napolitano way." I punctuated the air with an Italian hand gesture. "It's quick and easy to make. I make it all the time." I lied—hoping I could remember how.

"Sure. Even better." She didn't sound completely on board.

"I'll get you that head of lettuce."

I went to the garden and pulled out the largest head, twisted off the roots, grabbed several stems of basil for my pasta. With the melody of my new composition in my head, I realized my skin was tingling—like during an improvisation at the piano.

I handed her the lettuce. "Will this be enough?"

"Are you kidding?" She laughed. "That could feed an army."

Her voice didn't conceal her discomfort. Wisps of anxiety slipped out like phantasms.

"But please don't rush," she added. "When you get here, just ring the doorbell. I'll have the salad on the table."

"Alright."

I showered and dressed. The capellini pomodoro didn't take long: capellini pasta, chopped tomatoes, basil, diced garlic, and some olive oil, topped with Parmesan cheese, just as my grandmother had instructed. Before heading out the door, I splashed on some Brut and, suddenly, I felt like a teenager preparing for his first date.

I carried the pasta bowl covered with cellophane through the ficus hedges and rang Sonia's doorbell. I got no response. I rang it again. Waited. Nothing. I felt a sinking sensation. Maybe Don was right. Perhaps she really was crazy.

I was just about to leave when the door opened. "Marco. I'm sorry. I was upstairs. Come in." She seemed anxious. But I thought she sounded better, looked more clear-eyed. I smelled coffee.

"You'll have to excuse the mess," she said, picking up a few pieces of clothing and a purse. In truth, the place was *too* clean. "The pasta smells delicious. Go ahead and put it outside on the patio table. I'll start the salad."

It felt strange to walk through her space, go into her backyard, to stand near *the lady of the floodlit pool*'s pool. A true improvisation. All of it.

Back inside, except for the paintings under ceiling spots on her living room walls, the house felt cold and impersonal. I wondered if the paintings were her father's. Views of elderly peasants in front of rustic houses, forests of trees, various landscapes, a countryside full of sheep. The furniture in the room was sleek and black. All the appliances in the kitchen were stainless steel, like kitchens in restaurants. The refrigerator had no photos, no drawings or notes. Her bookshelves had no books, no knick-knacks, no photos, no personal items of any kind. Just a few expensive-looking bowls. She obviously didn't have children.

"Just as I was starting the salad, a friend called. She's getting a divorce. Her husband cheated on her, and she wanted my advice. I'll be damned if I knew what to tell her. Kill the son of a bitch," she said, laughing with a deadpan smile. Again, I thought of Don. "Is balsamic and olive oil okay with you? That's all I have. I rarely make salads at home." Sonia seemed unable to stop talking.

"I hope you don't mind I invited myself to dinner."

"Of course not," she said, slicing one of my tomatoes. "I should have invited you."

As she spoke, I was thinking how lovely she looked in her pink blouse and blue jeans. Her dark curly hair with streaks of gray flowing down her back. The smooth complexion of her olive-skinned face. It wasn't that she looked younger. She looked exactly her age, and that was attractive. I noticed her pungent perfume. Nothing like what the girls wore at parties on the beach.

"I like how you've decorated your house," I lied, again.

"Thanks. But this really isn't my taste. It's Yousuf's, my ex-husband. To make matters worse, he's an interior designer." She chuckled. "Imagine me trying to get in a design opinion. Anyway, in our culture, men make most of the decisions. At least he put in ceiling spots for the paintings that he resisted letting me hang. Not because he dislikes paintings in living rooms. He didn't think they were good enough." She stopped mixing the salad, looked at me, as if something had just occurred to her. "Someday, I'm going to tear this place apart. Start over." She smiled self-consciously. "I'll redecorate with antiques, old wood cabinets and rustic tables, armoires, folk art. Like homes in Armenia."

I thought of my grandparents' house. All the old wooden furniture, the armoires. New when they bought them.

"So, what would you like to drink? I can offer you a soda, Pepsi, I think it is, or some Perrier." She looked away. "I also have a bottle of Chardonnay if you'd like a glass."

Instinctively, I felt that helping her avoid her habit was not the friendship she needed tonight. It wasn't what I wanted either. But then, I didn't really know what I wanted. All I knew was that I was enjoying the evening. I felt Sonia should have a different experience than drinking her regular Chardonnay—alone.

"I have a bottle of Merlot that would go great with capellini pomodoro."

"Yes?" She smiled broadly. "Well, go get it."

I started for the door.

"Marco," she said, "wait," stopping me abruptly.

I worried. Was she going to back out?

"Would you mind if . . . we brought the food to your place?" She was looking out toward her patio. "We could eat outside on a blanket near your garden, have a picnic . . . I'm sick of being here." She looked at me. "Do you understand?"

"Yes. I do." It was the most sincere and genuine exchange we'd had. A chipping away at the veneer of civil neighborliness. "Actually, I've got a table and chairs I could set up outside. How's that?"

"That sounds wonderful."

"But you'd better bring your plates and silverware. Oh, and some wine glasses."

Sonia laughed. It was the first time I'd heard her *really* laugh.

Balancing the salad, glasses, and utensils on a tray, I led us through the ficus hedges. Sonia, with the pasta bowl, stumbled slightly on thick roots but saved herself. We giggled like two children about to set up a tea party. I realized I'd completely lost track of our difference in ages, our different generations. Intentions.

Entering my studio, Sonia set the pasta on the counter. "I like how you've fixed up the place. It's nice and cozy." She sat down on the bed covered by my red blanket. "Where did you get this great old wooden bed?"

"At the Antique Guild in the Helms Bakery building. Do you know it?"

"No. But I love antique furniture."

"I have to confess. I saw a copy of Van Gogh's *Bedroom in Arles*.

"Yes. I know the painting. Oh, I see it now."

"I loved how his bedroom made me feel. So . . . intimate. I really don't know much about art. But he's the painter I like best. His work I get."

"Well, you know enough to get Van Gogh. So, where's that Merlot?"

We set up the table and chairs outside next to the garden. I imagined the dim, unremarkable stars above Los Angeles glowing brighter—perhaps even swirling. Aromas from the vegetable garden wafted across the table. The honeysuckle was in full bloom.

"I've never done anything like this," Sonia said so matter-of-factly it hurt. She pulled out a Bic lighter from her jean pocket to light the votive candle I'd placed on the table, then began serving the pasta as I uncorked the Merlot and poured. "Thank you again, Marco."

"It's my pleasure, Sonia. I'm glad to get the chance to know you better." Raising my glass, I gave a toast. "Alla faccia di chi non ci può vedere."

"You speak Italian?"

"No. I wish I could. It's something my grandfather said at family dinners. It means something like to hell with anyone who can't see us or doesn't like us . . . or those who aren't at this table don't count. Something like that."

"I'll drink to that," she responded with attitude.

We clinked. Drank. I felt the wine going straight to my head. Or maybe it was the night.

"I have to be honest, Marco," she said, putting down her glass. "There *was* a moment when I thought . . . I wouldn't answer the door. I was lying on my bed struggling with the snap on my jeans, feeling foolish."

I imagined her lying on her back, lifting her hips, pulling at the snaps above her open zipper. A glimpse of her panties. Her thick black hair spread out behind her against the bedcover.

"Don't take this personally," she added. "I'm just not comfortable in social situations. I've never really been, even as a young woman. But you've been so nice. I forced myself off the bed."

"I'm glad you did. You had me worried. I would have been disappointed. I've enjoyed our conversations at the fence. Sitting together just makes it better."

"Yes. Well . . . if I weren't sitting here with you, I'd be headed to Ralphs to get more Chardonnay. I—"

"You don't have to explain to me."

I liked her frankness. Her honesty about herself. She knew I'd seen her drunk. Had seen her dumping bottles in the bin. I think she sensed I wasn't someone who judged.

"You're a very sweet man, Marco. I'm glad you took the place."

The pasta really *was* delicious. Everything seemed perfect about the evening.

"You mentioned once you danced." I stopped myself before saying "when you were younger." "Do you still?" I already knew the answer.

"No . . . I could, for exercise, I suppose. But . . . no, I don't. I was an art major in college."

"Really?"

She nodded her head, affirming. "My mother says I picked art because of my father, not because I had any real talent. It turned out, she was right."

"The paintings in your living room then, are they yours?"

"Some of them. Some are my father's, the ones she let me keep. I was so little when he died, but I insisted. His paintings comforted me more than the photos of me in his arms." She looked over at the garden. "But I did paint." She looked different when she talked of painting. Then she laughed. "I probably would have had more success trying to become an astronaut. At twenty-eight, my mother thought I'd never get married. I'd be her burden for life. I rarely dated. Ironically, she fixed me up with my ex-husband after she met him at the Armenian club. When he asked me to marry him, I just said yes. If only to get away from her, I suppose."

"From what you've said about your mother, it doesn't seem you had a very good relationship with her."

"Sadly, no. She's dead now. I always blamed her for my father's suicide. The way she shamed him. The divorce. Then I finally realized, she wasn't responsible for his death. He was a man too sensitive for the world, like Van Gogh. I thought he was strong. A survivor. But he wasn't. I tried to tell her at the hospital, but it was too late."

I thought we should steer the conversation away from all that. "So how did you end up in LA?"

"Oh. Well. My husband was offered a job here by his cousin who worked at an interior design company. I didn't want to leave Worchester. My friends and family. My home. The landscapes my father painted all around me." She thought a moment. I let the silence be. "Ironically, the dealer who got my father's paintings ended up making a lot of money with them. His work became popular in the years after he died. He became a local *cause célèbre*. I'm glad I insisted on keeping the ones I did." She looked at me. "Tell me, Marco, why do you like Van Gogh so much?"

"I don't know. Most paintings at museums leave me cold. Lines, slashes, colors, dots, squares, swirls of paint, splashes of color. But the day I saw Van Gogh's *Irises* at the Getty, everything changed. I bought a large book of his paintings in the gift shop. His stars. His sunflowers. Those wheatfields. Well, those I get. Reading of his life, I think of how sad and lonely he was. How much he wanted to be loved, but never was. To want love so badly. He married a prostitute with a child, just to not be alone. But it seems she only caused him more suffering. Probably cost him his ear too. But then, look at what all that loneliness and suffering created."

Sonia set down her fork. "Marco, sadness isn't necessary to create great art. Van Gogh knew this all too well. He didn't choose to be alone. Fate, his temperament, his choices gave him no other life but one of solitude and art. Yes, artists put their sadness into paint." She looked at me with a telling smile. "Some into their music. And so many die young because of it. Think of all the great Van Goghs we don't have, ending his life so young."

She took a sip of wine, only a sip. Set her glass down. "After I graduated from Boston College, my mother paid for me to go to Armenia, a kind of back-to-roots trip. I stayed with an aunt and some cousins for about a year. There was this boy in the village, a friend of one of my cousins, about my age—he fell in love with me. I liked him a lot. He was sweet and thoughtful. Not many like him." She smiled at me, then took another sip of wine. "A week before I was to leave, he proposed. Told me proudly of his family's farmland he would inherit, the acres that would all be his one day. His flock of sheep. He was so proud of the number of sheep he had." She chuckled. "You have no idea how smelly sheep are. Anyway, I hurt him when I turned him down. But not because of the sheep. I felt strongly that I wanted to paint, to know the world, to experience love. Funny, now, I think I passed up a better life . . . with those smelly sheep." She smiled. Grabbed a cigarette from her pack and lit up. "You're lucky you had such loving grandparents growing up."

"I am. Yes." I pulled my pipe from a jacket pocket and lit it with her lighter. "They were like second parents to me. It was tough when my grandfather died. It'll be worse when my grandmother goes."

Sonia exhaled. "My mother's parents were cold, formal people. Just how my mother turned out. I think I would have loved my father's parents. His family were all artists, musicians, intellectuals. Educated people. What about your father's parents?"

"Barely knew them." I let out a few puffs from my pipe, thinking of my father. "My father was born in Mexico. His parents died there when I was four or something."

"Oh. That's unfortunate. And Old Solomon. How's he treating you?"

"Great. I like him. He leaves me alone. First of the month, I just slip the rent check through his mail slot."

"He looks older, more feeble since his wife died."

"When did she die?"

"About a year ago. From breast cancer." Sonia looked at her cigarette. "He paid me to give her art lessons when he saw me painting outside. He converted this garage into her studio. I came twice a week. It didn't matter that she wasn't very good. It made her happy, so he was happy. He doted on her ... Imagine having someone who loves you like that. She was the kindest woman I ever met. She was very good to me after ... my husband left." She held something back. Instead, gave out a little laugh. "It's a miracle when two people find each other who are truly meant to be together, don't you think? When the universe allows such love to happen. It must be hard for him without her."

"You'd never know talking to him." I grabbed the bottle and filled our glasses.

"Thank you. Some people carry their sorrow privately. Others moan and complain to anyone who will listen." She took a sip of wine. The conversation was beginning to drag. She sat up. "Marco, this evening has been a real treat for me. But I should go. Let you get back to your piano."

"Oh, no. I'm not working tonight," I insisted. "I'm enjoying our conversation too much." I was about to compare our conversation with ones I had with girls my age but decided wisely not to. "Next time, I'll make you some homemade pasta."

"You know how to make homemade pasta?"

"My grandmother taught me. I was a strange kid. I loved rolling out dough. Feeding it into the cutting machine and making spaghetti. At my grandfather's wake, my grandmother handed me her old Columbus Modello e Marchio pasta cutter. Said I was the only grandchild who would appreciate it."

"You weren't strange. Just sensitive." Then, after a sip of wine, with a curious smile, Sonia asked, "Have you ever been in love, Marco?"

It was a question she must have debated asking all night. Perhaps this was her way to make things clear—that we were just being neighborly. I thought of the girl who moved to Paris.

"No. Not really." Seeing her skeptical smirk, I added, "Well, maybe once. But I'm not sure it was love. Or if I even know what love is." She smiled as if she'd trumped my ace. "Anyway, she moved to Paris." I drained my glass. "I think my parents ruined the whole damn business for me. Love seems crazy to me. All the fighting. They wouldn't talk to each other for weeks. Then, one morning I'd see them hugging and kissing. And they're still together." I decided not to mention my father's drinking. "When my father dropped me off at the airport after the funeral, he said, 'Careful, *mijo*. Love can destroy one's faith in God.'"

Sonia laughed out loud. "I already like your father. I understand what he means. I imagine he has a great sense of humor."

"He does."

"Marco, would you do something for me?"

"Sure."

"I've only heard your music through the window. Would you play something for me?"

"You don't have to ask that twice."

Sonia finished her wine. We carried the food, plates, and glasses inside.

The bottle was empty. Sonia didn't ask for another. She took her sandals off and sat on the bed—on the red blanket. I played the piece she had inspired.

As I played the last note, Sonia had tears in her eyes. She got up from the bed, came and sat next to me on the piano stool.

"You should see your face when you're playing. Makes me sad I don't feel that way about painting anymore . . . about anything, really."

The scent of her perfume. The closeness of her body. Her sunken, silent pain. Without thinking—I just did it. I leaned in and said, "Tell me if I should stop."

I kissed her. She received but did not give. Perhaps she was stunned but didn't want to hurt me. When I opened my eyes, she did not appear uncomfortable or embarrassed.

"I had to do that," I said. "I hope you don't mind—"

"You don't have to explain." She touched my face. "Marco, you are a lovely man. But . . . it's probably better that I go now. Do you know how old I am?"

"I have some idea. But it doesn't matter. I'm not thinking about that."

"You should. I'm forty-nine. I'll be fifty in two months." She had a serious look. "And you are, what? Twenty-eight, nine?"

I considered lying but decided on the truth. "I'm twenty-five."

She smiled. "Well, you've an old soul then." She looked out my window toward the garden. "I don't consider what happened inappropriate. Two people, regardless of age, who find something attractive about the other. What it is you find attractive about me, I don't know." And again, she smiled. "But you're so young and impressionable and—"

I kissed her mid-sentence. This time I felt her kiss me back. A resurrection in her body, a new breath, a new moment condensing already into some future memory.

Leaning back, I said, "Sonia, this wasn't planned. But it's what I want."

With that, she pulled my face close to hers and whispered, "Are you sure?"

"Absolutely."

She kissed me passionately—with force. Her body revived with a sudden surge of lust for an eager young man. Up close, I felt submerged in her pungent perfume, her full lips on mine, her confident hands touching me, her woman's body pressing against me. I even felt somewhat concerned if I had the experience to satisfy such a passionate woman. She grabbed my hand and led me to the bed. Made me sit and watch her unbutton her blouse.

Oh yes, Sonia. I remember . . . I remember you so well. How you removed your bra, your large breasts falling out, exposed. How you unsnapped your jeans, pulled them over your wide hips. How I saw the curve of your beautiful dancer's legs as you slid off your panties. You made no attempt to conceal yourself. You let me see everything, all that I needed to see. When you pulled my face into your breasts, I felt cradled in warm flesh, cushioned, comforted— perhaps I smelt the scent of fresh vegetables—no words were exchanged, nothing need be said. Pulling me up off the bed you began to undress me. In all my nakedness, you took a moment to look at me, for a future memory perhaps. So surprising this life, this momentary fulfillment of desire that was happening. You lay me back on the red blanket, in complete control. You took me that night. I followed, as all the vague and insignificant stars of an LA night swirled large and yellow in a lunacy of desire.

I awoke at sunrise. Sonia was not there. I felt loneliness, like I'd never felt before. I dressed and went through the ficus hedges, still hungry. A white envelope lay against her front door marked "Marco" in fine calligraphy.

Dear Marco,

I let you sleep. Last night was an awakening for me, the pasta, your tomatoes, your concert, your sweet tenderness—it was ideal. I hope it was for you too. I've gone away. I've been numb for so long. There's something I must do. I hope you will always feel good about our night together. Remember me.

Sonia

A month later, a Coldwell Banker for sale sign appeared on the front lawn. I had not heard from Sonia.

Not long after, I woke to voices in her driveway. Rushing out, I saw movers pushing dollies and carrying boxes to a moving van. A short, dark, middle-aged man with gray hair, dressed in slacks and a collared shirt was directing the movers. His accent was thick. His voice authoritative. He noticed me peeking through the hedges.

"Are you Marco?" he asked, walking toward me, adding awkwardly, "I'm husband of Sonia. You're the neighbor with the vegetable garden, I think, no?"

"Yes." I replied, "I am." I wished I'd worn shoes instead of slippers.

The man extended his big hand. "I'm Yousuf Tasjian."

"Nice to meet you."

"Sonia had many good things to say about you. Said you gave her tomatoes." A mover approached Yousuf with a question. He directed him to the master bedroom—the blue TV light room—it made me sad. "I'm glad you make good friends with Sonia."

"Yes. I enjoyed talking to her. How is she?"

Yousuf deliberated. "She is okay." A teenage boy and a younger girl came out of the house. "Come, her children. Meet Marco."

I was shocked. Sonia had children. So, this was her unspoken sadness.

"He's David," Yousuf said. The boy frowned but gave me a firm shake. "And she is Isabel."

She looked eleven, maybe twelve. A younger version of Sonia. She pointed to the studio. "You live in that house?"

"Yes. I do."

"It was a garage once."

"Really. Lucky for me they made it a studio."

"Lucky for my mother too, I guess." She smiled.

"Go now," Yousuf ordered. "Finish packing up Mother's clothes."

"I have to get another box out of the truck," David said. "It was nice meeting you. Come, Izzy." And he headed toward the moving van.

"Mother said you play the piano." Her smile unnerved me. "Too bad you can't play something for me. But I have to go." And she hurried off to join her brother.

"Thank you again, Marco." Yousuf and I shook hands.

Just then, a mover approached carrying a painting.

"Wait. Is that one of Sonia's paintings?" I asked.

"Yes," Yousuf said.

"Could I look at it a moment? I never saw any of her work."

"Of course." He motioned the mover to stop.

The painting was of a forest of trees, tree trunks in a crimson and yellow wood suggesting sunrise or perhaps an autumn scene. It was stunning. Like a Van Gogh, only more modern, I guess. But it communicated something to me more genuine than a forest, something more ideal.

"She's a wonderful painter, isn't she?"

"Yes," was all he said.

Some months later, sitting at the piano, I saw Mr. Solomon coming toward my front door. He had a large tube in his hand. "Hey, kiddo," he said through the open door. "This came for you. They left it on my porch."

I got up and took the package. "Thanks, Mr. Solomon."

"Wouldn't want it to get stolen. A lot of that going on these days."

I saw it was from Sonia Tasjian. No forwarding address. Only her name.

"So, you met Yousuf and the kids." Old Solomon didn't miss much. "You know, Sonia had it real rough for a long time. Did she tell you?"

"No. We just chatted."

Mr. Solomon squinted. "Well, she did. She was a heavy drinker. But you knew that. Right? After the baby was born, her husband had to bring the two older children over to Evelyn and me. It got pretty bad. Evelyn was my wife. She died."

"I'm sorry to hear that, Mr. Solomon. So, Sonia had another child?"

"Look, son, I'm not a judge. Just an observer. And it seems that only good things came out of all that giggling a while back." And he looked at me, more with commiseration than condemnation. "I liked Sonia. A lot. She was good to Evelyn. But I'm glad she's out of that house. Nothing but misery over there. They had that child too late. Children don't save marriages."

"Sonia never talked about her children."

"No? At two years old, the baby fell in the pool. Crawled through the open security gate. Yousuf found him. But it was too late. Terrible business."

"That's awful."

To think Sonia carried all that sorrow, inside—privately.

"Yousuf took the kids away," he continued. "But she wouldn't leave the house. Now, son, just some friendly advice. Forget all this. Let it alone. Go on with your *young* life." He went out the door, adding, "Sure like what you've done with the place." After a few steps he threw back, "Like your piano playing too."

Inside the tube, I found a rolled 18x26-inch print of Van Gogh's *Bedroom at Arles*. On the back she'd written,

> *Marco,*
> *Van Gogh said, "Don't take art or love too seriously."*
> *You'll always have a friend in Armenia with her sheep.*
> *Sonia*

"The museum will be closing in fifteen minutes," a guard announces, walking through the gallery. He looks straight at me, the strange dark man who's been sitting for some time on the gallery bench.

My fifty-year-old knees pop as I stand. I approach *Bedroom at Arles* for one last look. Lean in close. A detail in the brush stroke catches my eye—the folds in the red blanket, the color of the room. And I see it's not an intimate feeling I get, but one of melancholy. I wonder if Sonia ever made it to Armenia. I shudder to think she'd be seventy-five—if she's still alive.

Whatever happened to that red blanket? I think again, heading for the exit.

Forget it, I hear, passing Vincent's last self-portrait.

Outside, I select Marie's beautiful face on my cell, but the long-distance lines are jammed. I'll try again, later.

The Most Valuable Player
Jeremy Stelzner

Last year the franchise pulled in a cool $86 million in broadcasting revenue alone. You'd think the suits in the front office would spring for one of those portable deodorizers or at least a new air filter, but the press room still wreaked of mildewed carpeting and ancient BO. When Dan Coughlin slumped in, he shuffled slowly past the podium like a man half asleep.

He flopped himself down in his regular spot, nodding down the front row, silently acknowledging his fellow brothers in arms. They were the usual suspects. The *Times*, the *Herald*, the *Globe*, and the *Tribune*. All of their best beat reporters dressed in their cheap button-downs and hastily knotted neckties. They were all drenched in potent colognes meant to mask the hours spent in the rank sweat of post-game locker rooms. The group acknowledged Dan with melancholy eyes as if they'd all had the same thought at the same time. *My, how the mighty have fallen.*

Dan Coughlin was once a legend in the press room. He was *the* Dan Coughlin, the guy the other reporters in the front row doted on for his regional Murrow Award for Metro Desk Excellence. He was the guy they venerated for being a Pulitzer finalist for his coverage of forced gentrification in the neighborhoods bordering the Tractic International Colosseum. That Dan Coughlin marched through life with a fire in his belly that fueled his hunger for truth. But somewhere along the way, those long years of languishing in locker rooms took their tool, and that fire was extinguished.

The boys up front were bullshitting about that day's blowout loss at the hands of lowly Detroit when the team's VP of press relations, Virginia Onzin, entered the room. Unlike the paper boys, Virginia was not in a cheap suit. Rather, she stood tall in six-inch Valentino heels and a black Versace dress that cost more than Dan's monthly take-home pay. Virginia scanned the room suspiciously like a grade-school teacher supervising a class of booger-flicking, note-passing hooligans. Sweeping her silky blonde hair behind her ears, Virginia bent over and whispered to Dan, "Look, Dan, let's not make a thing out of it, but we need you to move on back to row eight."

"Row eight?" Dan asked, cocking his head around. There wasn't a single reporter occupying a seat past row five. "What gives?"

"Dan, please. Don't make a scene."

"Fellas, did you know about this?" he asked the other reporters.

His comrades shrugged.

It took a real effort for Dan to rise from his seat. Cross-country travel, fast food, and tight deadlines had taken their toll. He was tired, hungry, cranky, and he hadn't showered in three days. Dan took a secret whiff of his armpit while retreating, fearful the eviction was due to his stink.

When he got to the back of the room, he removed his tweed sports coat, the kind with the patches on the elbows, and tossed it on the empty chair next to him. He rolled up his sleeves. So this is what he gets. Thirty years at the paper and all he had to show for it was a 1996 Toyota Corolla and a seat in the back row.

Dan checked his watch. *Where the fuck is this guy? I'm gonna miss my deadline.* Sure enough, a text from Michelle, his editor, came through a moment later rife with exclamation points and enraged emojis.

The home screen on Dan's phone featured a picture of his estranged son blowing out the candles on his Spiderman birthday cake. His ex sent the picture after Dan missed the birthday party. He had been delayed at the Denver airport following the team's week-four overtime loss to San Jose. To make it up to the boy, Dan picked up a Superman Lego set in the airport gift shop that set him back a hundred and twelve bucks.

Watching his son rip through the wrapping paper, Dan thought for the briefest of moments that perhaps the extravagance of the gesture would repair the fractures in the foundation of their relationship. But when his son finally reached the prize, he looked up scornfully at his father and said, "Superman sucks."

Another fracture. They'd grown deeper and wider over the past few years. Too much time on the road. Too many missed holidays and T-ball games, and school plays. It was no way to father and Dan knew it. So did his son.

The muffled chitchat in the room died down. Everyone went quiet because they could tell that greatness was about to walk through the door. Anyone who's ever been around actors or musicians or politicians, or pro athletes, knows that such personalities tend to suck all the oxygen out of a room, leaving the rest of the mortals gasping for air. Dan Coughlin believed the journalist's job was to hold their breath and speak truth to power. Though if you'd asked him, he would have lectured you about how too many in the field were focused on forging powerful friendships. Then he probably would have preached to you about how journalism was turning into an industry overly concerned with likes, retweets, and engagement rates.

A moment later, a freshly shaven Rob Coleman sat down and adjusted the microphone. He ran his large hands through his thick brown locks. Coleman's perfectly angled facial features always reminded Dan of those marble statues so commonly found in the ancient world. Swagger practically radiated off him. Even all the way back in row eight, Dan could feel it.

"All right, folks. I've got time for a couple of questions," Rob said, toying around with a signed game ball.

All of the reporters flipped open their little notebooks and licked the tips of their pencils. These weren't kids fresh out of grad school. These were seasoned journalists like Dan, forced to pay their dues in musty locker rooms in towns like Oshkosh and Duluth and Stockton. They'd covered presidential campaigns and natural disasters. They'd been sent overseas to report from active war zones. They'd exposed countless financial crimes perpetrated by local politicians and most of them were on a first-name basis with the clerk at the city morgue. But when Rob Coleman settled in, even these old pros could feel the butterflies building.

After all, this wasn't just any old quarterback we're talking about here. This was *the* Rob Coleman. The Rob Coleman who was famously drafted in the twenty-third round out of Eastern Kentucky Tech. The six-time league MVP Rob Coleman. The Rob Coleman who led his team to ten league championships.

The American public fell for Coleman almost immediately. They nicknamed him Captain America. They flooded stores to purchase the products that he endorsed, and put aside his many faults and social faux pas, provided he continued to perform on the field.

Dan's editor, Michelle, told him that a hot story on Coleman, one that was bigger than just sports, one that belonged above the fold, would be a big win for the paper. She promised an end to this fucking beat and an end to the travel. No more missed birthdays. No more missed ball games and school plays. All Dan needed was that one hot story to get him back in the good graces of his boy.

In the front row, James DeVayle of the *Times* looked like something out of a Rockwell painting in his signature bowtie and fedora. Being from the *Times*, DeVayle was always afforded the first question. There was no need to even raise a hand. DeVayle flashed his familiar grin at the wily veteran, and Rob Coleman promptly responded.

"James, you're up first," Rob said.

"Thanks, Rob. It looked like you had a hard time getting comfortable out there. Just wondering what went wrong today?"

"Certainly wasn't ideal, James—tough conditions for sure. But we got a gritty effort from the guys, and I gotta thank God that we were able to get the job done," Rob said before patting himself on the back and pointing a finger up to the big guy in the sky.

"Get the job done?" DeVayle asked, befuddled.

"That's right, James. We killed it out there today. It's games like today. That's what all that practice is for. The offseason workouts, training camp, two-a-days, and the grind of all those preseason games. Oh yeah, say hi to Becky and the kids for me."

"Sure thing, Rob," DeVayle replied, shaking his head.

Each reporter looked around the room, totally baffled. They were so baffled, in fact, that they had all stopped writing, and these were guys who were constantly writing. Always. They wrote on Post-it notes, on bar napkins, on loose tissues, and on the palms of their sweaty hands. But they collectively had nothing. They glanced at one another, attempting to confirm through an offhand look that they'd heard correctly. Rob Coleman was a star. He didn't attend off-season workouts, he certainly didn't show up for two-a-days, and he hadn't played in a preseason game in over twenty years. But these minor inconsistencies in his statement were not what raised so many eyebrows. Did Rob Coleman just imply that they *won* the game?

"Who's next?"

Dan sat up and adjusted his tie. He'd been at the *Register* for his entire career, and the *Register* always got the second ask at the team's post-game pressers.

Rob scanned the room. He saw Dan with his hand raised in the back row. Rob looked him dead in the eye, shook his head, and said, "How about the *Herald*?"

The beat man for the *Herald* scooted up in his seat, shocked that his number had been called. He'd been covering these pressers for the past three seasons and had never been permitted to question the future Hall of Fame quarterback. He sat there for three whole seasons like a piece of staged IKEA furniture with a name no one could pronounce.

"Mr. Coleman, thank you, sir. I'm Dagstorp Norrviken from the *Herald*. I was wondering—"

"Sorry, what was that name?"

"Dagstorp Norrviken," he repeated.

"You new at the *Herald*?" Rob asked.

"No, sir, I've been covering the team for a while now," Norrviken admitted.

"Well, nice to meet you, Dogstop. Is it Dogstop?"

"Dagstorp," Norrviken corrected.

"How 'bout I just call you Doggie?" Rob asked, tossing the signed game ball from one hand to the other.

"Whatever you like, sir."

"What do you got for me today, Doggie?"

"The offensive line looked like Swiss cheese, Mr. Coleman. I think I'd be hard-pressed to find another game this year where you were under so much pressure. I mean, jeez. Twelve sacks. How are you feeling physically? And did you have any words for the rest of the offense after the game?" Norrviken asked.

"Wow. Just wow. You nailed it. All excellent questions, Doggie."

"Thanks, Mr. Coleman," Norrviken said, smiling.

"Call me Rob," he said.

Rob Coleman tossed the signed game ball toward the nervous reporter. Norrviken fumbled it some but was able to maintain control. He giggled a little. The very notion that *he*, a nobody reporter, was now on a first-name basis with *the* Rob Coleman, the GOAT, made him blush.

"I'm feeling pretty good. Looking forward to movie night with Impala and the kids. I'll head in for treatment in the morning and crush an ayahuasca tea. You know, start to get my mind and my body right for next week. As for the team, we'll do what we always do, get into the film room and get ready to destroy Dallas."

Squinting, Rob raised his hand over his eyes and called out, "Dan? Dan Coughlin? That you all the way back there?"

The room broke out in a collective chuckle.

"Yeah, it's me, Rob," Dan confessed with a heavy sigh. It was the sigh of a broken man.

"You run over somebody's dog or something? How'd you get tossed in the back row?"

"Ask Virginia."

Virginia, slighted by the accusation, put her phone back in her holster and stepped up to the podium. She whispered something into the quarterback's ear. Rob roared out in laughter.

"No need to get snippy, Dan. Those guys in the front office may look like nerds, but they can really hold a grudge. Better watch out there, Danny-boy."

"Well, I don't think they can move me back any farther," Dan said. When he turned to look behind him, he was at eye level with the crotches of a dozen cameramen who had their backs up against the wall of the press room.

"They can try."

Again, the room thundered with another robust round of laughter.

Rob was proud of himself. He doubled down. "I'll be here all night, ladies and gents. Don't forget to tip your waitress."

More laughter.

"Am I allowed to ask a question?" Dan interrupted.

"Fire away," Rob said, shooting pretend guns in Dan's direction.

"I'm sorry, Rob, but there's an elephant in the room, and I wouldn't be doing my job if I didn't—"

"Dan, please. We're all friends here."

"Do you believe that your relationship with former president Trottel is becoming a distraction to the team?"

"I'm sorry?" Rob leaned forward. He placed his elbows on the podium and scowled down at Dan.

"Come on, Rob. You've been traveling all over the country stumping for him. You're the only one on the team missing walkthroughs and first-squad reps. It's got to be a distraction when the offense comes to work and their all-pro quarterback, a sure-fire Hall of Famer, isn't even at the facility."

The room went quiet. Every single journalist held their breath. Half wanted to slap Dan across his smug face. The other half wanted to shake the hand of the man with the largest set of *cajones* on the Eastern seaboard.

"The president is a goddamned American patriot, Dan!" Coleman raged. Being a seasoned professional, Rob took a meditative breath and reset himself. "I'm a fan of Mr. Trottel, and that's all."

"You said the president, you meant the *former* president, right?" Dan asked.

"You say tomato. I say potato."

"Excuse me?"

Rob stood up and pointed at Dan as if he were about to launch into a furious tirade. But again, he cooled his jets and flashed that toothy grin that every American recognized from his Force Fuel sports drink commercials.

"It's an idiom, Dan. You believe that he's the *former* president—and I believe every American is allowed to believe whatever they want to believe. It's in the Constitution, Dan. Ever heard of it?"

Rob Coleman rolled his eyes and opened his phone. His home screen featured a picture of himself on the eighteenth tee box at Augusta National Golf Club. He scrolled around for a while silently, punching away while occasionally looking up at the press to make sure they were still watching him. Like a petulant child, he needed to make sure everyone in the room knew he was aggravated. None of the thirty-plus reporters asked a follow-up question. No one even spoke. The only sound was an occasional camera click.

"Rob?" Dan asked.

Silence.

Rob put down his phone, tightened his gorgeous jaw, leaned in, and stared harder. His gaze intended to burn right through Dan and melt him into a puddle of insignificant mush right there in the eighth row.

"Rob?" Dan asked again, but Rob had retrieved his phone and was typing again.

Finally, Rob held up a finger prompting Dan to wait, a suspicious twinkle in his eye. Rob was finishing up a message to his 126 million followers on social media. The post read, *"Dan Coughlin is a dick."*

The American icon returned his attention to the audience. He smiled at Dan, winked, and said, "I'm hearing from our guys that I've got time for one more question before Coach comes out."

"But, Rob," Dan begged, standing up.

"Again, Dan? You had your turn. Don't be such a crybaby," he said, still sulking like a horny teenage boy complaining to his girlfriend that blue balls are a legitimate medical affliction.

"I'm sorry, Rob."

"You know what, Dan? Call me Mr. Coleman."

Suddenly, the embers that had been cooling within Dan for the better part of the last decade ignited under a scorching need for truth. "Fine, Mr. Coleman—you never answered my question. Do you attribute today's thirty-point thrashing at the hands of Detroit, a division bottom dweller, to the fact that you were in Tulsa last night speaking at a campaign rally for Trottel?"

"Fake news, Dan."

"I'm sorry?"

"You got a problem with the good people of Tulsa, Dan?"

"Of course not," Dan said. But the more Rob deflected, the hotter Dan's coals of curiosity became.

"Good, I was never there."

Three large men in dark suits entered the room and huddled up around Virginia Onzin. She stared down Dan. Then, after getting his attention, Virginia ran her finger across her throat while mouthing the words *you're fucked, Dan.*

But Dan Coughlin wasn't scared; he'd spent a career standing his ground against tyrants. He'd asked the tough questions to despots. He'd criticized strongmen from fractured Eastern European nuclear powers. Dan wouldn't allow himself to be pushed around at the hands of an athlete, even one as revered as Rob Coleman.

"Yes, you were, Mr. Coleman. We've all seen tape of you there."

"Look, I'm *just* a football player, that's it," Rob said, unzipping his hoodie to reveal a Force Fuel T-shirt. Then Rob took a heavy swig from his fluorescent green Force Fuel sports drink and said, "Goddamn, this is good stuff. And no calories, if you can believe that. Now, if you've got a question about today's win, let's hear it. If you don't, just sit down."

The cameras behind Dan clicked while the reporters in the front row texted their editors, requesting more space in the morning edition.

"You lost," Dan said coldly.

"Good one, Dan. Hey, would you guys get a load of this joker?" Rob laughed, pointing at the fellas in the front row. He was smiling at them, but they didn't know if they should smile back. Like the spoiled children of divorced parents, they deliberated which side to take in order to elicit the greatest return.

"No, really, you lost."

"It's not about *me*, Dan. Rob Coleman is just one man, it was a team win."

"No, it wasn't. You're not hearing me. You know what? Let's go walk back on that field," Dan said. "The score's still up on the jumbotron."

"Score's wrong."

"Excuse me?"

"Dan, the jumbotron? Everyone knows you can't trust those numbers. We won 184–5." Rob spoke with such bravado; the words seemed to dance from his mouth.

"To five? That's insane, Mr. Coleman. How would Detroit even score five points?"

"Two safeties and an extra point."

"That's not what happened," Dan said, rolling his eyes.

"Alternative facts. And Dan, don't fucking roll your eyes at me."

"Mr. Coleman, with all due respect," and Dan did respect him. Dan always felt great joy watching him throw the pigskin around. Despite Rob Coleman's more recent enthusiastic political views, he was a hell of a football player.

"You say tomato. I say potato. My guys on the field, the trainers, coordinators, and coach, they all tell me the *real* score. I mean how can we really trust the scoreboard? Or the booing fans? Or ESPN? Or our own eyes?" he questioned.

In fact, the great Rob Coleman trusted very little. Of late, he had grown fond of traveling down the conspiracy theory rabbit hole, waxing poetic on social media about subterranean Jewish smack houses where enslaved puppy dogs and orphaned children had been brainwashed to cook meth for the cartels of the liberal intelligentsia.

"You sure you want to stick with your original statement, Mr. Coleman? I have you on the record here saying that the former president is not a distraction."

"The former president? Speak of the devil. He just texted me. Just now. At this very moment, Dan, you fucking simp,"

Rob said, his mind dancing with delight. "The president says *Congrats Rob. You destroyed those chumps. Great win. Hell of a game.*" Then Rob said, "I'm done," took off his mic, and spiked it to the ground like he'd just scored the winning touchdown. He stormed out of the press room as head coach Burt McKenzie waddled in.

Unlike his star quarterback, Coach McKenzie was a man of few words and many grunts. He was known as a gruff curmudgeon who wore ratty, mustard-stained sweatshirts with pictures of Looney Toons characters on gameday and always seemed to have a five o'clock shadow even moments after he shaved. The old man sat at the microphone and coughed up some heavy phlegm.

"Coach, has Coleman's relationship with the former president become a distraction?" Dan jumped right in without waiting to be acknowledged.

Coach McKenzie shrugged his shoulders.

The man looked fully uninspired and half drunk.

Dan was relentless. "Coach, where does the team go from here? Is there any pressure from ownership to start Johnny P?" he asked.

Coach shrugged his shoulders.

"Coach! Coach, Rob's been posting bizarre messages on social media about a secret moon base funded by the Turkish Illuminati. Do you think the Turkish Illuminati has built a secret moon base, and if so, what exactly is the function of such an installation?" he asked.

Coach shrugged his shoulders.

"Coach, any comment on Rob Coleman's statements that the team won today's game 184–5?" Dan asked. Each unanswered question only seemed to stoke his inquisitive fire.

"If Rob says that's the score—that's the score."

Dan shouted, "I have a job to do here, Coach."

"Jesus, he's our most valuable player. What do you want me to say?" McKenzie blubbered, the fat in his jowls jiggling.

"I just want the truth, Coach."

"The truth? What's the point, Dan? You've seen Rob's Twitter posts. You must've heard. There's no such thing as truth anymore."

Dan still didn't have his lede quote. He had to push harder.

"Coach, we get it. We all get it," Dan empathized while his colleagues in the front row scribbled away—the crew newly inspired by Dan's persistence. "The guy's talented, and he's won a lot of games for your ball club. But don't you think this talk is getting pretty dangerous? I mean, for Christ's sake, people actually believe this nonsense, and if we're being honest about it, Coach, he's not as sharp on the field as he was last season."

Dan Coughlin sat through enough of these pressers to know when his golden meatball would arrive. He could feel it coming. Rising from within the bloated old coach. That single line that would get him back on the front page, that would get him back to his boy.

"Look, fellas," Coach said, lowering his eyes. Here it comes. He shook his head while considering the ramifications of his next statement. "The guy's taken a lot of hits."

The camera flashes ignited, and Dan stood up triumphantly. He saluted Coach McKenzie and grabbed his jacket.

Virginia Onzin ran in front of the podium shouting out, "Hey, Coughlin! What do you think you're doing? We're not done here yet. Ownership is coming out with a statement."

"Not interested, I got my story," Dan said, striding toward the front of the room, his jacket in hand.

"That's it, Coughlin. I'm serious. Get back there and wait for ownership or else!" she yelled.

"Or else what, Virginia?"

"Or else you're finished with the team, Dan."

Dan stopped at the door.

Virginia walked over to him and leaned in real close. She whispered, "Sit back down or as soon as you walk out that door, I'll feed these boys a story about Dan Coughlin's *aggressively unprofessional* attempts to get an exclusive with the team's VP of press relations. I'll leave the phrasing vague and let them fill in the blanks. You guys are getting pretty good at conjecture."

"You say tomato. I say potato."

"What the fuck does that mean?"

Dan turned back toward his comrades. He winked and then flourished his jacket like a matador in an old Hemingway story, put it on, and left.

Anatomy of a Glacier
Cecilia Maddison

Moulin

A fall like that should have broken his neck.

Instead, Karl's femur had snapped like a wooden stick, and his body jangled with pain. Coaxing air back into the battered shuttlecock of his chest, he winced, taking stock. He lay suspended on the ledge of a cavernous chamber, and the skylight of blue from where he had fallen shone from an impossible height.

Jonny's earnest voice echoed down the moulin. "Hey, Karl, can you hear me? Talk to me. Tell me you're okay, buddy!"

The shrill, panic-stricken edge to his words tempted Karl to eke out his silence for a little longer. Anything to make Jonny sweat a little, to punish him for being the fortunate body on the ice sheet's surface. But the pain was too brutal for game-playing.

"I'm in a bad way," Karl called between gasps. The sheer walls amplified his words. They boomed and reverberated like a church organ in a fake display of might. "My thigh . . . clean break."

"No way!" Disbelief chimed in Jonny's voice.

"I need pain relief."

"Sure thing."

With gritted teeth, Karl rode out the silence, waiting for Jonny to sling the first-aid kit over the moulin's lip and drop it down. Somewhere far below he heard a rivulet of water trickling through a gully, snowfall from a thousand years ago journeying to the sea. A sudden, profound thirst overwhelmed him, and he wondered if the splintered bone had sliced a blood vessel. Then he recalled the strenuous climb, the effort of securing screws in ice as hard as granite, the bright sun beating down on his thermal layers. He'd been dehydrated before he even fell. Now he was acutely injured too.

"Karl?" called Jonny. "The first-aid kit's with you."

Karl raised himself onto his elbows. There was no sign of the backpack on the ledge. With a roar, he strained toward the side of the ledge, the drag on his useless leg sending stars spinning in his peripheral vision. Peering over, he saw an incongruent yellow blob punctuating the ice below. Karl hadn't shed tears since his childhood, but the sound bubbling from his lips was a sob.

"You think I can come down?" called Jonny. "Fix up some kind of harness?"

There was nothing that man would like more than to be a hero. A picture flashed through Karl's mind of Jonny's bashful grin as well-wishers clapped him on the back to congratulate him for saving his fellow researcher's life. Karl suppressed an urge to throw up.

"Be my guest. You've got a thirty-meter rope, and I'm a few meters below that. You could jump the rest and levitate me up."

Another silence.

"I'll fetch help then."

Karl didn't bother answering. The only way he would reach the surface was by being splinted and braced in a hoist. That was if the moulin's marker wasn't covered by drifting snow in the hours it would take for help to arrive. Meanwhile, chances were that even a sneeze would dislodge the ledge he balanced on and send him plummeting. There was no guarantee he would be found alive. Or found.

"Karl?"

"For Christ's sake," Karl hissed through clenched teeth. "What?"

"At least the samples are safe."

It was a hollow comfort. All the extracted ice cores were now in Jonny's sole possession, while Karl lay supine in a frozen hell. Colleagues had rightly pointed out that warned this section was unstable—it had claimed a sobering number of lives over the years. But after a warm spring and an accelerated melt rate, the opportunity to gather unique data was too rare to pass by.

It dawned on Karl that if he didn't make it, Jonny would be headlining next year's *Glaciology* journals, while he would be a mere footnote, a whispered tragedy. His hopes to revive a stagnant career with groundbreaking research had fallen with him through the ice.

"Jonny?" Karl called up to the patch of sky, his breath forming a frozen cloud of fear. The insignificance of his broken body in this terrible, stark place pressed down. "Wait! Jonny?"

But Karl was alone. A spotlight of sunshine poured through the moulin and inched across the walls of his tomb, marking out the hours before nightfall.

Moraine

From a distance, glaciers appear pristine; icy prisms that capture every-angled cool light. As a boy, traipsing behind his father one cold and barren walking holiday, Karl had been dismayed to discover that a glacier's snout is dirty, mixed with rubble razed from the underlying substrate. In time he learned the debris was an ancient story, a code to be unlocked, and his desire to decipher it was sparked. Now, a glacier held him in its empty heart, in an ironic, reciprocal gesture.

This was all Jonny's fault. It was as if he had planned it from the start: assuming the role of the cataloger, poring over serial numbers and labels. Karl had used his brute strength to hack away layers of snow and drill down ever deeper below the surface. His own hands had retrieved the plugs of prehistoric ice, placed them in the ziplock bags Jonny held open and stowed away. Bitter thoughts piled up like rubble, and doubts hailed down.

He imagined Jonny approaching the research station—a pitiful figure in the frigid gloom: distressed, fatigued. Perhaps he would stagger from the Ski-Doo and call for help in a tremulous voice. Maybe he would surrender the samples and let himself be guided inside the research station's warm glow. Then, Karl was certain, he would insist on overseeing their storage in the laboratory freezer, safe under lock and key. *Ever the conscientious scientist*, concerned colleagues would murmur. *He's still in shock—on autopilot*, they would fret. *It's what Karl would want, though.*

Jonny would have his solo-authored thesis written by spring.

Step by step, Karl reviewed the moments leading up to his fall, wracking his brain for mistakes. The patchy color on this particular stretch suggested pockets of air, and Karl had debated whether to proceed. Jonny's disappointment was palpable. He had offered to take the lead, reproachful of missing samples from this rarely accessed section.

"All this way to leave the data set incomplete?" he protested.

Karl dismissed the suggestion that Jonny should proceed alone as the lighter of the two—he lacked Karl's experience. But if the ugly, grit-pocked truth were to be told, Karl couldn't bear the thought of Jonny recounting to others how they had walked away. Against his better judgment, despite his instincts screaming no, he had advanced under Jonny's gleaming eyes.

The rope anchors were set deep in solid ice. Karl always tested their load before letting them bear his full weight. Always. It was common to lose footing, for the surface to crack and give way, but rare for screws to fully fail. Unless the ice shavings covering the fixtures had been dislodged while he was working. Brushed away by Jonny's hands—on purpose, perhaps. The sun would have heated up the metal fast, melting out the screws.

With a jolt, Karl relived the rope giving way and the flailing of crampons and ice ax to halt his descent. His heart lurched all over again. Not from the shock of the fall, but because there was nothing but dirt behind Jonny's cheerful façade. Of course, Jonny would feign distress retracing his steps with the rescue team, apparently desperate to find the moulin, and what a performance it would be. Secretly, he would gloat over Karl's demise before claiming their hypotheses as his own.

Pain throbbed through Karl's thigh and strobed through his pelvis. Hours had passed since his fall, and his muscles ached from shivering. As daylight faded, his chances of survival plunged with the temperature.

Arete

The brittle night sky was clear, and long-expired galaxies sparkled through the moulin's mouth. Karl's teeth chattered, although his fingers and toes were numb. As he slipped in and out of shallow sleep, faces and fragments of conversation drifted through his mind with vivid brilliance, heightened by his body's surging endorphins. After suppressing all thoughts of Julia these last few days, here she was, her image as clear as if she were sitting beside him. Refusing to leave, she gazed back at him, her face softened by that familiar wry smile, every bit as beautiful as the night they met.

It had been at one of those faculty-hosted evening events that academics only attend to rub shoulders with sponsors. Karl noticed Julia early on; she looked gawkish and out of place the way scientists often do when they dress up. Like Karl, she lingered close to the bar, evidently as horrified by the dance floor as he was. With little inclination to socialize, Karl ignored her, but she sidled on up.

"Hydrology," she announced by way of introduction.

"Glaciology," Karl replied.

"Dr. Nilsen, isn't it? Your work on ablation modeling inspired my undergraduate dissertation."

Heat flushed Karl's cheeks. It was true he'd once been hailed as a trailblazer, his research opening up new ways of understanding the impact of climate on ice reserves. It smarted that the zenith of his career had passed so soon.

"That was years ago. These days, it's a dated study." Karl stepped away, waving his empty glass in the other direction as if there were more important conversations to resume, despite the fact her attention warmed him far more than the scotch hitting his bloodstream.

"I disagree," she replied, her glance clocking the empty space behind him. "Your research isn't dated, it's seminal. Another drink?"

Later that night, after a collision of minds and bodies, Karl explored the landscape of her skin. His fingertips followed the jut of her hip bones and traced the ridge of her ribcage rising from the soft plain of her belly. He told her he was mapping out tectonic plates; she joked about the earth moving. He mapped her freckles and found Cassiopeia.

"We're made up of stardust and water," she told him. "It's all we are, in the end."

"And quite a lot of gas," he added.

Within a month she had moved in, bringing pot plants and scented candles to his spartan apartment, carving out a place in his life. Days became landscaped with unexpected peaks of joy.

Trembling, Karl reached out to touch Julia's cheek. His fingers closed over empty air. Behind the silhouette of his hand, distant stars twinkled.

Crevasse

The darkness birthed a new day, and the stars faded into a Krishna-colored dawn sky, but no god showed up to offer mercy. Karl's rebellious body still breathed, still hurt. He observed crafty notions of rescue creeping into the corners of his mind, and he cut them down with dark musings.

He and Julia were ticking along just fine, or so he'd thought. Immersed in their respective studies, they were a no-frills kind of couple, taking turns to cook and clean so they both had time for their own pursuits. His expectations were modest—after all, the surge of hormones and neurotransmitters that accompanies the passionate, early stages of a relationship are never sustained. The lack of attention Julia alluded to never meant he didn't care. They would have been fine if she didn't keep wanting *more*.

The last, catastrophic argument was triggered when Julia arranged drinks with friends before Karl flew out to the glacier. The modest list of invitees, comprised of a handful of Julia's acquaintances, seemed unnecessary to Karl, a superfluous commitment. It wasn't that Karl didn't have friends of his own—there were always one or two familiar faces at conferences—but he had neither time nor inclination for social rituals. When Julia pressed him to name someone he talked to outside of work, he reluctantly named Jonny.

"Great!" said Julia. "Jonny is guest of honor, alongside you. He's confirmed he'll be there."

Flustered, Karl clenched his fists and turned away.

"I won't go. I don't like small talk. And why would I want to see Jonny when I'm going to be working and sleeping alongside the wretched man anyway?"

"Stop pulling away." Julia moved in front of him, blocking his path. "It's not about Jonny. It's about us. Can't we do this one thing together? Every time I think we're getting somewhere, that we're moving forward as a couple, you freeze."

"I thought you were different," Karl countered. "You're needy and demanding, just like everyone else. Leave me alone."

That stare . . . as if she were only truly seeing Karl for the first time. It was obvious, even to Karl, that she didn't like whom she saw. As effortlessly as she had carved a place in his life, she gathered some clutter and left, announcing an intention to return for the rest of her belongings while he was away. Exhausted from his heart jumping at every beep and chirrup from his phone, Karl decided the fissure between them was simply too deep and barred her number.

He suspected Jonny would contact Julia to personally inform her about the accident. Maybe they would arrange to meet. She would weep, of course, for a life lost too soon and for what could have been. Sentimental nonsense. Karl imagined Jonny embracing her, stroking her hair to comfort her, maybe even noticing Cassiopeia. Later, Jonny would not only take the glory for their research, but he would also wriggle into Julia's affections. He'd become the emotionally available partner Julia pined for, offering soppy words of endearment—the type Karl cringed to hear. Her simpering friends would adore him.

With gritted teeth, Karl pulled himself a fraction closer to the edge in a bid to join his rucksack on the ice below, before swooning from agony. He may as well have been pinned in place by icicles. Tears froze on his lashes.

Terminus

Karl couldn't remember whether shivering increased basal metabolic rate by 75 percent or whether it raised core body temperature by 75 percent. It could be both statistics were true. Or neither. Simple facts and figures eluded him. He couldn't retrieve them from his brain. The pain had subsided, every other physical sensation too. His body was surrendering. The odds of him surviving the night had been stacked against him, but hadn't he endured? He noted this final achievement with an odd flicker of interest. It would have made a fine story to share over dinner, if things had turned out differently.

The sun, a few hours into its arc, once again beamed through the moulin. The spotlight of meager warmth on Karl's face thawed ice crystals nestling in his beard. Despite the freezing water trickling down his neck, he no longer shivered and lay sedated by a deep peace.

Once, as a child, his father had taken him fossicking. Huddled together on a windswept beach they had cracked open rocks with a hammer, wordlessly discarding disappointments at their feet. At last, one split apart to reveal a near-perfect ammonite. Karl cupped the spiraled imprints in his hands, marveling at the rare animation in his father's face, and blurted astonishment that life from millions of years ago was touching their own.

"Not quite," his father corrected. "The creature's death left the impression, not its life."

Karl studied the ridged whorls. "What about Mama? Did she leave an impression?"

It was a stupid question. Karl regretted it the moment it left his mouth. His father's face clouded as he gazed out to sea, a light rain pattering their hoods. "Low tide," he'd announced. "There may be, we might find belemnites."

Karl wondered what impression his own death would leave, whether a pulverized trace of it would one day be churned up by the glacier for future lives to wonder about. He would become part of the glacier's age-old history. If only he could fall asleep like this to the tinkle of meltwater, with sunshine pouring through the crimson lids of his closed eyes, and he could begin that journey. With angels singing.

"Karl? Buddy? You okay?"

Karl's eyes snapped open. In an instant, breathtaking pain flooded back into his body. A shadow fell across his face. His window to the sky was blocked by Jonny's padded backside as he was winched down with a green medical pack on his back. Jonny's jubilant exchange with the rescue team above boomed and echoed, and the excited neurons in Karl's damaged body pulsed.

"You bastard," croaked Karl through parched lips. "What took you so long?"

Jonny grinned, planting his feet tentatively on the ledge beside Karl, slipping rope through Karl's carabiner and tying half hitches in the slack. "We came as soon as we could. I knew you'd be in a foul mood, but for once, it's good to hear your voice."

"I thought you weren't coming back."

"Oh, I thought about it, Karl."

"Does Julia know I'm hurt?"

Jonny's smile never wavered. "You can tell her yourself."

"You should have seen the stars, Jonny. The brightest I've ever seen. It was like I was part of them."

"That's nice, buddy. We're all made up of stardust and water, right?"

"Don't forget the gas."

Karl wasn't sure if he spoke the words out loud or said them in his head. It didn't matter. An umbilical cord of rope connected him to another day, and the pool of sky above was so blue, so deep, he thought he might drown.

Recompose
Lee Woodman

I want to be dirt when I die—
not that I don't like cemeteries. I do.
But only because of the stories, not the bodies,
I want to be dirt when I die.

At the funeral home, they ask my friend
to identify her mother's embalmed colorless corpse.
No, I spurn the mahogany coffin, steel-lined,
to be lowered into a grave, encased by concrete.

I want to be dirt when I die—
no chemical perfumes, no open casket,
no taking up land that could be a playground,
a bird sanctuary, an orange grove.

I want to be covered with alfalfa and sawdust,
with tawny straw as a bed beneath my bones.
We'll dissolve together into bark-like pieces
to form an earthy floor, like pine needle mulch.

After all, the residue from the composting
will be given to families to throw over oceans,
where sediment may add silk to shore—
or to place under a peony bush like my mother's.

I want to be in the prayer hall of reconstitution,
not on an undertaker's table, nor burned to ashes—
because the price is too high,
because land and water are thirsting.

Let forest restoration folk spread me gently,
especially under willows and weeping firs.
Let me sink into the congregation of worms
and mushrooms; we'll send psalms aloft.

I want to be dirt when I die—
not that I don't like rituals. I do.
Bodies and bones become earth of the fields,
an epic higher than sky.

love letter to a weed
Jack Giaour

for the cleaning and redeeming of my dirt i've planted you
      in the image of myself   the soil recoils from you

the soil recoils from my little rake and hoe
      the pines turn and spill their dew on me and my little hoe

what i want is to see only you to see
      the rocks and wrinkled cliffs covered each summer with only you

when the forest drips with want and dew i'll look only upon you
      my tendriled heart aches for you

i have planted you to kill
      and be redeemed by the hollow echo of every other thing

my affection was all in the planting
      and if i never tend you you'll understand

it was always personal

Made in the USA
Las Vegas, NV
21 September 2024